Valiant

D1621069

HAL FOSTER — creator of the weekly masterpiece of art and high adventure, PRINCE VALIANT — is the world's most honored comic page artist:

1952: awarded the *"SilverLady"* of the Banshees

1957: awarded the *"Reuben"* of the National Cartoonists Society as the *"outstanding cartoonist of the year"*

1964: PRINCE VALIANT named *"best story strip"* by the National Cartoonists Society

1965: Hal Foster is elected to membership in the exclusive Royal Society of Arts of Great Britain (becoming one of the few American artists ever so honored)

The Royal Society of Arts is 210 years old. Founded in the time of Dr. Samuel Johnson "for the encouragement of Arts, Manufactures and Commerce," its roster has included some of the most distinguished names of the British Empire.

Presented on the front and back endpapers is the *1965 Prince Valiant Sales Brochure* published by King Features Syndicate. Brochures like this one were given to the syndicate's sales staff to mail or hand-deliver to newspaper editors in order to sell comics subscriptions. This brochure was produced after the National Cartoonists Society named *Prince Valiant* the "best story strip" in 1964, and Foster was elected to the Royal Society of Arts of Great Britain in 1965. Special thanks to Dean Mullaney for supplying this incredible piece of comics history.

PRINCE VALIANT

Special thanks to the SPECIAL COLLECTIONS RESEARCH CENTER of the SYRACUSE UNIVERSITY LIBRARY for providing the scans for the vast majority of the *Prince Valiant* strips, reproduced from original syndicate proof sheets, in this volume. Visit their website at http://library.syr.edu/find/scrc/

Prince Valiant Vol. 15: 1965–1966 Fantagraphics Books, Inc. 7563 Lake City Way NE, Seattle, WA 98115. Edited by Brian M. Kane. Editorial Liaison: Gary Groth. Series design by Adam Grano. Production by Sean David Williams. Restoration by Paul Baresh. Associate Publisher: Eric Reynolds. Publisher: Gary Groth. All comics © 2017 King Features Syndicate. "Sir Robert of Dell: The Prince Valiant Art of Bob Fujitani" ©2017 Brian M. Kane. "Not Just for Sundays: Prince Valiant's Adventures Beyond the Fourth Estate" copyright © 2017 Brian M. Kane. This edition copyright © 2017 Fantagraphics Books, Inc. All rights reserved. Permission to quote or reproduce material for reviews or notices must be obtained from Fantagraphics Books, in writing, at 7563 Lake City Way NE, Seattle, WA 98115. First edition: June 2017 ISBN: 978-1-68396-025-6. Library of Congress Control Number: 2016961052. Printed in China.

PRINCE VALIANT

VOL. 15: 1965-1966 — BY HAL FOSTER

PUBLISHED BY FANTAGRAPHICS BOOKS, INC., SEATTLE.

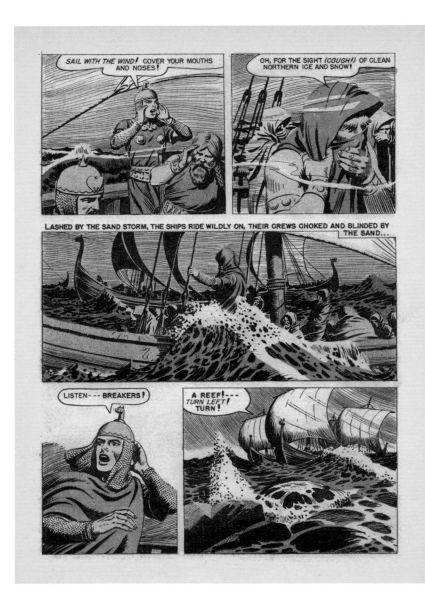

Bob Fujitani penciled and inked this four-page sequence featuring Prince Valiant. *Four Color* comics #900, May 1958 (Dell Publishing) was the last of seven issues showcasing original adventures of the Prince of Thule; all without Hal Foster's involvement.

SIR ROBERT of DELL:
The Prince Valiant Art of Bob Fujitani

By Brian M. Kane with Bob Fujitani

Robert "Bob" Fujitani (aka Fuje) was born on October 15, 1921 in Kripplebush, New York. Fujitani's Japanese-American father, Tom worked as a chef, while his English/Irish mother, Hannah (née Wells) stayed at home to raise Bob and his two brothers. When Fujitani was two-years-old the family moved to Greenwich, Connecticut where he has lived ever since. Fujitani began drawing in elementary school, and by the age of twelve was tenaciously copying Alex Raymond's *Jungle Jim* strip; fascinated by its beasts and exotic settings. In 1939, Fujitani went to the American School of Design in New York City, but after eighteen months his studies were interrupted by a call from his friend, Philip Eustice "Tex" Blaisdell, who asked, "Hey. You want a job?" That afternoon Will Eisner hired Fujitani to pencil stories for *Uncle Sam*, *Doll Man*, and *Hack O'Hara* at a rate of three pages a day for $5.00.

Besides Quality Comics, Fujitani worked for a variety of other publishers including MLJ Comics, Avon, Ace, Fawcett, Lev Gleason Publications, Holyoke Publishing, Atlas, Harvey, Hillman Periodicals, and Dell. Among his standout comic book titles during the 1940s-1960s were: *Hangman*, *Cat-Man*, *Flying Dutchman*, *Sky Wolf*, *Turok, Son of Stone* and *Doctor Solar, Man of the Atom*. It was at Dell that Fujitani was asked to pencil and ink the *Prince Valiant* movie adaptation for *Four Color* comics; technically making him second artist to illustrate the adventures of the Prince of Thule. Sales of *Prince Valiant's* first non-reprint comic book appearance were so impressive that Fujitani was hired to illustrate six more original stories over the next four years. Additionally, Fujitani worked on comic strips, ghosting on *Judge Wright*, *Mandrake the Magician*, and *Rip Kirby* for John Prentice, but it was his long stint co-developing *Flash Gordon* with Dan Barry that represents his largest body of work.

BMK: *I know that Tex Blaisdell was friends with you at the American School of Design, and helped you get into comics, but did you know that in the 1960s he was a background artist for Hal Foster on* Prince Valiant?

BF: Really? He was a year older than me. He had already graduated and was working for Eisner when he called me. So I went down there and Eisner hired me, but it was Tex who got me the job.

BMK: *How long did you work for Eisner?*

BF: Only about four months.

Right: Bob Fujitani with his wife, Ruth, and their dog, Fred.

BMK: *Oh. I've read in some places that it was the Eisner Studio could be pretty grueling work at times.*

BF: No. I loved it. You learned to get it down to a system.

BMK: *How did you end up going from Eisner's to Dell Comics?*

BF: What happened is that while I was at Eisner's, Harry Lucey called me. He was doing a comic book called the *Hangman*. He asked me if I could do some penciling for him. Harry was paying me $5.00 a page, and I could do 3 or 4 pages a day, but Eisner was only paying me $5.00 a day salary, so I started freelancing. After that Harry went into the Service, and I took it over drawing it completely.

BMK: *How did you end up working on the* Prince Valiant *books for Dell?*

BF: I did a lot of work for [Matthew Hilt] Matt Murphy who was the editor at Western Publishing. I did a whole series of *Lassie* books. Anything that came along like *Turok*. I did a number of those, and things like *Lowell Thomas [High Adventure]* about the reporter that went to Africa. So one day Matt just called me and asked me to do *Prince Valiant*.

†*Lowell Thomas High Adventure appeared in* Four Color #949 *and* 1001.

BMK: *Just like that.*

BF: Yeah. I did so many of them. I have them here in my house.

BMK: *Do you have any of the original artwork?*

BF: No.

BMK: *Did you have any contact with Foster?*

BF: No. Nothing.

BMK: *With the* Prince Valiants *who came up with the stories?*

BF: It was [Paul Sylvan] Newman. He wrote a lot of stories I worked on like *Turok* and *Lassie*.

BMK: *Did you receive full scripts first?*

BF: Yeah. That's how it worked. They gave me a script of the story and that was it.

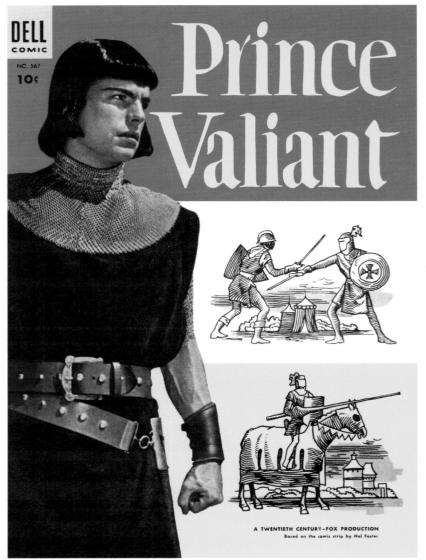

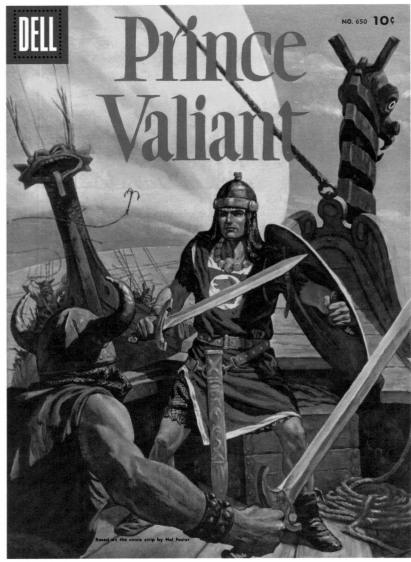

DELL COMIC
NO. 567
10¢

Prince Valiant

A TWENTIETH CENTURY-FOX PRODUCTION
Based on the comic strip by Hal Foster

DELL
NO. 650 10¢

Prince Valiant

Based on the comic strip by Hal Foster

BMK: *What do you remember from working on those? I recall reading that you liked Raymond's figures better than Foster's. How much of your approach on the comic book was Raymond's style, and how much was Foster's?*

BF: I actually never tried to imitate someone's style. It just seemed natural for me to draw realistically. I would try to keep the characters looking like the originals; by the artists that came before me. With *Flash Gordon* so many guys worked on that thing so Flash had changed drastically. So all I tried to do was the best drawing I could do. I never really worried about technique. I think with *Prince Valiant* though I did try to indicate Hal Foster's approach a little bit. I didn't study it for style, but I looked at it to see the way he modeled Prince Valiant. The other characters I just tried to make them the way I thought they should look. That's about it.

BMK: *Is there anything else you'd like to add.*

BF: Did I ever tell you how I got holy hell with *Prince Valiant*?

BMK: *No.*

BF: Our local newspaper, *The Greenwich Times*, which is owned by Hearst now, runs *Prince Valiant* every Sunday. They're killing it now. They have a whole page, but they're running it at a fourth of a page. Even the bigfoot comics, which don't require any space at all, have more space than *Prince Valiant*. That strip depends on size because they are always trying to make a scene of ships at sea and big fights. It's crazy. It's ridiculous. Anyway, so they interviewed me, and the reporter asked me what work I had done, so I told her I worked on the *Prince Valiant* comic book, and the *Flash Gordon* comic strip for a number of years. The next day when it came out in the newspaper it said that I did the *Prince Valiant* newspaper strip. Now down in Cos Cob [, Connecticut] lived John Cullen Murphy who took over *Prince Valiant* after Foster left it, and he'd been doing it for years. Anyway, Mrs. Murphy, this was after her husband had passed, called me and she was furious and said, "How dare you say that you did *Prince Valiant* when my husband was doing it?" So I explained to her what I told the reporter, but she wasn't too satisfied. She thought I was some kind of imposter trying to get glory from her husband's work. I

think Al Williamson was the guy who should have done *Prince Valiant*.

BMK: *Al once told me, "You don't follow an act like Foster."*

BF: Even though Dan Barry and I were doing *Flash Gordon*, it really should have been Al on that strip. You know, Dan and the other guys and even myself all departed from Alex Raymond's style—many times over—but Al did classic Raymond stuff; beautiful stuff.

BMK: *How did you end up working with Dan Barry on the* Flash Gordon *comic strip?*

BF: He was in Europe. He had gone over to Austria to avoid Income Tax. If he did the strip over there he got a big tax break. So one day he wrote me a letter and asked if I'd be interested in taking over *Flash Gordon*. [laughs] He was thinking about retiring and becoming a painter. Now I had known him before this, so I said "Sure. I'd be interested." So then he sent me some pencils for the dailies. At that time Mac Raboy was doing the Sunday pages. So I inked the strips and delivered them to Ben Oda who was the letterer. Ben was lettering a lot of strips at that time. So I'd drive over the Tappan Zee Bridge out to Englewood every Monday where Ben lived and deliver the pages. After a bit I started penciling the strips and he'd ink a few of them. One day he said, "Do the whole thing." because he was more interested in painting.

So I was doing [*Flash Gordon*] for a number of years until Dan returned from Europe. He stayed with me for about four months,

Above left: *Four Color* #567, June 1954 (Dell Publishing, 1942 series) featuring *Prince Valiant* [Dell Code # P.V.O.S. #567-546].
Cover: Photo of Robert Wagner as Prince Valiant
Story: "Prince Valiant" adapted by Paul S. Newman from the screenplay by Dudley Nichols
Pencils & inks: Bob Fujitani

Above right: *Four Color* #650, September 1955 (Dell Publishing, 1942 series) featuring *Prince Valiant* [Dell Code # P.V.O.S. #650-559].
Cover: Artist unknown. Possibly Don Spaulding
Story: "Prince Valiant: Hostage to Treachery" by Paul S. Newman
Pencils & inks: Bob Fujitani

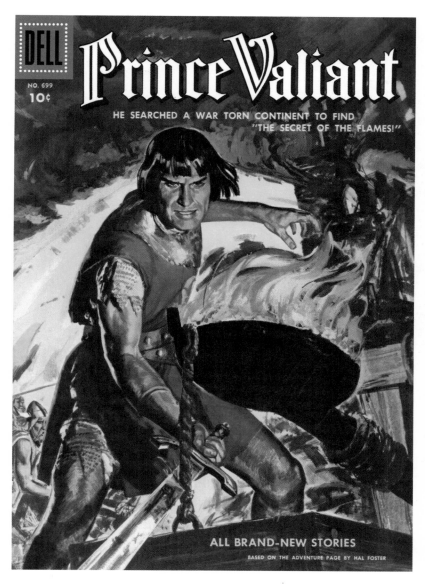

and we worked together in my studio. After that Dan moved up to Kent, Connecticut where he was exhibiting his paintings. Then Dino De Laurentiis decided to do a movie of Flash Gordon. [De Laurentiis] wanted us to do some of the publicity posters and pamphlets, so Dan got all excited. "This is our big chance," he said. "We'll do a good job on the posters for Dino." Dan was on a first-name basis with him. So Dan got so excited, and he said, "We can open a studio and between the two of us we can turn these things out." He wanted to form a partnership that would include everything; the strip, the movie, anything in the future, and we'd split everything 50/50.

Everything was going fine with the poster, but it was hard for two guys to work on a painting. It's easy for two guys to work on a strip; one guy would pencil it and one guy would ink. So we managed to do a triptych poster with one large scene in the middle and two smaller ones on the sides. Dan said, "You lay-out the whole thing, and I'll paint the large one in the middle, and you paint the smaller ones." Well, that was fine with me. So we were working on it, and [Dan] was calling me twice a day to check up, and then he quit calling. Almost a week went by, so I called him and said, "Dan, what's happening here. Are you sick? Do you need some help?" Then there was a long silence and he said, "We have to talk." And I said, "Talk about what?" He said, "I've been breaking my ass going to Newark two or three times a week to have conferences with Dino. It's costing me a lot of money. I had to buy a couple of new suits. I had to take

the secretary out." I could feel it coming, so I said, "What do you want from me?" He said, "I think our partnership has to be 60/40 because this is costing me too much money."

BMK: *Really?*

BF: Well that "60/40" brought up other dealings I had, so I said, "Look, Dan, as far as I'm concerned you can have 100% because it's just a matter of principle. I don't mind 60/40, but the idea was that you kept it 50/50. But now when you see the possibility this thing maybe worth a lot more you changed your mind. We argued for a while until finally, in the heat of the argument I told him to just take the whole thing and just shove it because I was out.

So we didn't talk for quite a while and then one day he called me and said, "What about the strip?" So I told him he could do the strip all by himself also. So he said, "Can you help with the strip until I can get someone else." That was it. I did a couple more weeks and that was it. We never talked after that.

BMK: *Unfortunately it's not that uncommon, is it?*

BF: No. It brought back some vivid memories because I had the same deal with [Robert] Bob Bernstein [for a book called *Eerie Comics*] way back and he also insisted on a 50/50 contract. [Bob] had a brother-in-law who was a lawyer who drew up a contract. Then when we finally landed a big deal he got quiet. We were walking down Lexington Avenue from 58th Street where his cousin lived, and I said, "Bob, what's the matter?" He said, "Let's get a cup of coffee. We have to talk." I said, "Talk about what?" He said, "This is going to involve a lot of money." I said, "So?" Then he said, "I really busted my balls on this and I took a lot of my time, but you didn't put so much time in. You just sat at home at your desk." And I thought, "Here it goes." So we went into an automat and sat down, and I said, "Well, whatever it is, Bob, spit it out." He said, "I want to tear up the contract and make the partnership 60/40." I said, "Bob, you can have 100% because I'm out." That was a long time before this *Flash Gordon* thing.

With some of these guys everything is hunky-dory until they see the possibilities. Even my wife's cousin wanted to do a strip and wanted me to do the preliminary drawings for him.

Above left: *Four Color* #699, April 1956 (Dell Publishing, 1942 series) featuring *Prince Valiant* [Dell Code # P.V.O.S. #699-564].
Cover: Franco Picchioni
Story: "Prince Valiant: The Quest for Greek Fire" by Paul S. Newman
Pencils & inks: Bob Fujitani

Above right: *Four Color* #719, August 1956 (Dell Publishing, 1942 series) featuring *Prince Valiant* [Dell Code # P.V.O.S. #719-568].
Cover: Sam Savitt
Story: "Prince Valiant: Peril of the Round Table" by Paul S. Newman
Pencils & inks: Bob Fujitani

He wanted to give me a percentage of the profits, and I said, "No. I'll do the samples for the presentation, but I want to be paid for them." He paid me, but then he called me one day and said, "This thing is really hot, and it's probably gonna sell. Who knows how much money will be in it." I asked, "Will I get any of the profits?" And he said, "No. I paid you and that's it." So just kiddingly I said, "Not even 1% or 2% of the profits?" And he said, "Nope. I paid you. You didn't want to go in on it, so that's it." A little time went by and he called me again and said, "Can I come down and talk to you?" and I said, "Sure." So he came down and we went into my studio and he said, "I'm having a big lawsuit. I hired one of these big law firms in New York, and we're suing a Japanese company who it seems stole my idea. What I really wanted to talk to you about is have you gone to Japan lately?" Can you imagine that?

BMK: *Wow. What was the property?*

BF: *Mechano.*† It was about a giant robot. He insinuated that I went to Japan, took his idea and sold it to the Japanese. The only thing that I ever regretted was that I didn't take him by the scruff of the neck and throw him out. He was my wife's cousin. Anyway, as soon as they see the money things change.

Note to designer. Put the following blue footnote at the bottom of the column featuring the previous caption. Change blue footnote to black, and delete green text from article.

† At the time Bernstein believed his idea for *Mechano* was appropriated for Mitsuteru Yokoyama's *Tetsujin 28-go*, or *Gigantor* as it was renamed for American audiences.

BMK: *After Dell where did you go?*

BF: Well, I was still working on *Flash Gordon*.

BMK: *But no more comic book work.*

BF: No. I don't think so. But I also did some work for John Prentice on *Rip Kirby*.

BMK: *How did that come about?*

BF: I was at a National Cartoonists Society dinner and he came up to me and asked me if I could help him with the strip. I said, "Sure." And the next day he called me to do some work. So I worked for him for a while.

BMK: *While you were also working on* Flash Gordon.

BF: That's right. I'd go to John's office to drop off the strips then one day I caught him outside the office. He told me he couldn't talk because he wasn't feeling well and on his way to the doctors. That was the day the doctor diagnosed him with the flu and lung cancer. After that we never met at his office; only at his home. I'd go there to drop off the strips and he'd be dressed in a bathrobe. He lasted only about a month. After John died I continued working on the strip until it ended. I'd take the strips over to Leonard Starr's house and he'd Xerox them for King [Features] then give me the originals. I still have the last couple weeks of the strips.

BMK: *The original strips?*

BF: Yeah, they're around here in the house. When I took them to John he just kept them, but Starr gave them back to me.

BMK: *So after* Rip Kirby *you still kept working on* Flash Gordon *until your falling out with Dan Barry?*

BF: Yeah. That's right.

BMK: *And what did you work on after that?*

BF: Nothing. I quit. That was it.

BMK: *Do you miss it.*

BF: Not anymore. I have good memories. I had fun and I'm proud of the work I did. ✠

Above left: *Four Color* #788, April 1957 (Dell Publishing, 1942 series) featuring *Prince Valiant* [Dell Code # P.V.O.S. #788-574].
Cover: Morris "Mo" Gollub
Story: "Prince Valiant: Trial By Arms" by Paul S. Newman
Pencils & inks: Bob Fujitani

Above middle: Four Color #849, December 1957 (Dell Publishing, 1942 series) featuring Prince Valiant [Dell Code # P.V.O.S. #849-5712].
Cover: Artist unknown
Story: "Prince Valiant: Quest For The Grail" by Paul S. Newman
Pencils & inks: Bob Fujitani

Above right: Four Color #900, May 1958 (Dell Publishing, 1942 series) featuring Prince Valiant [Dell Code # P.V.O.S. #900-585].
Cover: George Wilson
Story: "Prince Valiant: Island of Thunder" by Paul S. Newman
Pencils & inks: Bob Fujitani

Special thanks to: Jim Amash, Roy Thomas, John Morrow, Axel M. Wulff, Rick Norwood, Dwight Radford, and Kevin Chickanis for their help in preparing this article.

References

Amash, Jim (2003). "'Fuje' for Thought!" *Alter Ego*, Vol. 3, No. 23, April, pp. 3-20. Raleigh, North Carolina: TwoMorrows.
Matthew Hilt Murphy's middle name retrieved from his obituary printed in *The Journal News*, December 6, 2014.
Paul Sylvan Newman's middle name obtained from the *U.S., Social Security Applications and Claims Index, 1936-2007.*

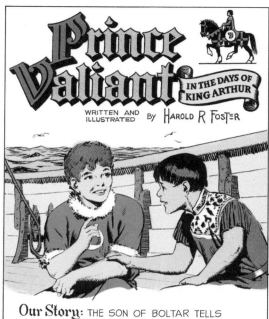

Prince Valiant
IN THE DAYS OF KING ARTHUR
WRITTEN AND ILLUSTRATED BY HAROLD R FOSTER

Our Story: THE SON OF BOLTAR TELLS PRINCE ARN OF A PROMISE MADE LONG AGO TO A PEOPLE WHO LIVED BEYOND THE WIDE SEA. "MY PEOPLE BELIEVED YOUR MOTHER TO BE THE SUN GODDESS, AND SHE PROMISED THAT ONE DAY YOU WOULD RETURN TO THEM. WILL YOU?"

"I REMEMBER THE STORY AS MY MOTHER TOLD IT," ANSWERS ARN. "ULFRUN, THE SEA HAWK, CAST HIS EYES UPON MY MOTHER AND DESIRED HER ABOVE ALL THINGS. HE STOLE HER FROM THE CASTLE."

"IN HIS GREAT WARSHIP HE SAILED WESTWARD, TOWARD UNKNOWN SEAS, AND WHEN THE RED SAILS OF MY SIRE'S SHIP SHOWED ON THE HORIZON HE LAUGHED, FOR NO ONE DARED FOLLOW WHERE HE, THE SEA HAWK, LED."

"THROUGH MIST AND RAIN ICELAND WAS DISCOVERED, BUT BECAUSE OF MOTHER'S FAIR HAIR AND GRAY EYES IT SEEMED UNIMPORTANT. ONLY BY ROWING INTO A WIND COULD ULFRUN OUTDISTANCE THE SAILING SHIP. BUT SOON THE RED SAILS WOULD BE AGAIN IN SIGHT."

"NO LONGER WAS ULFRUN LEADING HIS ENEMY TO DEFEAT; HE WAS FLEEING! LOVE TURNED TO HATE. HE STRUCK HIS CAPTIVE DOWN AND DREW HIS SWORD. HER SEWING WAS SPILLED UPON THE DECK, BABY CLOTHES. THEN ULFRUN KNEW PRINCE VALIANT WOULD NEVER GIVE UP THE CHASE!"

"LAND! AND THE GREAT UNKNOWN SEA HAD BEEN CROSSED. UP A HUGE RIVER, NEVER FAR APART, THEY WENT UNTIL STOPPED AT LAST BY NIAGARA. THE CHASE ENDED IN A CLASH OF SWORDS."

"ULFRUN FLED, BUT MY SIRE FOUND HIM AT THE EDGE OF THE CHASM AND DREW THE 'SINGING SWORD'."

1456   1-3-65

"MY PARENTS WERE UNITED. 'I FOUND THIS BEFORE I LEFT AND KNEW I MUST FOLLOW YOU TO THE VERY END'."

NEXT WEEK—**Tillicum's Story**

HAL FOSTER

Prince Valiant
IN THE DAYS OF KING ARTHUR
WRITTEN AND ILLUSTRATED BY HAROLD R FOSTER

Our Story: *"AND THAT,"* CONCLUDES PRINCE ARN, *"IS THE STORY AS MY MOTHER TOLD IT, OF HOW MY PARENTS CROSSED THE UNKNOWN SEA AND CAME TO THE STRANGE LAND WHERE YOUR MOTHER, TILLICUM, LIVED WITH HER PEOPLE."*

HATHA, SON OF BOLTAR, TAKES UP THE TALE: *"WHEN THE VIKING SHIP LANDED, OUR PEOPLE GAZED IN AWE. NEVER HAD THEY SEEN A WOMAN WITH HAIR LIKE SUNLIGHT ON RIPENING GRAIN, EYES GREY AS THE RAIN. THEY CALLED HER THE SUN-WOMAN AND WORSHIPPED HER AS 'BRINGER OF HARVESTS'."*

"WHEN IT BECAME KNOWN THAT THE SUN-WOMAN WAS ABOUT TO BEAR A CHILD, THE CHIEFS ASSEMBLED AND BROUGHT MANY GIFTS, ONE OF WHICH WAS TILLICUM, MY MOTHER, AND SHE WAS BOUND TO SERVE THE 'BRINGER OF HARVESTS' FOREVERMORE."

"THE HARVEST WAS GOOD THAT AUTUMN, AND DURING THE WINTER GAME WAS PLENTIFUL, SO THAT THERE WAS NO FAMINE WHEN SPRING CAME. AND THAT SPRING YOU, ARN, WERE BORN AND THE STALWART VIKINGS WHO SERVED YOUR MOTHER HAILED YOU AS A FUTURE CHIEFTAIN."

"WHEN THE SHIP WAS MADE READY FOR THE PERILOUS JOURNEY BACK ACROSS THE GREAT SEA OUR PEOPLE CRIED; 'IF THE SUN-WOMAN LEAVES, WHO WILL BRING FERTILITY TO OUR PLANTING, RIPENESS TO OUR GRAIN?'"

"'IT IS NOT BY ANY GIFT FROM ME THAT YOU WILL PROSPER BUT BY YOUR OWN WISDOM AND INDUSTRY. AND WHO KNOWS, SOME DAY MY SON MAY RETURN AND LEAD YOU TO GREATNESS!'"

1457

HAL FOSTER

"THEN I AM HONOR BOUND TO RETURN ACROSS THE SEA AND FULFILL MY MOTHER'S PROMISE," CRIES ARN, *"AND YOU MUST COME WITH ME, HATHA!"*

NEXT WEEK— **The Oath Remembered**

1-10-64

Prince Valiant
IN THE DAYS OF KING ARTHUR
WRITTEN AND ILLUSTRATED BY HAROLD R FOSTER

Our Story: PRINCE ARN IS FIRED BY A GREAT AMBITION TO CROSS THE WILD SEA TO THE PLACE OF HIS BIRTH BESIDE THE GREAT FALLS THE NATIVES CALL NIAGARA.

BUT IT WILL BE SOME TIME BEFORE HE CAN DISCUSS HIS PLANS, FOR A FEAST IS BEING HELD TO CELEBRATE THE VICTORY OVER SKOGUL ODERSON AND HIS RUFFIAN ARMY, AND VIKINGSHOLM ROCKS WITH THE NOISE.

FROM A SMALL BALCONY THE ROYAL FAMILY SURVEYS THE WRECKAGE OF THE DINING HALL. "VICTORY HAS ITS PRICE," SAYS THE KING RUEFULLY. "OUR COFFERS HAVE BEEN EMPTIED FOR FOOD AND DRINK AND VIKINGSHOLM DEVASTATED IN THE INTERESTS OF HOSPITALITY."

AT LAST ARN IS ABLE TO TELL HIS PARENTS OF HIS GREAT DESIRE TO VISIT THE LAND BEYOND THE SEA AND FULFILL HIS MOTHER'S PROMISE. HATHA TOO BEGS HIS PARENTS, BOLTAR AND TILLICUM, TO LET HIM SEE THE LAND FROM WHICH HIS MOTHER CAME.

"I DID NOT TELL YOU OF THE PROMISE I MADE," ANSWERS ALETA ANXIOUSLY, "FOR YOU ARE SO YOUNG. I INTENDED TO WAIT UNTIL YOU WERE MORE MATURE, BUT NOW THAT YOU KNOW YOU WILL NOT BE CONTENT TILL MY PROMISE IS FULFILLED."

1458   1-17

"SUMMER IS ENDING, YOU CANNOT START UNTIL SPRING. SO SPEND THE WINTER WITH US, LEARN TO SPEAK OUR TONGUE AND THE WAYS OF OUR PEOPLE."

AS THEY ROUND THE HEADLAND ON THEIR WAY TO BOLTAR'S STEAD ARN GAZES ACROSS THE WILD, GRAY, ENDLESS OCEAN. HE HAS A MOMENT OF MISGIVING. "HAVE I THE WISDOM AND THE COURAGE TO CARRY ME THROUGH THIS QUEST?"

NEXT WEEK—Boltarstead

Prince Valiant
IN THE DAYS OF KING ARTHUR
WRITTEN AND ILLUSTRATED BY HAROLD R. FOSTER

Our Story: TO FULFILL A PROMISE MADE BY HIS MOTHER, PRINCE ARN ASKS PERMISSION TO VOYAGE ACROSS THE WIDE SEAS TO THE PLACE WHERE HE WAS BORN, A PLACE THE NATIVES CALL 'NIAGARA'. NOW THAT HIS PARENTS HAVE GIVEN THEIR PERMISSION HE IS BESET WITH DOUBTS: IS HE ABLE TO COMMAND, HAS HE THE WISDOM, THE EXPERIENCE, WILL HE FALTER DURING THE PERILOUS JOURNEY?

ARN HAS LITTLE TIME LEFT TO WORRY. WHEN BOLTAR LANDS HIS DRAGONSHIP BENEATH HIS FORTRESS-LIKE FARMSTEAD ARN FINDS EVERY WAKING HOUR FILLED WITH RESPONSIBILITIES.

GUNDAR HARL'S SAILING SHIP THAT MADE THE JOURNEY FOURTEEN YEARS AGO IS MADE READY. PROVISIONS, TOOLS, TRADE GOODS, WEAPONS AND ALL THE NECESSARY ITEMS FOR THE ADVENTURE MUST BE GATHERED BEFORE SPRING.

AUTUMN HAS BEEN A TIME FOR HAWKING OR RIDING OUT WITH HIS HOUNDS, BUT NOT NOW. NOW ARN MUST LEARN A STRANGE LANGUAGE AND STRANGER CUSTOMS.

SEAFARERS HAVE NEITHER COMPASS NOR SEXTANT TO AID THEIR NAVIGATION. THE NORTH STAR IS THEIR GUIDE AT NIGHT, BY DAY THE DIRECTION OF THE SUN'S SHADOW AT NOON, THE LENGTH OF THE SHADOW INDICATING THE LATITUDE.

BOLTAR'S SHIPS ARE DRAWN UP AND PREPARED FOR WINTER. GEAR IS REPAIRED AND STORED, AND THE VIKINGS, THE YEAR'S ROVING AT AN END, LEAVE FOR THEIR HOMES.

ARN TRIES TO RECRUIT SOME OF THEM FOR HIS GREAT ADVENTURE, BUT THEY ARE TOO ANXIOUS TO BE HOME WITH THEIR FAMILIES TO GIVE HIM HEED.

1459   1-24

HAL FOSTER

VALIANT WARRIORS WILL FOLLOW HIS FATHER, SEEK TO SERVE BOLTAR THE SEA-KING, BUT WHO WILL DARE PERIL FOR A BOY?

NEXT WEEK— Recruiting

Prince Valiant

IN THE DAYS OF KING ARTHUR

WRITTEN AND ILLUSTRATED BY HAROLD R FOSTER

Our Story: THE FIRST FROST...AND THE WOODS ARE BRIGHT WITH AUTUMN COLORS. ARN GAZES WISTFULLY AT THE SLEEK LINES OF GUNDAR HARL'S SAILING SHIP AND WONDERS HOW MANY OF ITS CREW WILL CONSENT TO SAIL ON THE GREAT ADVENTURE PLANNED FOR THE SPRING.

GUNDAR OFFERS LITTLE COMFORT: "MY CREW HAVE BECOME RICH BY OUR TRADING VENTURES, THEY MAY NOT CARE TO SAIL THE UNKNOWN SEA WITHOUT THE ASSURANCE OF GOOD PROFITS."

"I DOUBT IF ANY OF MY WARRIORS WILL VOLUNTEER FOR THE VOYAGE," BOLTAR ROARS IN HIS NORMAL VOICE, "YOU MAY ASK THEM, BUT THEY ARE USED TO ROVING, FIGHTING AND PLUNDER."

THEN TILLICUM RISES: "I, TILLICUM, WIFE OF BOLTAR, MOTHER OF HATHA, SAIL WITH GUNDAR IN THE SPRING TO MY HOMELAND, TO PRINCE ARN'S BIRTHPLACE. WE DO NOT WANT MEN OF VIOLENCE SEEKING PLUNDER, BUT THOSE WHO WILL TRADE IN FAIRNESS FOR RICH FURS, ORNAMENTS OF GOLD AND COPPER."

"LOOK, HATHA, YOUR MOTHER'S WORDS ARE HAVING EFFECT, NOT AMONG THE OLDER MEN WHO STICK TO OLD WAYS, BUT TO THE ADVENTUROUS YOUTHS!"

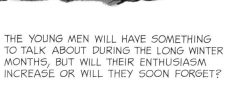

THE YOUNG MEN WILL HAVE SOMETHING TO TALK ABOUT DURING THE LONG WINTER MONTHS, BUT WILL THEIR ENTHUSIASM INCREASE OR WILL THEY SOON FORGET?

1460   1-31-65

THE RESTLESS SEA GIVES WARNING OF WINTER GALES TO COME, BUT PRINCE ARN HAS AN IDEA AND SETS SAIL IN A FRAIL BOAT FOR VIKINGSHOLM.

NEXT WEEK— The Petition

Our Story: THE AMBITIOUS VOYAGE PRINCE ARN HAS SET HIS HEART ON FACES FAILURE, FOR THE VIKING SEAFARERS ARE ONLY INTERESTED IN RAIDING AND PLUNDER. IN A SMALL SKIFF ARN SETS OUT FOR VIKINGSHOLM WITH A FAIR WIND.

WHEN HE TURNS INTO THE FJORD THE WIND IS AGAINST HIM, SO HE TAKES TO THE OARS. ALL THROUGH THE NIGHT HE ROWS. THE WIND GOES DOWN BUT THE BLISTERS GROW.

IT IS MID-MORNING WHEN HE REACHES VIKINGSHOLM. KING AGUAR IS HOLDING COURT, AND ARN REQUESTS THE CHAMBER-LAIN TO ANNOUNCE HIM.

THE KING IS SURPRISED THAT HIS OWN GRANDSON APPEARS AS A PETITIONER. "WHAT CAN WE DO FOR YOU, PRINCE ARN?"
"IS IT NOT TRUE," ARN ASKS, "THAT YEARS AGO YOU OFFERED A REWARD TO ANY OF YOUR SUBJECTS WHO DISCOVERED NEW LANDS AND OPENED NEW TRADE ROUTES?"

"YES, SUCH IS THE LAW. THE TITLE OF EARL AND WIDE LANDS GO TO THE LEADER, AND EACH MEMBER OF THE CREW RECEIVES A FARM AND A FULL PURSE. BUT WHY DO YOU COME AS A PETITIONER WHEN YOU KNOW YOUR FAMILY WILL GIVE ALL THE HELP YOU NEED?"

"BECAUSE THIS IS MY ADVENTURE, SIRE," ARN REPLIES PROUDLY, "AND I ASK NO FAVORS, ONLY WHAT IS RIGHTFULLY MINE."

1461   2-7

ANOTHER OBSTACLE HAS BEEN CLEARED FROM THE HIGH ROAD TO ADVENTURE, BUT AT A PRICE: HE MUST LEAVE BEHIND ALL THE LOVE AND TENDERNESS HE HAS TAKEN FOR GRANTED THROUGH THE YEARS.

WITH THE DAWN ARN IS ON HIS WAY, AND THE WIND HOLDS FAIR FOR THE RUN DOWN THE TRONDHEIMFJORD.

NEXT WEEK—The Wreck

Our Story: THE WIND IS BRISK AND PRINCE ARN'S LITTLE CRAFT SAILS SWIFTLY ALONG IN THE SHELTER OF THE MANY ISLANDS. ONLY WHEN HE ROUNDS THE HEADLAND THAT GUARDS THE ENTRANCE OF THE FJORD WHERE BOLTAR LIVES IS HE FACED WITH THE FULL FORCE OF THE OPEN SEA.

AND HERE THE SAIL RIPS. FLAPPING WILDLY, IT THREATENS TO TEAR THE BOAT APART UNTIL ARN UNSHIPS THE USELESS MAST AND HEAVES IT OVERBOARD.

BY THE TIME HE GETS THE OARS OUT, WIND AND WAVE HAVE SWEPT THE LIGHT CRAFT PERILOUSLY CLOSE TO THE ROCKS.

INCH BY INCH HE IS LOSING GROUND. TO KEEP UP THE STRUGGLE ANY LONGER WILL LEAVE HIM TOO EXHAUSTED TO SAVE HIMSELF. DELIBERATELY HE RIDES THE NEXT BREAKER TOWARD THE MENACING ROCKS.

THE WAVE EXPLODES AGAINST THE ROCKS IN A WELTER OF FOAM, AND WHEN IT RECEDES THE SHATTERED SKIFF HANGS FOR A MOMENT ON A LEDGE.

ARN CLIMBS OUT OF REACH OF THE CLUTCHING BREAKERS AND LOOKS BACK. AS HE WATCHES THE POWER OF THE SEA TEAR HIS BOAT TO SPLINTERS, HE IS TREMBLING. HE HAS BEEN TOO BUSY TO FEEL FEAR UNTIL NOW.

HE FINDS A SHELTERED SPOT AND, WHILE HIS BODY IS STILL WARM FROM HIS EXERTIONS, WRINGS THE WATER FROM HIS CLOTHES.

NIGHT IS NEAR AND THERE IS A CHILL IN THE WIND THAT PROMISES FROST. HE SETS OUT TO FIND SHELTER, FIRE AND FOOD.

NEXT WEEK— Recruits

2-14-65   1462

Prince Valiant
IN THE DAYS OF KING ARTHUR
WRITTEN AND ILLUSTRATED BY Harold R Foster

Our Story: PRINCE ARN HAS SURVIVED SHIPWRECK AND THE ANGER OF THE SEA, BUT IS DOUBTFUL IF HE CAN SURVIVE THE CHILL NIGHT WIND. ALREADY HIS DAMP CLOTHING IS STIFF WITH ICE.

HE LIFTS HIS HEAD AND TAKES A DEEP BREATH; YES, FAINT BUT UNMISTAKABLE, THE SMELL OF WOOD SMOKE.

FOLLOWING UPWIND HE CAN NOW SMELL CATTLE. THEN A DOG BARKS AND ARN SHOUTS A GREETING. A DOOR OPENS AND FLOODS THE DARKNESS WITH LIGHT.

IT IS UNSAFE TO APPROACH A VIKING HOUSE AT NIGHT, SO ARN STANDS OUTSIDE AND GIVES HIS NAME AND HIS REASON FOR BEING THERE. HE IS BIDDEN TO ENTER BY A DOORWAY SO CONSTRUCTED THAT A VISITOR, FOR THE MOMENT, IS HELPLESS.

ARN TELLS THEM OF HIS ADVENTURE AND HOW HE SAVED HIMSELF, AND THE VIKINGS NOD THEIR HEADS KNOWINGLY; THIS LAD IS ONE OF THE 'LUCKY ONES'. WHATEVER HE UNDERTAKES WILL END FAVORABLY.

THEN HE TELLS OF THE GREAT ADVENTURE HE HAS PLANNED FOR THE SPRING. "WE SAIL THE WIDE SEA WESTWARD UNTIL WE COME TO THE NEW LAND. THE KING WILL REWARD WITH A FARM AND A FULL PURSE ALL WHO RETURN."

IN THE MORNING A BOAT IS LAUNCHED AND ARN IS ROWED ACROSS THE FJORD TO BOLTAR'S STRONGHOLD. AND THE YOUNG CARLS ASK HIM MANY QUESTIONS ABOUT HIS PROPOSED VOYAGE AND THE REWARDS. ARN IS HOPEFUL. PERHAPS HE CAN GET A CREW AFTER ALL.

NEXT WEEK— The Salesman

© King Features Syndicate, Inc., 1965. World rights reserved.

1463   2-21   HAL FOSTER

Prince Valiant
IN THE DAYS OF KING ARTHUR

WRITTEN AND ILLUSTRATED BY HAROLD R FOSTER

Our Story: PRINCE ARN RETURNS TO BOLTAR'S STRONGHOLD AND THE BOATMEN TELL OF HIS MIRACULOUS ESCAPE FROM THE HUNGRY SEA. THEY HAIL HIM AS ONE OF THE 'LUCKY ONES' WHOSE UNDERTAKINGS WILL PROSPER.

HE TELLS OF THE SUCCESS OF HIS MISSION; "KING AGUAR HAS REAFFIRMED HIS PROMISE OF A FARM AND A FULL PURSE TO ALL WHO DISCOVER NEW LANDS OR NEW TRADE ROUTES FOR THULE." THIS SOUNDS GOOD TO SOME OF THE YOUNG MEN FROM THE BOAT AND THEY ASK TO JOIN THE ADVENTURE PLANNED FOR THE SPRING.

WHEN DARKNESS FALLS THE SKALD OFTTIMES TAKES HIS HARP AND SINGS A HERO-POEM, AND A GREAT FAVORITE WITH THE VIKINGS IS THE SAGA OF PRINCE VALIANT AND HOW HE SAILED TO THE WORLD'S EDGE TO RESCUE THE FAIR ALETA FROM ULFRUN, THE SEAHAWK.

"IT IS A TRULY GREAT POEM YOU HAVE COMPOSED, NOBLE SKALD, BUT IT LACKS A LAST VERSE: THE PROMISE THE LADY ALETA MADE THAT HER FIRST-BORN WOULD RETURN TO THAT FAR LAND. I, PRINCE ARN, AM THAT FIRST-BORN AND, WITH THE SPRING, I WILL RETURN TO FULFILL THAT VOW."

THE SKALD BECOMES A PUBLIC-RELATIONS MAN AND SETS FORTH ON THE LONG OVERLAND JOURNEY TO VIKINGSHOLM. AND HE IS WELCOMED AT EVERY STEAD AND STRONGHOLD, FOR A SKALD HOLDS MUCH HONOR AMONG THE WINTER-BOUND VIKINGS.

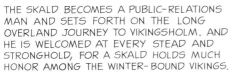

THE FAR-WANDERING VIKINGS LISTEN TO THE WILD MUSIC AND DREAM OF ADVENTURE AND STRANGE NEW LANDS TO RAID. AFTER A PAUSE THE SKALD AGAIN PLUCKS THE STRINGS AND SINGS THE LAST VERSE CALLED 'THE CHALLENGE AND THE FULFILLING'. THEN HE TELLS OF THE KING'S REWARD, OF THE GOLD AND FURS TO BE HAD BY ALL WHO DARE THE VOYAGE.

HAL FOSTER

2-28 1464

NEXT WEEK— The Workshop

Prince Valiant
IN THE DAYS OF KING ARTHUR
WRITTEN AND ILLUSTRATED BY HAROLD R FOSTER

Our Story: THROUGH THE EVER-DEEPENING SNOW THE SKALD GOES FROM ONE LONELY FARM TO ANOTHER SINGING THE OLD HERO SAGAS, BUT HE ALWAYS MANAGES TO END THE RECITAL WITH THE 'POEM OF FULFILLMENT' AND HOW PRINCE ARN, WITH THE COMING OF SPRING, WILL JOURNEY TO THE WORLD'S END BECAUSE OF HIS MOTHER'S VOW.

SOON ADVENTUROUS YOUNG VIKINGS ARE BREASTING THE DRIFTS TO COME TO BOLTAR'S STRONGHOLD AND SEEK A PLACE ON THE SHIP AND THE KING'S REWARD.

TILLICUM, WIFE OF BOLTAR, IS THE REAL MANAGER OF THE EXPEDITION. ALL THROUGH THE LONG WINTER SHE HAS TAUGHT ARN THE TONGUE OF HER DISTANT PEOPLE AND THE SIGN LANGUAGE USED AMONG THE MANY TRIBES.

THE RECRUITS ARE SET TO WORK MAKING THEIR OWN TRADE GOODS, AXES, FISHHOOKS, KNIVES AND SPEAR HEADS, FOR SHE KNOWS THE NEEDS OF HER PEOPLE.

AND SHE KEEPS THE WOMEN AT THE LOOMS AND DYEING VATS LONG HOURS MAKING THE BRIGHT COLORS AND DESIGNS THAT WILL DELIGHT SAVAGE EYES..

3-7-65

THE SPRING EQUINOX COMES AND GOES, BUT STILL BOLTAR'S STRONGHOLD STANDS MANTLED AND SILENT AS IF WINTER WILL NEVER END.

#1465

THEN ONE MORNING ARN THROWS BACK THE SHUTTERS AND HEARS WATER DRIPPING FROM THE EAVES, AND DOWN BY THE SHORE MEN ARE TAKING THE WINTER COVER FROM GUNDAR HARL'S SAILING SHIP!

NEXT WEEK—The Great Day

Prince Valiant

IN THE DAYS OF KING ARTHUR

WRITTEN AND ILLUSTRATED BY HAROLD R FOSTER

Our Story: AT LAST THE DAY ARRIVES WHEN GUNDAR HARL'S SAILING VESSEL IS MADE STAUNCH AND TIGHT, AND FROM MILES AROUND MEN COME TO HELP IN THE LAUNCHING.

THE GREAT MOUNTAIN OF SUPPLIES AND TRADE GOODS IS CAREFULLY STORED, WATER CASKS FILLED, FOR SHOULD THEY MEET UNFAVORABLE WINDS THEY MIGHT SPEND MONTHS AT SEA.

ON THE EVE OF DEPARTURE PRINCE VALIANT AND ALETA ARRIVE TO BID GODSPEED TO THEIR SON. FOR YEARS ALETA HAS SMILED AS VAL WENT GAILY OFF INTO DANGER, NOW SHE MUST PUT ON A BRAVE FRONT AS HER YOUNG EAGLE TAKES WING.

BOLTAR HOLDS A FAREWELL BANQUET AND HIS GREAT HALL IS FILLED WITH YOUNG VIKINGS EAGER TO ENLIST ON THE ADVENTURE. PRINCE ARN SPEAKS: "OUR COMPANIONS HAVE BEEN CHOSEN, BUT IF THERE ARE ANY AMONG YOU WHOSE COURAGE GROWS FAINT AT THE THOUGHT OF UNKNOWN SHORES AND LONG MONTHS AT SEA, SPEAK NOW WHILE OTHERS ARE EAGER TO TAKE YOUR PLACE."

DRAGONSHIPS ESCORT THE SAILING VESSEL OUT TO SEA. FOR IT IS SPRING AND THE SEA RAIDERS ARE OUT, MOVING SOUTHWARD FOR A SUMMER OF ADVENTURE AND PROFIT, RECOGNIZING NO LAW BUT THEIR OWN.

ALL THE LONG WINTER THERE HAS BEEN TALK OF PRINCE ARN'S VOYAGE AND THE GREAT STORE OF TRADE GOODS IN HIS SHIP'S HOLD. SVERE HODER HAS DECIDED TO MAKE A TRY FOR HER.

WHEN THE ESCORT SHIPS TURN BACK SVERE STARTS IN PURSUIT. HE DOES NOT KNOW THAT, UNLIKE AN OARED VESSEL, A SAILING SHIP NEED NOT STOP FOR THE NIGHT.

3-14   #1466

HAL FOSTER

BUT CHANCE FAVORS HIM. WITH THE DAWN THE WIND DIES AND THE GREAT SAILS OF GUNDAR HARL'S VESSEL FLAP IDLY. AS THEIR PRIZE COMES IN SIGHT SVERE'S WEARY OARSMEN TAKE HEART.

NEXT WEEK— **Liquid Fire**

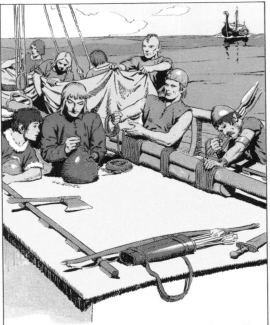

Our Story: THE DRAGONSHIP COMES FOAMING OVER THE GLASSY SEA, THE FIERCE SHOUTS OF THE RAIDERS GROWING LOUDER AS THEY WORK THEMSELVES INTO A BATTLE FRENZY. PRINCE ARN IS SURPRISED AT THE PREPARATIONS GUNDAR MAKES TO MEET THE ATTACK.

TWO SPARS ARE BOUND TOGETHER TO MAKE ONE LONG ONE. THEN GUNDAR BRINGS OUT HIS SECRET WEAPON, A LEATHERN FLASK, FROM WHICH HE REMOVES THE STOPPER AND INSERTS A LIGHTED WICK.

A FRIGHTENING MOMENT: THE SAILING SHIP ROCKS ON THE OILY SWELLS, ITS SAILS FLAPPING IDLY AS THE ENEMY DRAWS EVER CLOSER, WEAPONS CLASHING ON SHIELDS.

"IS THAT LITTLE FLASK AND THE ARCHERS OUR ONLY DEFENSE?" ASKS ARN.
"I BROUGHT THAT FLASK BACK FROM MY LAST VOYAGE TO THE INLAND SEA," ANSWERS GUNDAR. "IT IS CALLED GREEK FIRE. WATCH IT!"

THE LONG SPAR DROPS ON THE PIRATES' DECK, HOLDING THE TWO VESSELS APART, WHILE FROM THE FLASK BRIGHT RIVULETS OF FLAME RUN ACROSS THE DECK.

WATER WILL NOT QUENCH THE FIRE, FOR THE OIL FLOATS ON THE SURFACE AND HOT FLAMES FOLLOW WHEREVER THE WATER RUNS. PROTECTED BY THE HIGH BULWARK OF THE SAILING SHIP THE ARCHERS ADD TO THE GROWING PANIC.

THE FLAMES BURN OUT AND THE DRAGONSHIP FREES ITSELF. "HAVE YOU ANY MORE GREEK FIRE?" ASKS ARN.
"NO," ANSWERS GUNDAR, "THIS IS ONLY WATER, BUT ITS PRESENCE WILL DISCOURAGE FURTHER ATTACK."

NEXT WEEK—Escape

3-21   #1467

Prince Valiant
IN THE DAYS OF KING ARTHUR
WRITTEN AND ILLUSTRATED BY Harold R Foster

Our Story: THE TWO SHIPS STAND APART, SVERE HODER TRYING TO REPAIR THE DAMAGE HIS DRAGONSHIP HAS SUFFERED FROM THE GREEK FIRE, AND THE SAILING VESSEL ROCKING SLOWLY ON A WINDLESS SEA.
THEN THE MOON RISES BEHIND TATTERED, SWIFT-MOVING CLOUDS. "HOIST THE SAILS," COMMANDS GUNDAR, "FOR SOON THERE WILL BE WIND ENOUGH."

A FITFUL BREEZE FILLS THE SAILS AND SOON THE PIRATES ARE LOST IN THE DARK. BY DAWN THE WIND HAS SETTLED INTO A NORTHWEST GALE.

DAYS PASS BEFORE THE GALE BLOWS ITSELF OUT. BY THIS TIME THEY ARE SO FAR TO THE SOUTH THAT GUNDAR SAILS FOR THE SHETLAND ISLANDS. "IT WAS FROM HERE THAT YOUR FATHER, PRINCE VALIANT, AND I BEGAN OUR JOURNEY ACROSS THE UNKNOWN SEA," SAYS GUNDAR TO ARN. "SO I KNOW THE ROUTE."

HEADWINDS DELAY THEM ON THE NEXT LEG OF THEIR JOURNEY AND IT HAS BEEN A MONTH SINCE THEY LEFT THEIR HOME PORT. WHEN THE FAEROE ISLANDS COME IN SIGHT FUEL FOR THEIR COOKING FIRES HAS BEEN EXHAUSTED, AS THERE WERE NO TREES ON THE SHETLANDS.

WHILE THE WATER CASKS ARE BEING FILLED A SCOUT REPORTS: "THERE ARE NO TREES ON THESE INFERNAL ISLANDS."

#1468

BUT ANOTHER SAILOR COMBING THE BEACH HAS A BETTER REPORT: A STRANDED WHALE RIPENING IN THE SUN AND THE BLEACHED TIMBERS OF A STORM-BATTERED LONGSHIP.
"BRING THE RENDERING POT," ORDERS GUNDAR. "IF WE LACK WOOD WE CAN AT LEAST BURN WHALE OIL."

NEXT WEEK— Ripe Harvest

HAL FOSTER

3-28

Our Story: THE YOUNG NORSEMEN STRIP THE BLUBBER FROM THE STRANDED WHALE. THEY WORK RAPIDLY TO GET THE JOB DONE, FOR THE CARCASS HAS LAIN TOO LONG IN THE SUN AND BECOME OVER-RIPE.

THE BLEACHED TIMBERS OF THE ANCIENT WRECK ARE SALVAGED, FOR NO ONE KNOWS HOW LONG IT WILL BE BEFORE THEIR SUPPLY OF FUEL FOR THE COOKING FIRES CAN BE REPLACED.

A FEW CHIPS OF WOOD IN A PAN OF OIL PROVIDE A HOT FIRE AND ALSO A CLOUD OF BLACK SMOKE THAT COVERS THE GALLEY WITH OILY SOOT. EVEN THE FOOD TASTES OF IT.

"OUR NEXT LANDFALL IS UNCERTAIN," SAYS GUNDAR, "FOR WHEN PRINCE VALIANT AND I SAILED THIS WAY WE WERE CHASING ULFRUN AND CHANGED OUR COURSE OFTEN. WE HAVE TO GUESS AT OUR DIRECTIONS."

THE WIND BLOWS FAIR AND THE GREAT SQUARE SAIL IS SET AND, FOR THE SPACE OF A WEEK, THE SHIP RUNS SWIFTLY BEFORE THE WIND.

ALL DAY A MYSTERIOUS WHITE CLOUD HAS HUNG MOTIONLESS IN THE SKY, GROWING LARGER HOUR AFTER HOUR AS THEY APPROACH. AT LAST GUNDAR EXCLAIMS: "IT IS A GLACIER-TOPPED MOUNTAIN! I RECOGNIZE IT AS OUR LANDFALL." THE SHIP IS APPROACHING ICELAND.

NEXT WEEK— *The Wonders of the New Land*

#1469   4-4

Prince Valiant
IN THE DAYS OF KING ARTHUR
WRITTEN AND ILLUSTRATED BY Harold R Foster

Our Story: ON THAT WILD CHASE TO RESCUE QUEEN ALETA PRINCE VALIANT AND GUNDAR PASSED THIS LAND FOURTEEN YEARS AGO BUT DID NOT LAND. THE SHIP MOVES SLOWLY UP THE COAST SEARCHING FOR A SAFE HARBOR. FROM THE MOUNTAINS GLACIERS RUN DOWN TO THE SHALLOW SEA.

AT LAST AN ANCHORAGE IS FOUND IN A RIVER'S MOUTH. THE DRAGON FIGUREHEAD IS SET UP IN THE PROW TO INSTILL FEAR IN THE NATIVES, SHOULD THERE BE ANY.

PRINCE ARN AND HATHA SET OUT TO EXPLORE THE NEW LAND, TAKING TWO WARRIORS ALONG IN CASE THEY MEET WITH DANGER. LUSH MEADOWS COVER THE COASTAL PLAIN.....

.....BUT FARTHER INLAND IS A WEIRD AND FRIGHTENING LAND. LAKES OF HOT MUD BOIL AND BUBBLE, FUMAROLES BELCH FORTH EVIL-SMELLING GASES, HISSING GEYSERS THROW BOILING WATER ALOFT.

TO ARN THIS IS A NATURAL WONDERLAND, EACH DAY BRINGING NEW SURPRISES... GLACIERS, LAVA FLOWS, STEAM VENTS, SALMON RIVERS, BUT NO TREES.

#1470

BUT TO THE TWO GUARDS IT IS THE END OF THE WORLD, A PLACE WHERE TROLLS AND DEMONS SHAKE THE EARTH AND BREATHE STEAM HORRIBLY.

4-11

HAL FOSTER

ON THEIR RETURN ARN AND HATHA REPORT THEIR FINDINGS TO GUNDAR AND TILLICUM. BUT THE TWO GUARDS TELL THE CREW OF THE AWFUL THINGS THEY HAVE SEEN, AND THE TALE LOSES NONE OF ITS TERRORS IN THE TELLING.
NEXT WEEK: Enter: Fear.

Our Story: PRINCE ARN AND HATHA MAKE A REPORT ON THEIR EXPLORATIONS. "*THERE IS PLENTY OF SALMON IN THE RIVERS, AND THE LAKES ARE ALIVE WITH WATERFOWL, BUT EXCEPT FOR WILLOW BUSHES AND SOME STUNTED BIRCH TREES THERE IS NO WOOD FOR OUR COOKING FIRES.*"

THE TWO WARRIORS WHO ACCOMPANIED THEM DO NOT WANT TO APPEAR TIMID, SO THEY GREATLY EXAGGERATE THE TERRORS THEY SAW.

SEALS ARE PLENTIFUL, SO GUNDAR SENDS OUT THE HUNTERS AND SETS UP A RENDERING KETTLE. IF WOOD IS SCARCE, THEY WILL HAVE TO BURN SEAL OIL IN THE GALLEY.

VOLCANIC LANDS ARE SUBJECT TO EARTH TREMORS. NOW SUCH A QUAKE DEMOLISHES THE TALL CAIRN GUNDAR HAD RAISED CLAIMING THIS LAND FOR THE KING OF THULE. THE STORIES THE MEN HAVE HEARD TURN FEAR INTO PANIC.

BRAVE YOUNG WARRIORS WHO WOULD GO INTO BATTLE LAUGHING FEAR ONLY THE UNKNOWN AND RUSH FOR THE BOAT. TILLICUM MEETS THEM: "*IT WILL MAKE POOR TELLING AROUND THE HOME FIRE ON WINTER NIGHTS THAT BRAVE WARRIORS LEFT IN FRIGHT, LEAVING ALL THEIR GEAR BEHIND WHILE AS YET NONE HAD RECEIVED A HURT.*"

SHAMEFACED, THEY RETRIEVE THE CAULDRON, THE NETS AND TOOLS, AND ROW OUT TO THE SHIP.

#1471

ALL IS STOWED AND READY AS THEY AWAIT THE FULL TIDE. TILLICUM'S BLACK EYES SEARCH EACH FACE: "*YOU VOLUNTEERED FOR THIS VOYAGE INTO THE UNKNOWN BUT FALTERED WHEN FACED WITH THE UNKNOWN. A CRIPPLED SEA-CAPTAIN, TWO BOYS AND A WOMAN WILL SEE THIS ADVENTURE THROUGH. CAN YOU DO LESS?*"

NEXT WEEK— The Bad Apples

4-18

Our Story: THE SHIP IS TOWED FROM ITS ANCHORAGE AND, WHEN BEYOND THE HEADLAND, SAILS ARE HOISTED AND THE MOST PERILOUS LEG OF THE VOYAGE BEGINS.

GUNDAR STUDIES THE NOTES TAKEN ON THE FORMER JOURNEY. IT WILL BE AT LEAST A MONTH BEFORE THEY COME TO A LAND WHERE THERE IS FOOD, FUEL AND WATER.

ARN AND HATHA WATCH ICELAND RECEDING INTO THE DISTANCE. THEY ARE STILL EXCITED ABOUT THE WONDERS THEY SAW ON THEIR EXPLORATIONS.

BUT OLIN AND KARL, THE TWO WARRIORS WHO ACCOMPANIED THEM, TAKE A DIFFERENT VIEW. HISSING HOT SPRINGS, ROARING GEYSERS THROWING BOILING WATER HIGH IN THE AIR, LAKES OF BUBBLING MUD AND SUCH WONDERS CAN ONLY BE THE WORK OF TROLLS AND DEMONS.

FEAR IS CONTAGIOUS AND SOON THE WHOLE CREW IS INFECTED BY THE EXAGGERATED TALES. WHEN THE BLACKNESS OF NIGHT IS FILLED WITH A STRANGE, ROARING, GRINDING NOISE, PANIC IS NEAR.

DAWN REVEALS THE CAUSE. BORN ON A STRONG CURRENT A RIVER OF ICE IS CHURNING SOUTHWARD, BARRING THEIR SHIP FROM LANDING ON THE SHORES OF A LAND OF TOWERING, ICE-CAPPED MOUNTAINS AND GLITTERING GLACIERS. GREENLAND, BUT THEY CALL IT GLACIERLAND.

4-25

© King Features Syndicate, Inc., 1965. World rights reserved.

"WE MUST FIND A LANDING. THERE IS NOT ENOUGH WATER IN OUR CASKS TO CARRY US TO THE NEXT LANDFALL," SAYS GUNDAR SERIOUSLY, "AND OUR CREW IS IN NO MOOD TO FACE AN ADDED HARDSHIP."

NEXT WEEK— *A Leader Arises*

#1472

Prince Valiant

IN THE DAYS OF KING ARTHUR

WRITTEN AND ILLUSTRATED BY HAROLD R. FOSTER

Our Story: DAYS PASS AND STILL THE GRINDING ICE PACK DENIES THEM PASSAGE TO THE MOUNTAINOUS SHORE.
THEN A WARM CURRENT COMES IN FROM THE EAST AND WITH IT THE GREAT GRAY FOG, BLOTTING OUT THE DISTANT LAND.

ON SO SMALL A VESSEL NOTHING IS HIDDEN, AND THE SULLEN CREW ARE WELL AWARE THAT THEIR WATER SUPPLY IS DANGEROUSLY LOW.

WHEN THE FOG LIFTS, GREENLAND IS NO LONGER IN SIGHT, THE PACK ICE HAS VANISHED, AND IN ITS STEAD HUGE ICEBERGS DRIFT IN THE CURRENT.
"THE ICE PACK IS FROZEN SEA WATER, BUT THE BERGS ARE FROM GLACIERS," SAYS ARN, *"AND GLACIERS ARE COMPOSED OF ICE FROM SNOW WATER, THEREFORE FRESH."*

"LAUNCH THE BOATS," ARN COMMANDS. THOUGH LEADER OF THIS VOYAGE, HE HAS, UNTIL NOW, ALLOWED GUNDAR TO GIVE THE ORDERS. THE RINGLEADERS, OLIN AND KARL, WHISPER TO THE MUTINOUS CREW AND THEY HESITATE.

THE REFUSAL TO OBEY HIS FIRST ORDER BRINGS A SUBTLE CHANGE IN THE YOUNG LAD. HE IS DESCENDED FROM KINGS AND QUEENS, GREAT LEADERS AND WARRIORS, AND ARN HAS INHERITED SOMETHING OF EACH. AT THIS MOMENT HE TAKES COMMAND.

"OLIN! KARL! UNLASH THE BOAT!" THOUGH HE SPEAKS QUIETLY THERE IS CONFIDENCE IN HIS VOICE AND HE IS OBEYED, AND AT THAT MOMENT BOYHOOD VANISHES. ARN HAS BECOME A YOUNG MAN.

5-2

HAL FOSTER

A MOUNTAIN OF FRESH WATER, BUT HOW TO GET IT? WAVES POUND ITS BASE AND FALLING ICE THUNDERS DOWN ITS SIDES.

NEXT WEEK— **Cold Comfort**

#1473

Prince Valiant
IN THE DAYS OF KING ARTHUR
WRITTEN AND ILLUSTRATED BY HAROLD R FOSTER

Our Story: GETTING FRESH WATER FROM AN ICEBERG IS NO EASY MATTER. WAVES THUNDER AGAINST ITS BASE AND FALLING ICE CRASHES DOWN ITS SIDES. ARN BREAKS UP THESE SMALLER PIECES WITH A SPEAR, AND HIS MEN, HANDS NUMB WITH COLD, FUMBLE THE SLIPPERY PIECES INTO THE BOAT.

IT IS NOON BEFORE THE TOSSING BOAT IS FILLED AND ROWED BACK TO THE SHIP. AT THIS RATE IT WILL TAKE A WEEK TO FILL THE CASKS, AND IT IS NOT LIKELY THE GOOD WEATHER WILL HOLD THAT LONG.

ARN TAKES THE LARGEST SEINE NET, SURROUNDS A LARGE PIECE OF THE BERG, AND TAKES THE LINES BACK TO THE SHIP SO ALL HANDS CAN BRING IT ALONGSIDE.

THE WHOLE CREW SET TO WORK, TOO BUSY NOW TO THINK OF MUTINY, AND SOON THE DECK IS FILLED WITH GLITTERING ICE.

© King Features Syndicate, Inc., 1965. World rights reserved.

THE NEXT DAY IS STILL BRIGHT AND ARN BRINGS UP FROM THE SAIL LOCKER A NEW SAIL AS YET UNTAINTED BY SEA WATER. A VIKING CREW SPEND THE DAY MAKING ICE CUBES, BUT THEY ARE REWARDED AS A WARM SUN ON A WHITE SAIL FILLS THE WATER CASKS.

THE PROUD VIKINGS WHO WERE NEAR MUTINY WHEN GIVEN ORDERS BY A BOY NOW RECOGNIZE ARN AS A LEADER BORN, AND REMEMBER HE IS ONE OF THE 'LUCKY ONES.' HATHA HAS LOST A PLAYMATE BUT GAINED A LEADER. GUNDAR REMARKS: "I HAVE BEEN WAITING FOR THIS," AND TILLICUM, WHO HAD BEEN HIS FAITHFUL NURSE, SAYS NOTHING, BUT PRIDE SHINES IN HER DARK EYES.

OLIN AND KARL, WHO HAD FOMENTED THE DISCONTENT, NOW CHANGE THEIR TUNE. THEY STILL TELL OF THE TERRORS OF GEYSERS AND HOT SPRINGS, BUT ADD THAT ARN WALKED CALMLY AMONG THESE DANGERS UNAFRAID.

#1474   NEXT WEEK — The Familiar Coast   5-9

Prince Valiant
IN THE DAYS OF KING ARTHUR

WRITTEN AND ILLUSTRATED BY HAROLD R FOSTER

Our Story: THE WIND BLOWS STEADILY FROM THE NORTHWEST WITH RAIN SQUALLS AND FOG. IT IS HOPED NO ICEBERG WILL DRIFT UNSEEN INTO THEIR COURSE.

THEN ONE DAY THE LOOKOUT GIVES A GLAD CRY AND POINTS TO A TANGLE OF DRIFTWOOD. LAND CANNOT BE FAR AWAY.

WHEN AT LAST LAND IS SIGHTED GUNDAR SHAKES HIS HEAD. THIS COAST IS NOT AS HE REMEMBERED IT.

ARN GOES ASHORE AND SEES A VAST TUNDRA, MUSKEG AND STUNTED TREES.

GUNDAR RECOGNIZES THIS AS A FAR NORTHERN COUNTRY. "*THE COAST SEEMS TO BEND AWAY TO THE SOUTH,*" HE SAYS. "*WE MUST FOLLOW IT UNTIL WE REACH A WARMER CLIMATE.*"

AFTER SEVERAL DAYS OF SAILING ALONG THE DESOLATE LABRADOR COAST GUNDAR EXCLAIMS: "*THERE IS THE STRAIT (BELLE ISLE) THROUGH WHICH WE PASSED FOURTEEN YEARS AGO!*"

5-16

FOR SEVERAL DAYS THE VIKINGS CAMP ON THE SHORE OF NEWFOUNDLAND, HUNTING, FISHING AND GATHERING A SUPPLY OF FIREWOOD. DURING THE PAST MONTH ALL COOKING HAD BEEN DONE OVER A FIRE OF RANCID WHALE OIL UNTIL THE WHOLE SHIP REEKED. THEY MAKE THEIR STAY ONE LONG BANQUET.

NEXT WEEK— **Indian Signs**

#1475

Prince Valiant

IN THE DAYS OF KING ARTHUR

WRITTEN AND ILLUSTRATED BY HAROLD R. FOSTER

Our Story: THE UNCHARTED SEA HAS BEEN CROSSED WITHOUT ENCOUNTERING ANY REAL DANGER, BUT DURING THE LONG JOURNEY UNCERTAINTY HAD BRED FEAR AND FEAR HAD BROUGHT THE CREW CLOSE TO MUTINY. NOW THAT LAND HAS BEEN REACHED AND THEIR COURSE KNOWN THE TENSION IS LIFTED.

THERE IS PLENTY OF FRESH WATER, THE SEA YIELDS ITS FISH, AND HUNTING PARTIES RETURN WITH VENISON. ALL THOUGHTS OF MUTINY ARE IN THE PAST AND BEST FORGOTTEN.

UNTIL NOW THEY HAVE SEEN NO SIGN OF NATIVES, BUT A HUNTING PARTY COMES ACROSS A CAMPING PLACE THAT HAS BEEN BUT LATELY VACATED, FOR THE ASHES OF THEIR FIRE ARE STILL WARM. THEY TELL OF THEIR FIND TO TILLICUM.

"THIS BIT OF POTTERY INDICATES THEY CAME FROM UPRIVER, FOR THE NORTHERN TRIBES DO NOT MAKE POTTERY. IT WAS NOT A WAR PARTY, FOR THERE WERE LODGE POLES FOR ONLY THREE SHELTERS. THE FIREPLACE WAS STILL WARM SO THEY WERE HERE WHEN WE CAME TO ANCHOR. EVEN NOW THEY ARE WATCHING US."

IT IS EVEN AS SHE SAID, AND AS THE INDIANS GAZE IN AWE AT THE HUGE WINGED CANOE THE FEARSOME DRAGON FIGUREHEAD COMES DOWN. DOES THIS MEAN THE STRANGERS COME IN PEACE?

TILLICUM BRINGS OUT THE COSTUME SHE HAS MADE TO IMPRESS THE INDIANS. "PRINCE ARN, THIS IS YOUR FIRST TEST. REMEMBER, YOU ARE THE SON OF 'THE SUN-WOMAN, BRINGER-OF-HARVESTS', COME TO FULFILL HER PROMISE. IF THIS TRIBE DOES NOT KNOW THE TONGUE I TAUGHT YOU, USE THE SIGN LANGUAGE. THE REST IS UP TO YOU."

NEXT WEEK— The Meeting

1476

5-23

Prince Valiant
IN THE DAYS OF KING ARTHUR
WRITTEN AND ILLUSTRATED BY Harold R Foster

Our Story: PRINCE ARN IS ROWED ASHORE TO MAKE HIS FIRST CONTACT WITH THE NATIVES. HE GOES UNARMED IN THE SMALL BOAT, WEARING A COSTUME TILLICUM HAS DESIGNED TO IMPRESS HER PEOPLE.

BUT ON THE SEAWARD SIDE OF THE SHIP THE BIGGER BOAT IS FILLED WITH ARMED AND READY YOUNG VIKINGS IN CASE OF TROUBLE.

FROM THE FOREST KEEN EYES WATCH THE APPROACH AND NOTE EVERY ASTONISHING DETAIL.

THE INDIANS GAZE IN AWE AT THE COMMANDING FIGURE IN THE BOW. IN ALL THEIR LANDS THEY CANNOT MATCH SUCH COLORS AS HE WEARS. EVEN THOUGH HE COMES UNARMED AND MAKES THE SIGN OF PEACE, THEY HESITATE. SUCH WONDERS THEY HAVE NOT HEARD OF EVEN FROM THEIR STORYTELLERS.

ARN STEPS ASHORE AND ADDRESSES THE INDIANS, BUT THEY DO NOT UNDERSTAND UNTIL ONE OLDSTER STEPS FORWARD AS INTERPRETER. WHEN THEY HEAR ARN'S STORY THEY NOD THEIR HEADS. YES, THEY HAVE HEARD THE LEGEND OF THE SUN-WOMAN AND THE PROMISE SHE MADE.

SIGNS OF FRIENDSHIP ARE MADE, GIFTS EXCHANGED, AND ARN RETURNS TO THE SHIP.

5-30

FOR A LONG TIME TILLICUM STANDS IN THE PROW, MOTIONLESS. WHEN SHE COMES DOWN SHE IS SMILING. *"THE TRIBES ALONG OUR WAY WILL RECEIVE US IN PEACE,"* SHE ANNOUNCES.

#1477

FOR SHE HAS SEEN A RUNNER LEAVE THE INDIAN CAMP CARRYING THE MESSENGER'S STAFF TO INSURE HIM SAFE PASSAGE.

NEXT WEEK—*The Gathering of the Tribes*

Prince Valiant
IN THE DAYS OF KING ARTHUR
WRITTEN AND ILLUSTRATED BY HAROLD R FOSTER

Our Story: AS THEY CRUISE DOWN THE COAST GUNDAR HARL TASTES THE WATER EACH DAY. FINALLY HE EXCLAIMS: "THE WATER IS FRESH. WE ARE ENTERING THE RIVER MOUTH."

SOON BOTH BANKS ARE VISIBLE AT THE SAME TIME AND THE CURRENT SLOWS THEIR PROGRESS.

TILLICUM IS WORRIED. "WE HAVE PASSED THE HUNTING GROUNDS OF MANY TRIBES BUT HAVE BEEN GREETED BY NONE. THIS CAN BUT MEAN THEY ARE GATHERING UPSTREAM FOR A MEETING. WE MUST PASS ANOTHER TEST."

THE DECKHOUSE IS REMOVED AND THE TRADE GOODS STORED THERE ARE STOWED IN THE SPACE BELOW ONCE FILLED WITH FOODSTUFFS. OARPORTS ARE UNCOVERED AND THE SWEEPS PUT IN PLACE, FOR BOTH SAIL AND OAR MUST CONTEND WITH THE CURRENT.

ON A ROCKY POINT THE INDIANS ARE ASSEMBLED TO MEET THEM. "WHAT DO YOU SEE, TILLICUM?" ASKS ARN. "CHIEFTAINS, MEDICINE MEN, COUNCIL ELDERS, BUT NO WOMEN OR CHILDREN. WE WILL MEET WITH THEM ASHORE WITH A GUARD OF FULLY-ARMED VIKINGS."

"WEAR THIS SHIRT OF MAIL UNDER YOUR TUNIC, ARN, BUT NO HELMET. YOUR HAIR IS YOUR BEST PROTECTION."

ARN STEPS ASHORE, HIS RED HAIR FLAMING IN THE SUNLIGHT, THE POLISHED ARMS OF HIS BODYGUARD GLEAMING.

A WHITE-HAIRED OLD MEDICINE MAN EXCLAIMS: "FOURTEEN SUMMERS AGO I BEHELD THE 'SUN WOMAN, BRINGER-OF-HARVESTS'. THIS TRULY IS HER MAN-CHILD!"

NEXT WEEK— Treachery!

1478   6-6

Prince Valiant
IN THE DAYS OF KING ARTHUR
WRITTEN AND ILLUSTRATED BY HAROLD R FOSTER

Our Story: PRINCE ARN GOES ASHORE TO MEET THE ASSEMBLED INDIANS AND GREETS THEM WITH THE SIGN OF PEACE. THEY RETURN HIS GESTURE BUT REMAIN ON THE LEDGE ABOVE, SO THAT HE MUST TALK UP TO THEM.

IT WOULD NEVER DO FOR THE 'SUN-WOMAN'S' SON TO STAND IN AN INFERIOR POSITION FOR A PARLEY. HE MOUNTS TO THE LEDGE, WALKS THROUGH THE AMAZED NATIVES, AND TAKES A POSITION ON A HIGHER LEDGE WITH THE SUN BEHIND HIM.

"I AM 'ARN-OF-THE-NEW-DAY', SON OF THE 'SUN-WOMAN, BRINGER OF HARVESTS', COME AMONG YOU TO FULFILL MY MOTHER'S PROPHECY."

THEY GAZE AT ARN IN SILENT AMAZEMENT. NEVER HAVE THEY SEEN GARMENTS SO RICH, A SKIN SO WHITE. AND THE WAY TILLICUM HAS ARRANGED HIS HAIR MAKES IT FAIRLY GLOW IN THE SUNLIGHT.

"WE MUST KEEP THIS DAWN-BOY. WITH HIM AS A MEMBER OF OUR TRIBE WE WILL STRIKE FEAR INTO OUR ENEMIES AND RULE FROM THE ICE TO THE BIG WATERS (GREAT LAKES)."
ONE OF THE ELDERS TOUCHES HIS ARM: "THINK WELL, GREAT CHIEFTAIN. FOURTEEN WINTERS AGO MY TRIBE MADE WAR ON SUCH MIGHTY WARRIORS. THEY ARE TERRIBLE IN BATTLE AND THEIR BODIES TURN ASIDE OUR WEAPONS."

BUT THE AMBITIOUS CHIEF HAS ALREADY WHISPERED AN ORDER AND SEVERAL BRAVES APPROACH ON THE PRETEXT OF EXAMINING ARN'S RICH GARMENTS. A SUDDEN SHOVE SENDS ARN FLYING INTO THE GRIP OF THE WAITING WARRIORS BELOW.

"TAKE THE CHIEFTAIN ALIVE!" SHOUTS ARN AS HE STRUGGLES TO DRAW HIS SWORD.

NEXT WEEK— **The Hostage**

#1479   6-13

Prince Valiant
IN THE DAYS OF KING ARTHUR
WRITTEN AND ILLUSTRATED BY HAROLD R FOSTER

Our Story: TREACHERY EXPLODES QUICKLY AND PRINCE ARN FINDS HIMSELF HELD IN A SINEWY GRIP. HE TRIES TO DRAW HIS SWORD, BUT CANNOT BREAK THE HOLD ON HIS RIGHT ARM.

WITH HIS LEFT HAND HE REACHES BACK FOR HIS SAXEKNIFE. ONCE, TWICE, THRICE HE STABS VICIOUSLY, AND HIS GROANING ADVERSARY LOSES HIS GRIP, AND ARN DRAWS HIS SWORD.

THE INDIANS FIGHT BRAVELY, BUT WAR CLUB, TOMAHAWK AND FLINT-TIPPED SPEAR SHATTER ON SHIELD AND IRON HELMET AS THE VIKING GUARD MOVES FORWARD LIKE REAPERS IN A FIELD OF RIPENING CORN.

TO THIS MEETING HAD COME THE HEAD MEN, ELDERS OF THE COUNCIL AND CHIEFTAINS OF THE TRIBE, BUT AT DAY'S END THE TRIBE WILL BE WITHOUT LEADERS.
THE GREAT CHIEF IS BROUGHT BEFORE ARN. HE EXPECTS THE USUAL DEATH BY TORTURE, INSTEAD HE IS TREATED WITH CONTEMPT.
"REMOVE ALL INSIGNIA OF HIS RANK AND TAKE HIM TO THE BOAT."

SOME OF THE BATTERED SURVIVORS ARE BROUGHT IN. "I, ARN, FIRST-BORN OF THE 'SUN-WOMAN', CAME TO YOU IN PEACE BEARING GIFTS. YOUR GIFT TO ME WAS TREACHERY. NOW COUNT YOUR DEAD AND TELL YOUR NEIGHBORS OF THE PRICE YOU PAID."

MANY WONDERS DOES THE CHIEF BEHOLD AS THE WINGED CANOE RESUMES ITS COURSE. HE IS NOT BOUND, IN FACT THE HUGE BLUE-EYED WARRIORS WITH THE YELLOW HAIR IGNORE HIM COMPLETELY.

AND STRANGEST OF ALL IS THAT A WOMAN IS ALLOWED TO SIT AT THEIR COUNCIL.... AND TWO BOYS!
"OUR FORTUNES DEPEND UPON THE NEXT MEETING," TILLICUM ANNOUNCES. "RUNNERS WILL PRECEDE US UPRIVER TELLING OF OUR APPROACH."

NEXT WEEK— Council Island

1480

6-20

Our Story: AS THE SHIP GETS UNDER WAY THE CAPTIVE CHIEFTAIN BEHOLDS MANY WONDERS AND REGRETS THE TREACHERY THAT MADE THESE FAIR-HAIRED WARRIORS HIS ENEMIES.

SHORN OF ALL HIS REGALIA HE STANDS ALONE AMID THE ACTIVITIES OF THE SAILORS. NO ONE PAYS THE SLIGHTEST ATTENTION TO HIM. THIS IS TORMENT INDEED FOR A ONCE-GREAT CHIEFTAIN.

THEY SAIL ON FOR A FEW MORE DAYS BEFORE THEY AGAIN MEET ANY NATIVES. "HERE COMES A CANOE TO ARRANGE A PARLEY," SAYS TILLICUM. "PUT ON YOUR CEREMONIAL COSTUME, ARN. THE FARTHER UPRIVER WE GO THE BETTER THESE PEOPLE WILL UNDERSTAND THE DIALECT I TAUGHT YOU."

ARN HAS LITTLE TROUBLE UNDERSTANDING THE WORDS OF THE MESSENGER. A MEETING IS REQUESTED, HOSTAGES TO BE EXCHANGED TO GUARANTEE SAFETY. THE SITE CHOSEN IS AN ISLAND. "MY GUARD WILL BE TEN WARRIORS," ANNOUNCES ARN. "YOU MAY BRING A HUNDRED BRAVES."

"WELL SAID, ARN," SMILES GUNDAR. "THAT WILL SHOW THEM ONE OF OUR MEN IS WORTH TEN OF THEIRS."
"AND YOU, GREAT CHIEF-WITHOUT-HONOR," SAYS ARN, POINTING, "WILL BE A HOSTAGE TO LET THEM KNOW THAT NO ONE SHOULD DARE AROUSE OUR WRATH."

THE SAILS ARE FURLED AND, ON TILLICUM'S SUGGESTION, THEY ROW ALONG NEAR THE SHORE TO MAKE SURE NO FLEET OF CANOES IS READY FOR A SURPRISE ATTACK.

6-27   1481

A MURMUR OF SURPRISE COMES FROM THE ASSEMBLED INDIANS AS THE HUGE WARRIORS WITH THE YELLOW HAIR STEP ASHORE, THEIR ARMOR GLEAMING. BUT MORE WONDROUS STILL IS THAT THEIR LEADER IS A BOY, A BOY WITH WHITE SKIN AND HAIR THE COLOR OF THE SETTING SUN.

NEXT WEEK— In the Balance

Prince Valiant

IN THE DAYS OF KING ARTHUR

WRITTEN AND ILLUSTRATED BY HAROLD R FOSTER

Our Story: THIS IS THE MOST IMPORTANT MEETING WITH THE INDIANS, AND PRINCE ARN MUST WIN THEIR RESPECT AND FRIENDSHIP. FOR THIS TRIBE ROAMS THE FORESTS AS FAR AS THE ISLAND OF THE MOUNTAIN (MONTREAL) AND THEIR HELP WILL BE VITAL IN SURMOUNTING THE RAPIDS ABOVE (LACHINE).

"AS HOSTAGE WE GIVE YOU TILLICUM, ONE WISE IN COUNCIL, THE WIFE OF BOLTAR, THE GREAT SEA KING," ANNOUNCES ARN, "ALSO HER SON, HATHA. IN EXCHANGE YOU ARE TO SURRENDER TEN CHIEFTAINS' SONS."

TILLICUM IS TAKEN BY CANOE TO THE VILLAGE, WHERE SHE CREATES A SENSATION, FOR SHE FAIRLY GLITTERS WITH JEWELS AND GOLD ORNAMENTS. BOLTAR HAS BEEN GENEROUS AND HAS LAVISHED UPON HIS WIFE THE LOOT OF MANY A WALLED CITY.

THE INDIAN HOSTAGES ARE ROWED TO THE SHIP, AND MANY A TALE WILL THEY TELL OF THE WHITE MAN'S CANOE WHERE EVERYTHING IS HUGE BEYOND UNDERSTANDING.

NOW ARN PLAYS HIS ACE. CALLING HIS CAPTIVE HE SAYS: "YOU ARE FREE TO GO, O CHIEFTAIN-WITHOUT-HONOR, FOR IT IS NOT GOOD FOR A TRIBE TO BE WITHOUT A LEADER, EVEN ONE WHO HAS SO LITTLE WISDOM."

THE MEETING LASTS WELL INTO THE NIGHT AND MANY TIMES ARN WISHES THAT TILLICUM WERE AT HIS SIDE TO ADVISE HIM. BUT HE REMEMBERS MOST OF HER SUGGESTIONS: THE PRIVILEGE TO TRADE AND TO HUNT, AND HELP AT THE RAPIDS. ARN PROMISES TO CONTROL THE TERRIBLE RAGE OF HIS WARRIORS, AND ALL ENDS IN PEACE AND FRIENDSHIP.

NEXT WEEK— The First Hurdle

#1482

7-4

Prince Valiant IN THE DAYS OF KING ARTHUR

WRITTEN AND ILLUSTRATED BY HAROLD R FOSTER

Our Story: WHEN QUEEN ALETA WITH HER FIRST-BORN LEFT THIS LAND FOURTEEN YEARS AGO THE NATIVES OBJECTED, FOR THEY BELIEVED HER TO BE 'THE SUN WOMAN, BRINGER-OF-HARVESTS,' AND SHE HAD SAID: "IT IS NOT BY ANY GIFT FROM ME THAT YOU WILL PROSPER, BUT BY YOUR OWN TOIL AND WISDOM. PERHAPS SOME DAY MY SON WILL RETURN AND LEAD YOU TO GREATNESS."

AND NOW PRINCE ARN HAS COME TO FULFILL HIS MOTHER'S PROMISE AND GIVE REALITY TO THE LEGEND THAT HAS BEEN GROWING THROUGH THE YEARS. "I GO TO YOUR CAMP TO ESCORT OUR HOSTAGES BACK TO THE SHIP. YOU, MY FRIENDS, MAY PADDLE OUT TO OUR VESSEL AND RETRIEVE YOUR SONS, AND SEE THE GREAT CANOE THAT HAS BROUGHT US OVER THE WIDE SEAS."

ARN FINDS TILLICUM GLITTERING WITH JEWELS, TALKING TO A CIRCLE OF AWESTRUCK SQUAWS. SOME OF THE ELDERS GATHERED GREAT WISDOM THROUGH THE YEARS, AND THOUGH THEY WERE ALLOWED NO VOICE IN COUNCIL, THEY HAD MUCH INFLUENCE WITHIN THE FAMILY. NOW THEY WILL HAVE GREAT WONDERS TO TELL AROUND THE FIRE.

AS THEY ARE BEING ROWED BACK TO THE SHIP, ARN ASKS: "ARE THE INDIANS READY TO ACCEPT THE GIFT WE BRING THEM?" "THEY TRUST AND RESPECT US," ANSWERS TILLICUM, "BUT WILL THEY ABANDON THE OLD WAYS FOR THE NEW? IT IS WORTH A TRY."

THE GIFT HE BRINGS WILL FREE THEM FROM LATE WINTER FAMINE AND THE CEASELESS WANDERING OVER THEIR HUNTING GROUNDS. VILLAGES, EVEN TOWNS, WILL SPRING UP.

HIS GIFT? A BAG OF GRAIN, A MILLSTONE AND A PLOW.

NEXT WEEK- **The Harvest**

#1483   7-11-65

Our Story: ART AND SCIENCE WILL FLOURISH ONLY IF THE PEOPLE ARE FREED FROM THE UNCEASING BATTLE FOR SURVIVAL. ARN BRINGS FORTH THE GIFT THAT WILL CHANGE ALL THIS AND BANISH THE SPECTRE OF FAMINE.

HE DEMONSTRATES HOW TO GRIND THE GRAIN INTO COARSE FLOUR WHICH THE COOK BAKES INTO BANNOCK, AND THE CHIEFS ARE INVITED TO TASTE IT. IT IS SOMETHING NEW, DELICIOUS, AND THE HEADMEN ARE ENTHUSIASTIC TO POSSESS THE SECRET.

FOR TWO OR THREE DAYS ARN AND HIS MEN INSTRUCT THE INDIANS IN PLOWING, PLANTING, HARVESTING, STORING, GRINDING AND COOKING *"SAVE ENOUGH GRAIN FOR NEXT YEAR'S PLANTING,"* HE CONCLUDES, *"AND THERE WILL BE NO FAMINE EVEN WHEN GAME IS SCARCE AND THE LAKES FROZEN."*

THE PLOWING TURNS INTO A FUN GAME, GIVING THE YOUNG BUCKS A CHANCE TO SHOW THEIR STRENGTH AND COMPETE AGAINST EACH OTHER.

BUT SOON THEY TIRE OF IT. WHY WORK SO HARD, THE HARVEST TIME IS MANY MOONS AWAY, SO WHAT IS THE HURRY? LEAVING THE FIELD BUT HALF PLOWED THEY SET OUT FOR THE HUNTING GROUNDS WHERE THE RESULTS ARE IMMEDIATE.

WITH ONLY HALF A FIELD PLOWED, ALL THIS GRAIN WILL NOT BE NEEDED. THE CHIEFS GRIND UP A LITTLE, BUT THE FIRST TASTE CALLS FOR MORE, AND SOON THEY HAVE A POTLATCH AND EVERY GRAIN IS EATEN.

WHEN THE FIRST SPRING THAW TURNS THE SNOW TO SLUSH, AND THE RIVERS LEAVE THEIR BANKS, FAMINE AND DISEASE PAY THEIR USUAL VISIT. WHAT ELSE? THIS HAS BEEN THEIR WAY OF LIFE FOR CENTURIES.

PRINCE ARN HAD GONE HIS WAY WITH THE PLEASANT FEELING THAT HE HAD SHOWN A PRIMITIVE PEOPLE THE ROAD TO PLENTY AND THE BEGINNING OF CIVILIZATION.

NEXT WEEK— **Passengers**

7-18   1484

Prince Valiant
IN THE DAYS OF KING ARTHUR
WRITTEN AND ILLUSTRATED BY HAROLD R FOSTER

Our Story: THE TRIBAL CHIEFTAINS COME ABOARD THE SHIP TO GET THEIR SONS WHO HAVE ACTED AS HOSTAGES DURING THE MEETING. SOME OF THE INDIAN LADS BEG TO SAIL WITH THE WHITE MEN AS FAR AS THE BOUNDARY OF THEIR TRIBE'S DOMAIN.

THE BOYS PROVE THEIR WORTH IN SUPPLYING VENISON. WHEN THE SHIP ANCHORS FOR THE NIGHT THEY PADDLE ASHORE IN THEIR CANOES AND SELDOM RETURN EMPTY-HANDED.

PRINCE ARN JOINS IN THE HUNTING, CONFIDENT THAT HIS SKILL WITH THE BOW WILL NOT BE INFERIOR TO HIS COMPANIONS'.

HE IS AMAZED AT THE SKILL WITH WHICH THEY STALK THEIR GAME. THEY SHOOT FROM A CROUCHED POSITION WITH DEADLY ACCURACY AT CLOSE RANGE, AND SHOULD A TWIG DEFLECT THE ARROW, HAVE TIME TO SHOOT ANOTHER. TO GET THE FULL POWER OF HIS LONGER BOW ARN SUDDENLY STANDS ERECT AND, AS THIS IS THE RANGE HE HAS PRACTICED MOST, SELDOM MISSES.

IT IS THE BIRCHBARK CANOE THAT GIVES HIM THE GREATEST THRILL. IT GLIDES EASILY WITH SO LITTLE EFFORT AND STEERS WITH THE SLIGHTEST TWIST OF THE PADDLE.

HE MUST HAVE ONE OF HIS OWN TO EXPLORE THE MANY RIVERS AND BROOKS THAT FLOW INTO THE MIGHTY ST. LAWRENCE. HE CONSULTS TILLICUM ON THE INDIAN METHOD OF BARGAINING.

ARN ASKS THE INDIAN LADS TO TAKE HIM TO A VILLAGE WHERE HE MIGHT PURCHASE A CANOE. THEY TAKE HIM UP A SMALL RIVER FAR FROM THE BIG WATERS AND THE DANGER OF RAIDS FROM ROVING BANDS.
NEXT WEEK — The Salesman

7-25   1485

Our Story: AS THEY APPROACH THE VILLAGE ALL THE WOMEN AND CHILDREN QUIETLY VANISH INTO THE WOODS. A CHIEFTAIN STEPS DOWN TO THE LANDING AND THE BRAVES STAND ARMED AND READY BEFORE THEIR TEPEES.

ARN MAKES THE SIGN OF PEACE AND THE CHIEFTAIN RETURNS THE GESTURE, SO THEY LAND. THESE PEOPLE HAVE HEARD THE LEGEND OF THE 'SUN WOMAN' AND OF HOW HER SON WOULD RETURN, BUT THEY ARE WIDE-EYED WITH WONDER AT SIGHT OF THE WHITE-SKINNED BOY WITH HAIR OF FLAME.

WHEN ARN MAKES IT KNOWN HE WISHES TO TRADE FOR A CANOE, SOME OF THE BRAVES STEP UP AND OFFER WORN-OUT WRECKS, EXTOLLING THEIR VIRTUES AND GIVING THEM SUCH NAMES AS 'SWIFT ARROW,' 'FLYING DUCK', ETC.

BUT ARN HAS ALREADY SEEN THE CANOE HE WANTS. ITS OWNER HESITATES TO PART WITH SO BEAUTIFUL A PIECE OF CRAFTSMANSHIP AND COLDLY REFUSES THE STEEL KNIFE ARN OFFERS. ONE AT A TIME THE ITEMS IN HIS VALISE ARE DISPLAYED. THE INDIAN'S FACE REMAINS IMPASSIVE, BUT ARN IS WATCHING HIS HANDS.

BY THIS TIME THE WHOLE VILLAGE HAS GATHERED TO WATCH THE CONTEST, FOR SHREWDNESS IN TRADING IS CONSIDERED A VIRTUE. WHEN ARN BRINGS OUT A STRING OF GLITTERING BEADS HIS OPPONENT'S HANDS MOVE IN A CLUTCHING GESTURE. ARN GATHERS UP THE BEADS, ALLOWING THE SUN TO SPARKLE ON THE BRIGHT COLORS, THEN, WITH A SHRUG, PUTS THEM AWAY.

"I WANTED YOUR CANOE AND OFFERED TOO MUCH, BUT MY GENEROSITY CANNOT EQUAL YOUR GREED. THERE ARE OTHER CANOES." ARN STANDS AND STRETCHES. "WAIT," SAYS THE INDIAN.

1486   8-1

AT SUNDOWN HE PADDLES BACK TO THE SHIP. NOT ONLY HAS HE THE CANOE, BUT TWO PADDLES, A WOVEN BLANKET AND BEADED MOCCASINS HAVE BEEN THROWN IN.

THE INDIANS WATCH HIM GO AND NOD THEIR HEADS IN APPROVAL. THIS FIRSTBORN OF THE 'SUN WOMAN' HAS WON THEIR RESPECT AT THE MANLY ART OF TRADING.

NEXT WEEK— **The Braggart**

Our Story: A BLUSTERING WIND BLOWS OUT OF THE NORTHEAST BRINGING MIST AND RAIN, BUT THE NORTHMEN REJOICE, FOR THE SAILS ARE FILLED AND GUNDAR HARL'S SHIP GLIDES UPSTREAM WITHOUT TOILING AT THE SWEEPS.

ARN IS ANXIOUS TO TRY OUT HIS NEW CANOE, SO ON THE FIRST FINE AFTERNOON HE ORDERS IT LAUNCHED. ONE OF THE INDIAN BOYS WHO IS A GUEST ABOARD ADVISES: "IT IS TOO WINDY FOR SMALL CANOE AND SMALL KNOWLEDGE."

BUT WITH THE OVERCONFIDENCE OF YOUTH ARN PUSHES OFF. THE WIND IMMEDIATELY CATCHES THE FRONT END OF THE CANOE AND SWINGS IT DOWNWIND, AND STRUGGLE AS HE MIGHT, ARN CANNOT BRING IT BACK.

TWO MILES DOWNSTREAM HE GAINS THE SHORE. NOW, HOW TO GET BACK? HE STUDIES HIS CANOE. IT IS EASIEST TO PADDLE FROM THE END SEAT WHERE THE CRAFT IS NARROW, BUT THAT RAISES THE FRONT TOO HIGH. THE MIDDLE SEAT IS TO BALANCE IT FOR CARRYING ON PORTAGES. THE THIRD SEAT LOOKS PROMISING. HE STARTS OFF WITH A BIG STONE IN FRONT TO KEEP THE END DOWN.

WITH EACH STROKE HE LEARNS SOMETHING ABOUT CANOES. IF HE RESTS BUT A MOMENT IT TURNS SIDEWAYS AND THREATENS TO SWAMP. THE WAVES MAKE THE BOW BOUNCE AND THE STONE POUNDS DANGEROUSLY. ARN IS SURE HIS CANOE HAS THE SOUL OF A MISCHIEVOUS IMP.

WHEN HE REACHES THE SHIP HE IS IN NO MOOD FOR JOKING. "IS WHITE BOY NOT STRONG ENOUGH TO MAKE LITTLE CANOE OBEY?" CHIDES, A YOUNG INDIAN. "IF YOU ARE SO STRONG, I WILL RACE YOU TO THE TOP OF THE MAST," SNAPS ARN

1487   8-8

WITH THE SKILL OF LONG PRACTICE ARN WALKS UP THE SHROUDS AND IS BACK ON DECK WHILE HIS OPPONENT IS STILL STRUGGLING UPWARD, MUCH TO THE AMUSEMENT OF HIS COMPANIONS

TILLICUM SHAKES HER HEAD IN DISAPPROVAL. "YOU SHOULD HAVE ASKED HIM TO SHOW YOU HOW TO HANDLE A CANOE, AND MADE A FRIEND. INSTEAD YOU HUMILIATED HIM BEFORE HIS FRIENDS, AND MADE AN ENEMY."
NEXT WEEK— The Meeting Place

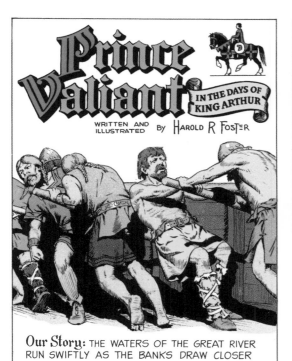

Prince Valiant
IN THE DAYS OF KING ARTHUR
WRITTEN AND ILLUSTRATED BY Harold R Foster

Our Story: THE WATERS OF THE GREAT RIVER RUN SWIFTLY AS THE BANKS DRAW CLOSER TOGETHER. PROGRESS IS SLOW, BUT THEY ARE IN NO HURRY. IT IS TIME FOR THE INDIANS TO FULFILL THEIR PROMISE.

THE MORNING SUN FLASHES ON A HUNDRED WET PADDLES AS A GREAT FLEET OF CANOES WENDS ITS WAY CLOSE TO THE SHORE, TAKING ADVANTAGE OF EVERY EDDY AND BACKWATER.
THE INDIAN LADS WHO ARE GUESTS ABOARD ARE WILD WITH EXCITEMENT AS THEY POINT OUT PARENTS, FRIENDS AND CHIEFTAINS.

"ALL IS WELL," SAYS TILLICUM, "THE TRIBE WE HAD COUNCIL WITH HAS KEPT FAITH WITH US AND WILL HELP HAUL OUR VESSEL OVER THE RAPIDS."

AT THE ISLE OF THE MOUNTAIN EVERY SWEEP, OAR AND PADDLE HAS TO BE PUT TO WORK TO MAKE HEADWAY. THE SHIP SEEMS DOUBLY HUGE AND CLUMSY COMPARED WITH THE INDIANS' LIGHT CANOES WHICH CAN FIND SLACK WATER NEAR THE SHORE.

AT LAST GUNDAR HARL BRINGS HIS VESSEL TO ANCHOR IN THE SHELTER OF A TONGUE OF LAND BEYOND WHICH THE LACHINE RAPIDS FOAM AND ROAR.
HERE THE WHOLE TRIBE OF FRIENDLY NATIVES IS ENCAMPED READY TO MAKE A HOLIDAY OF THE PROBLEM OF "LINING" THE SHIP UP TO THE CALM WATER ABOVE.

8-15 © King Features Syndicate, Inc., 1965. World rights reserved. 1488

HAL FOSTER

PRINCE ARN SITS WITH TILLICUM WELL INTO THE NIGHT. ONCE HE THOUGHT OF HER ONLY AS HIS NURSEMAID, BUT NOW HE FINDS HER COUNSEL INDISPENSABLE AND RELIES ON HER WISDOM AND KNOWLEDGE OF INDIAN WAYS.

NEXT WEEK— On the Towline

Prince Valiant
IN THE DAYS OF KING ARTHUR
WRITTEN AND ILLUSTRATED BY HAROLD R FOSTER

Our Story: DRESSED IN HIS CEREMONIAL ROBES PRINCE ARN GOES TO THE CAMP TO ARRANGE TO HAVE THE SHIP LINED UP THE RAPIDS. THE INDIANS LEAD A HARSH AND LONELY LIFE AND ARE SO STARVED FOR ENTERTAINMENT THAT THEY TURN EVERY EVENT INTO A CEREMONY.

A PROPHECY HAS BEEN FULFILLED. THE FLAME-HAIRED SON OF THE 'SUN-WOMAN' HAS COME ON THE GREAT WINGED CANOE, AND THE FIERCE WARRIORS WITH THE YELLOW HAIR ARE HIS SERVANTS. MANY COUNCILS ARE CALLED, CEREMONY FOLLOWS CEREMONY UNTIL AT LAST THE HUNTERS REPORT THAT THERE IS NO MORE FOOD LEFT WITHIN THE NEARBY FORESTS.

AT LAST THE GREAT DAY DAWNS. THE TOW ROPE IS LAID OUT AND THE SLINGS ATTACHED, AND THE SHOUTING INDIANS TAKE THEIR PLACES. TO THE THROBBING OF TOM-TOMS AND THE CHANTING OF THE MEDICINE MEN THE BRAVES THROW THEIR STRENGTH AGAINST THE SLINGS, AND THE HEAVY VESSEL SLOWLY MOVES AGAINST THE CURRENT. THIS WILL BE THE GREATEST, MOST INTERESTING EVENT IN THEIR LIVES, AND THEY WILL HAVE TALES TO TELL AROUND THE FIRE FOR MANY A YEAR.

NEXT WEEK—**The Birth of an Idea**

1489

KAL FOSTER
8-22

Prince Valiant

IN THE DAYS OF KING ARTHUR

WRITTEN AND ILLUSTRATED BY Harold R Foster

Our Story: THE SHIP IS LINED UP THE LACHINE RAPIDS AND ANCHORS IN THE CALM WATER ABOVE. THE VESSEL IS THE BIGGEST MAN-MADE THING THE INDIANS HAVE EVER SEEN, AND AS SOON AS THEY CATCH THEIR BREATH THEY GIVE WAY TO THEIR EXCITEMENT WITH WILD YELLS AND BOASTING.

TOWING THE GREAT WINGED CANOE IS A NEVER-TO-BE-FORGOTTEN EVENT IN THE LIVES OF THE INDIANS, BUT WHEN IT COMES TO BRINGING THE CARGO OVER THE PORTAGE THEIR INTEREST FLAGS, AND ONE BY ONE THEY TAKE TO THEIR CANOES FOR THE HOMEWARD TRIP, LEAVING THE HEAVY WORK TO THE NORTHMEN ALONE.

SEVERAL CANOES ARRIVE FROM UPSTREAM, LED BY A GREAT CHIEFTAIN: "MY HEART IS GLAD AT SIGHT OF MY FATHER," SAYS TILLICUM. "MAY YOU WALK IN PEACE, MY DAUGHTER," RETURNS THE CHIEF, "YOUR PEOPLE WILL BE HAPPY AT YOUR SAFE RETURN."

FROM TILLICUM'S FATHER ARN LEARNS MANY THINGS. THE ISLAND OF THE MOUNTAIN IS TREATY GROUND WHERE TRIBES FROM THE FOUR WINDS COME TO TRADE ONCE A YEAR. FROM THE GREAT WATERS COME THE HURONS; BY WAY OF THE RIVER JUST ABOVE, THE OTTAWAS BRING THEIR GOODS; AND JUST BELOW HERE IS A CANOE ROUTE THAT REACHES ALL THE WAY TO THE GREAT SALT SEA.

NOW ARN HAS A GREAT DREAM: TO EXPLORE A NEW ROUTE TO THE SEA.

14-90   8-29

HE TELLS GUNDAR OF HIS IDEA. "WHEN WE RETURN YOU WILL TAKE THE SHIP TO THE SEA AND FOLLOW THE COAST SOUTHWARD AND I WILL FOLLOW THE INLAND ROUTE AND WE WILL MEET."

ARN WOULD LOVE TO LAUNCH HIS CANOE AND EXPLORE THE THOUSAND ISLANDS, BUT WHILE THE WIND HOLDS FAVORABLE HE DARES NOT CAUSE ANY DELAY.

NEXT WEEK: **Arn's Birthplace**

Prince Valiant

IN THE DAYS OF KING ARTHUR

WRITTEN AND ILLUSTRATED BY HAROLD R FOSTER

Our Story: WITH PRINCE ARN ACTING AS INTERPRETER, TILLICUM'S FATHER DIRECTS THE WAY THROUGH THE THOUSAND ISLANDS. HE KNOWS THESE WATERS WELL, HAVING OFTEN COME TO THE TREATY GROUNDS.

LAKE ONTARIO — AND FOR THE FIRST TIME SINCE LEAVING THE OCEAN THEY CAN SAIL DAY AND NIGHT, AND SOON REACH THE UPPER END.

HERE THEY ARE MET BY A GREAT GATHERING OF INDIANS. FOR IT WAS AMONG THESE PEOPLE THAT PRINCE VALIANT AND ALETA LIVED, WHERE ALETA WAS BELIEVED TO BE THE 'SUN-GODDESS, BRINGER-OF-HARVESTS,' AND WHERE ARN WAS BORN.

ARN IS CONDUCTED TO THE PLACE OF HIS BIRTH. THE COMFORTABLE, WELL-INSULATED DWELLING THE INDIANS HAD BUILT FOR HIS MOTHER HAS LONG SINCE ROTTED, BUT THE PLACE IS REGARDED AS SACRED, AND PROTECTED BY SYMBOLS.

THE GREAT LOG HOUSE THE VIKINGS HAD ERECTED STILL STANDS, BUT TIME HAS DESTROYED ITS USEFULNESS.
"IT IS BEYOND REPAIR," GUNDAR HARL REMARKS. "WE WILL HAVE TO BUILD ANOTHER, BUT SMALLER. AS I REMEMBER, THAT WAS THE DRAFTIEST PLACE I EVER SPENT A WINTER IN."

ARN SPENDS LONG HOURS WITH THE CHIEF, TELLING ABOUT HIS DREAM OF BRINGING TRADE, PROSPERITY AND FINALLY CIVILIZATION TO THE TRIBES.

"HAS THE BOY THE WISDOM TO CARRY OUT HIS DREAMS?" THE CHIEF ASKS HIS DAUGHTER, TILLICUM.
"HE IS EARNEST, FATHER, AND HAS GREAT WISDOM FOR HIS YEARS, BUT HIS YEARS ARE FEW."

HIS MOTHER HAD PROPHESIED HER SON WOULD BRING GREATNESS; IF ARN THINKS TRADE AND WEALTH ARE GREATNESS, IT MUST BE REMEMBERED THAT HE IS VERY YOUNG.

NEXT WEEK: **Arn's First Lesson**

1491

9-5

Prince Valiant
IN THE DAYS OF KING ARTHUR
WRITTEN AND ILLUSTRATED BY HAROLD R FOSTER

Our Story: PRINCE ARN IS VERY EARNEST AS HE TRIES TO CONVINCE THE CHIEFTAIN THAT PERMANENT TOWNS, CULTIVATION OF THE LAND, AND LAWS SUCH AS KING ARTHUR HAS LAID DOWN WOULD BENEFIT THE WHOLE TRIBE. "SEE," HE CRIES, "HERE COME SOME OF OUR HUNTERS NOW."

"BY CO-OPERATING AND WORKING TOGETHER AS A TEAM THEY RETURN WITH A GREAT QUANTITY OF GAME." THE CHIEF SMILES: "COME, AND I WILL SHOW YOU THE COST OF THEIR SUCCESS."

HE LEADS THE WAY TO A LUSH MEADOW. "YESTERDAY MANY DEER BROWSED HERE. YOUR HUNTERS LAY HIDDEN BY THE GAME TRAILS WHILE OTHERS WITH LOUD CRIES DROVE THE DEER TO THEM. IT WILL BE MANY MOONS ERE THE FRIGHTENED SURVIVORS RETURN."

"NOW WE WILL SEE HOW MY PEOPLE HUNT," AND HE LEADS THE WAY TO A ROCKY POINT MANY MILES DISTANT. AFTER A LONG WAIT THREE INDIANS ARE SEEN AT THE EDGE OF THE CLEARING, THEN THEY DISAPPEAR IN THE LONG GRASS.

A MOOSE APPEARS AND STANDS MOTIONLESS FOR SOME TIME, TESTING THE AIR WITH WIDE NOSTRILS, THEN BEGINS TO FEED. SUDDENLY THE ANIMAL DROPS AND THE INDIANS APPEAR A FEW YARDS AWAY, AND WITHIN MINUTES HAVE CUT UP THE CARCASS AND RETURNED THE WAY THEY CAME.

"SEE, YOUNG CHIEFTAIN, MY PEOPLE HAVE TAKEN ONLY WHAT THEY NEED AND HAVE NOT DISTURBED THEIR HUNTING GROUND. THE CROWS WILL CLEAN UP WHAT IS LEFT."

ARN SEEKS COUNSEL WITH TILLICUM AS USUAL. "MY PEOPLE KNOW NOT GREED, THEY TAKE FROM THE LAND WHAT THEY NEED, AND LEAVE NO WRECKAGE IN THEIR PASSING."

© King Features Syndicate, Inc., 1965. World rights reserved.

"WHILE MY PEOPLE GLORY IN MARCHING ARMIES, CONQUEST AND PLUNDER," MUSES ARN. "I AM CONFUSED."
"WAIT," ADVISES TILLICUM, "AND LEARN."

NEXT WEEK—Waiting and Learning

9-12

1492

Prince Valiant

IN THE DAYS OF KING ARTHUR

WRITTEN AND ILLUSTRATED BY HAROLD R FOSTER

Our Story: THE SHIP THAT HAS BROUGHT THEM ACROSS THE WIDE SEA IS SAFELY MOORED IN A SHELTERED COVE AND THE NORSEMEN BUILD SHELTERS ON SHORE. THEY FIND IT BETTER TO PUT UP WITH THE BLACK FLIES AND MOSQUITOES THAN THE CRAMPED QUARTERS THEY HAVE SHARED FOR SO LONG.

IT IS TIME TO BUILD A HOUSE FOR THE COMING WINTER AND ARN SUGGESTS TEARING DOWN THE OLD ONE AND CONSTRUCTING A NEW ONE. "NO," ANSWERS THE CHIEF, "THAT PLACE IS SACRED, A SHRINE TO THE 'SUN WOMAN', YOUR MOTHER. I HAVE SET ASIDE A SITE FOR YOU."

THE INDIANS LOOK ON IN AMAZEMENT AS THE NORSEMEN CLEAR THE FOREST AND ERECT THEIR LOG HOUSE. TO FELL A LARGE TREE IS LONG AND TEDIOUS WORK FOR THE INDIANS, WHILE THE KEEN AXES OF THULE CLEAVE THROUGH IN MINUTES!

THE VIKINGS SNEER AT THE FRAIL, CROWDED INDIAN DWELLINGS. THEY WANT SOMETHING SOLID TO STAND AGAINST STORM AND SIEGE, AND SMOKY ENOUGH INSIDE TO DISCOURAGE THE MOSQUITOES.
ARN TURNS TO THE CHIEF: "YOU COULD BUILD SUCH HOUSES, MANY HOUSES, AND FORM A COMMUNITY SAFE FROM ATTACK."

THE CHIEF SMILES: "THE WHITE MAN COUNTS HIS WEALTH IN POSSESSIONS. YOU ARE BOUND TO YOUR POSSESSIONS. MY PEOPLE COUNT THEIR WEALTH IN THEIR SKILL AS HUNTERS, THEIR WISDOM IN COUNCIL. WHILE YOU ARE TETHERED TO YOUR GREAT CANOE AND HUGE HOUSE WE CAN MOVE TO NEW HUNTING GROUNDS WITHIN THE HOUR."

AS USUAL ARN TAKES HIS PROBLEM TO TILLICUM. "I HAVE TRIED TO SHOW YOUR PEOPLE NEW METHODS, NEW WAYS, BUT THEY PREFER THE OLD WAYS. AND," HE ADMITS, "WITH GOOD REASON."
"THE RABBIT CANNOT BUILD A NEST OR THE BIRD DIG A BURROW," ANSWERS TILLICUM.

"THEN HOW AM I TO FULFILL MY MOTHER'S PROPHECY AND BRING GREATNESS TO THE TRIBE?" HE ASKS. "WAIT," ADVISES TILLICUM, "AND LEARN."

ARN GOES FISHING, NOT TO CATCH FISH, BUT TO BE ALONE WHILE HE WRESTLES WITH A PROBLEM, ONE HE MUST SOLVE HIMSELF.

NEXT WEEK—War Clouds

9-19

1493

Our Story: PRINCE ARN HAS SOUGHT ADVICE FROM TILLICUM AND ONCE AGAIN SHE HAS SAID: "WAIT AND LEARN." WISE COUNSEL, NO DOUBT, BUT ARN IS YOUNG AND THEREFORE IMPATIENT. HIS MOTHER HAD PROMISED HE WOULD BRING GREATNESS TO THE TRIBE, BUT THE INDIANS PREFER THEIR OWN WAYS.

"AND WHY NOT? THEIR WAYS SUIT THE LIFE THEY LEAD. WITH FEW POSSESSIONS THEY ENJOY A FREEDOM UNKNOWN. ACROSS THE SEA."

"A FOOL AM I TO THINK THAT A CHANGE IS FOR THE BETTER. THEIR CHIEFS MEET IN COUNCIL AND THE WISDOM OF MANY FORMS THEIR DECISIONS, WHILE OUR KINGS HOLD ALL POWER AND THEIR THRONES ARE SURROUNDED BY MANY WHO LUST FOR THAT POWER."

"THEY LIVE IN THE GREAT QUIET FORESTS, CLOSE TO NATURE. PERHAPS THAT IS WHY MY WARLIKE VIKINGS ARE SO INVINCIBLE AGAINST THEM!"
A BABBLE OF VOICES FROM THE NEARBY VILLAGE SWELLS INTO WILD SHOUTING AND THE DRUMS BEGIN TO THROB.

A WAR PARTY OF YOUNG MEN HAS RETURNED FROM A SUCCESSFUL RAID, BRINGING WITH THEM THE GRISLY TROPHIES OF THEIR VICTORY. THEY DANCE WILDLY TO THE RHYTHM OF THE TOMTOMS, EACH ONE ACTING OUT THE PART HE PLAYED IN THE FIGHT.

NOW THE GREAT CHIEF NAMES EACH ONE 'WARRIOR' WITH PERMISSION TO DON WAR PAINT AND WEAR AN EAGLE FEATHER.

THEN HE CALLS ARN AND GUNDAR: "THIS MEANS WAR WITH THE TRIBE TO THE SOUTH. YOU AND YOUR MEN WILL BE INVOLVED, SO PREPARE FOR THE ATTACK. TILLICUM WILL TELL YOU IN WHAT MANNER OUR PEOPLE FIGHT, SO YOU CAN READY YOUR DEFENSES AND PLAN YOUR ATTACK."
NEXT WEEK – 'Many Canoes Come'

1494

9-26

Our Story: BECAUSE SEVERAL YOUNG MEN WISHED TO WIN THE TITLE OF 'BRAVE AND WARRIOR' THEY ATTACKED AND SLEW A HUNTING PARTY THAT HAD STRAYED ONTO THE TRIBE'S HUNTING GROUNDS. NOW WAR WITH THEIR NEIGHBORS IS CERTAIN, AND TILLICUM EXPLAINS TO THE NORTHMEN THE INDIAN METHODS OF WARFARE: STEALTH, SURPRISE, SLAUGHTER, AND THE TORTURE OF PRISONERS.

THE CHIEF SENDS OUT SCOUTS AND RUNNERS, AND THE ARROW MAKERS SET TO WORK. THERE SEEM TO BE NO OTHER PREPARATIONS TO MEET ATTACK.

AT PRINCE ARN'S SUGGESTION A TOWER IS RAISED ON EACH CORNER OF THE UNFINISHED LOG HOUSE, SO ARCHERS CAN COMMAND EACH WALL.

AND A BALCONY IS HASTILY RAISED INSIDE TO REPEL ANY ATTEMPT TO SCALE THE WALLS. WHEN THE STORE OF ARMS IS BROUGHT UP FROM THEIR SHIP ALL IS READY.

NONE OF THE SCOUTS HAS REPORTED ANY SIGN OF THE ENEMY, SO ARN DECIDES TO HAVE A DAY'S HUNTING. TILLICUM HAS SOMETHING TO SAY ABOUT IT:

"YOU WILL WEAR YOUR CHAIN-MAIL SHIRT AND THIS JERKIN. YOUR OWN CLOTHES ARE TOO CONSPICUOUS. AND COVER YOUR RED HAIR WITH THIS HOOD."
THOUGH SHE SMILES, ARN KNOWS FROM LONG EXPERIENCE THAT IT IS USELESS TO ARGUE WITH HIS NURSE.

AN HOUR LATER THE FIRST SCOUT RETURNS. THE ENEMY HAVE CROSSED THE GREAT RIVER IN MANY CANOES AND ARE CAMPED TWO DAYS' MARCH AWAY!

NEXT WEEK—A Dangerous Game

1495

© King Features Syndicate, Inc., 1965. World rights reserved.

10-3

Prince Valiant
IN THE DAYS OF KING ARTHUR
WRITTEN AND ILLUSTRATED BY HAROLD R FOSTER

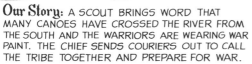

Our Story: A SCOUT BRINGS WORD THAT MANY CANOES HAVE CROSSED THE RIVER FROM THE SOUTH AND THE WARRIORS ARE WEARING WAR PAINT. THE CHIEF SENDS COURIERS OUT TO CALL THE TRIBE TOGETHER AND PREPARE FOR WAR.

ARN PADDLES UP A SMALL RIVER SEARCHING FOR GAME. THERE ARE MANY PORTAGES, AND THE SHIRT OF MAIL TILLICUM PERSUADED HIM TO WEAR IS HOT, HEAVY AND SCRATCHY.

AT THE NEXT PORTAGE HE SEES TWO INDIANS CROSSING. HE SWINGS HIS CANOE AROUND AND PADDLES LIKE MAD...FOR THEY ARE IN FULL WAR PAINT.

"BLESS YOU, TILLICUM," HE GASPS AS AN ARROW THUDS AGAINST HIS BACK AND DROPS INTO THE CANOE.

TWO INDIANS IN A CANOE CAN TRAVEL FASTER THAN ONE BOY. ARN TIPS HIS CANOE TO FILL IT WITH WATER AND SINKS IT WITH LARGE STONES. HE HAS BARELY TIME TO HIDE BEFORE THE INDIANS GLIDE BY.

THE NEXT PORTAGE IS A LONG ONE AND THEY EXPECT TO RUN DOWN THEIR QUARRY BEFORE HE REACHES THE OTHER END. ABOVE THE ROAR OF THE RAPIDS ARN CAN HEAR THEIR WAR CRIES.

BUT THEIR VICTIM HAS VANISHED WITHOUT A TRACE. AND THEN, AFTER A LONG SEARCH, THEY RETURN TO FIND THEIR CANOE HAS ALSO DISAPPEARED.

FROM ACROSS THE RIVER WHERE HE HAS CONCEALED THEIR CANOE ARN WATCHES THE INDIANS. HE HAS LEFT THE ARROW WITH ITS BROKEN POINT TO ADD TO THEIR WORRIES.

NEXT WEEK—The Long Night

Prince Valiant

IN THE DAYS OF KING ARTHUR

WRITTEN AND ILLUSTRATED BY HAROLD R FOSTER

Our Story: ARN IS QUITE PLEASED WITH HIMSELF. HE HAS OUTWITTED THE TWO INDIANS WHO WOULD HAVE KILLED HIM HAD IT NOT BEEN FOR HIS SHIRT-OF-MAIL. HIS CANOE WITH STONES IN IT IS SUNKEN ON THE FAR SIDE OF THE RIVER, AND HE HAS DONE THE SAME WITH THE INDIANS' CANOE.

THE QUIET OF THE EVENING BRINGS OUT THE MOSQUITOES IN SWARMS, AND STILL THE HOSTILE INDIANS LINGER ON THE PORTAGE HE MUST CROSS TO GET BACK.

FINALLY THE INDIANS MOVE UP THE PATH, AND ON A FLAT SPACE BUILD A SHELTER AND A SMUDGE FIRE. CAN IT BE THAT THEY ARE EXPECTING SOME OF THEIR FRIENDS TO COME ALONG? ARN FEELS LESS SMART.

IN THE DEAD OF NIGHT HE UNDRESSES AND RAISES THE INDIANS' CANOE, AND AS SILENTLY AS POSSIBLE SWIMS IT ACROSS THE RIVER.

THE INDIANS HAVE MOVED BACK FROM THE END OF THE PORTAGE WHERE SUCH STRANGE THINGS HAPPENED. THE ARROW WITH THE BROKEN POINT THAT SHOULD HAVE KILLED THEIR VICTIM AND THE DISAPPEARANCE OF THEIR CANOE ARE FRIGHTENING MYSTERIES. QUIETLY ARN RETURNS THEIR CANOE.

THEN HE RETRIEVES HIS OWN CANOE, CROSSES THE RIVER, AND AGAIN SINKS IT. THE DAWN IS CHILL AND HE IS GLAD TO GET DRESSED AGAIN.

MORNING, AND TWO AMAZED AND TERRIFIED BRAVES FIND THEIR CANOE HAS RETURNED AS MYSTERIOUSLY AS IT VANISHED! AND WHERE IS THE ONE AGAINST WHOSE BODY THEIR WELL-AIMED ARROW BROKE?

1497   10-17

THE INDIANS PADDLE BACK THE WAY THEY CAME, FEARFULLY EXPECTING THEIR CRAFT TO DISAPPEAR FROM UNDER THEM. ARN RAISES HIS CANOE FOR THE JOURNEY HOME.

NEXT WEEK— **The Approaching Storm**

HAL FOSTER

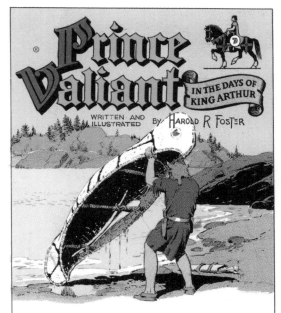

Prince Valiant
IN THE DAYS OF KING ARTHUR
WRITTEN AND ILLUSTRATED BY HAROLD R FOSTER

Our Story: THE TWO INDIAN SCOUTS HE HAS OUTWITTED HAVE LEFT AND ARN RAISES HIS SUNKEN CANOE FOR A FAST TRIP HOME. BUT SOMETHING HAS HAPPENED, THE CANOE THAT HAD BEEN SO LIGHT AND EASY TO HANDLE IS NOW A HEAVY BURDEN.

IT HAS BEEN UNDER WATER ALL NIGHT AND THE UNPAINTED WOOD HAS SOAKED UP SO MUCH MOISTURE THAT ARN CAN BARELY CARRY IT. HE HOPES THE SCOUTS WILL NOT RETURN.

"THANKS FOR ADVISING ME TO WEAR MY ARMOR, ELSE I WOULD HAVE BEEN KILLED." THEN HE TELLS TILLICUM OF HIS MEETING WITH THE WAR-PAINTED INDIANS.

THE NUMBER OF WARRIORS INCREASES BY THE HOUR AS THE TRIBE GATHERS. THE ENEMY IS APPROACHING STEALTHILY, BUT IT IS UNKNOWN WHEN AND FROM WHICH DIRECTION THE ATTACK WILL COME. THE WAR OF NERVES HAS COMMENCED.

AT NIGHT THE WOMEN AND CHILDREN ARE TAKEN TO A SAFE PLACE BY CANOE AND GUNDAR HARL'S SHIP, FOR IN TRIBAL WARS NO ONE IS SPARED AND THE FATE OF CAPTIVES IS QUITE UNPLEASANT.

BECAUSE HE HAS LOST A HAND AND A FOOT GUNDAR IS NOT A WARRIOR, BUT HIS TRADING VENTURES HAVE TAKEN HIM TO FAR PLACES IN A TURBULENT WORLD AND HE HAS LEARNED MUCH OF WARFARE. THE HALF-FINISHED DWELLING HAS BEEN TURNED INTO A FORTRESS SINCE THE FIRST RUMOR OF WAR.

EVEN NOW ENEMY SCOUTS ARE LOOKING IN GREAT ASTONISHMENT AT THE WHITE MAN'S STRANGE TEPEE.

NEXT WEEK— **Drums at Dawn**

1498

10-24

Our Story: THE NORTHMEN HAVE DONE ALL THEY CAN TO TURN THEIR HALF-FINISHED DWELLING INTO A FORTRESS IN EXPECTATION OF THE COMING TRIBAL WAR. THEIR INDIAN FRIENDS HAVE MADE NO PREPARATIONS EXCEPT TO SEND THE WOMEN AND CHILDREN AWAY.

THE WAR DRUMS THROB, WAR CRIES ARE SCREAMED, AND THE BRAVES DANCE THEMSELVES INTO BATTLE FRENZY. GUNDAR GOES TO THE CHIEF WITH A PLAN OF BATTLE, BUT THE CHIEF SHAKES HIS HEAD....

..."MY WARRIORS MUST FIGHT MAN TO MAN TO PROVE THEIR MANHOOD, EACH TO HIS OWN PRIVATE WAR. IT IS THEIR WAY. ONCE THE BLOOD LUST IS UPON THEM THEY OBEY NO LAW EXCEPT TO KILL."

THE OMINOUS QUIET OF DAWN IS SHATTERED BY THE SCREAMING OF WAR CRIES, AND THE ENEMY BREAKS OUT OF THE DARK FOREST. DEATH OR VICTORY! ASIDE FROM A FEW PRISONERS FOR SLAVES OR FOR TORTURE, THERE IS NO THOUGHT OF PLUNDER, FOR THE INDIANS HAVE FEW POSSESSIONS.

FROM WITHIN THE FORTRESS ARCHERS TAKE A STEADY TOLL OF THE ENEMY, BUT SOON THE FIGHTING IS SO CONFUSED IT IS IMPOSSIBLE TO TELL FRIEND FROM FOE.

THE FURY MOUNTS AS THE BATTLE SWAYS BACK AND FORTH. EACH SIDE SEEMS TO BE ABLE TO RECOGNIZE A FOE AND, WATCHING, ARN REMEMBERS THE MARKINGS ON THE FACES OF THE SCOUTS WHO SOUGHT TO KILL HIM.

HE SHOUTS THIS INFORMATION TO HIS COMPANIONS, AND THEY ARE ABLE TO IDENTIFY THEIR TARGETS.

THIS HARASSMENT BRINGS CRIES OF RAGE FROM THE ENEMY, AND THEIR ATTENTION IS DIRECTED TO THE GREAT WOODEN TEPEE.

NEXT WEEK— The Shield Wall

10-31

1499

Prince Valiant
IN THE DAYS OF KING ARTHUR
WRITTEN AND ILLUSTRATED BY HAROLD R FOSTER

Our Story: THE BATTLE SWAYS BACK AND FORTH, WITH THE TRIBE FROM ACROSS THE RIVER SLOWLY GAINING THE ADVANTAGE. FROM WITHIN THEIR BARRICADED LOG HOUSE THE NORTHMEN CANNOT DISTINGUISH FRIEND FROM FOE.....

.... BUT WHEN THE FIGHTING COMES CLOSER THEY CAN TELL THE FOE BY THE WAR-PAINT MARKINGS, AND LOOSE A DEADLY SHOWER OF ARROWS.

THE ATTACKING INDIANS TURN THEIR ATTENTION TO THE FORTRESS AND STORM UP THE ROUGH LOGS LIKE SQUIRRELS, TO BE MET WITH A DELUGE OF ROCKS AND TIMBERS.

"OUR FRIENDS ARE NOT DOING SO WELL, ARN. LOOK, THE ENEMY HAS GAINED THEIR VILLAGE, AND THE WIGWAMS ARE IN FLAMES. SOUND THE CHARGE!"

AT THE BACK OF THE BUILDING IS A LARGE HINGED FRAME. THIS IS PUSHED OUTWARD AND FALLS IN PLACE WITH A CRASH, AND THE NORTHMEN COME STORMING DOWN, SHOUTING THEIR WAR CRIES.

IN 'V' FORMATION BEHIND THEIR SHIELD-WALL THE WELL-TRAINED VETERANS PRESS FORWARD, THEIR AWFUL AXES GLEAMING AS THEY RISE AND FALL, WHILE IN THE SECOND ROW SPEARMEN THRUST BETWEEN THE SHIELDS.

11-7   1500

A WARRIOR, MAD WITH THE BLOOD LUST, BREAKS THROUGH THE SHIELD-WALL, AND PRINCE ARN TURNS FROM THE LINE TO GIVE BATTLE.

NEXT WEEK—The Warrior and The Boy

Prince Valiant
IN THE DAYS OF KING ARTHUR
WRITTEN AND ILLUSTRATED BY HAROLD R FOSTER

Our Story: THE BATTLE GOES CRASHING BY, LEAVING PRINCE ARN FACING A BATTLE-CRAZED WARRIOR. "MAY I PROVE WORTHY OF MY SIRE'S TRAINING," PRAYS ARN AS THE WILD-EYED BRAVE ADVANCES SOFTLY.

ARN STEPS ASIDE FROM THE SUDDEN RUSH AND MOMENTARILY HAS HIM OFF BALANCE.

BENDING LOW BEHIND THE SHIELD, HE AVOIDS THE EXPECTED BLOW FROM THE TOMAHAWK AND SLASHES WITH HIS SWORD AT THE EXPOSED LEGS.

WITH A CRY OF PAIN AND RAGE THE BRAVE PLACES BOTH HANDS ON THE SHIELD AND, WITH A GREAT SHOVE, SENDS ARN SPINNING TO THE GROUND. HE LIMPS IN FOR AN EASY KILL, FOR ARN IS SITTING ON HIS OWN SHIELD.

HOOKING ONE FOOT BEHIND HIS ADVERSARY'S ANKLE ARN DELIVERS A MIGHTY KICK AT HIS KNEE WITH THE OTHER.

WITH BOTH LEGS USELESS THE INDIAN IS HELPLESS AND ARN DOES WHAT IS NECESSARY. CRUEL? NO! AN ACT OF MERCY, FOR WELL HE KNOWS THE TORTURES IN STORE SHOULD HE BE TAKEN PRISONER. "MAY THE RED GODS WELCOME THE SPIRIT OF A BRAVE WARRIOR," WHISPERS ARN.

11-14   1504

THE DAY ENDS WITH VICTORY, BUT THERE IS LITTLE REJOICING. THE FINE FRENZY OF BATTLE IS GONE AND SO TOO ARE MANY FRIENDS AND RELATIVES. NEW-MADE WIDOWS WEEP AMID THE RUINS OF THE BURNT-OUT VILLAGE.

NEXT WEEK— The Worriers

HAL FOSTER

WRITTEN AND ILLUSTRATED BY HAROLD R FOSTER

Our Story: THE BATTLE IS OVER, THE ENEMY SCATTERED. NOW THE WOMEN AND CHILDREN RETURN AND THE VICTORY CHANTS CEASE AND THE SOUND OF WEEPING IS HEARD AS NEW-MADE WIDOWS AND ORPHANS MOURN THEIR LOSS.

IN FAR-OFF THULE PRINCE VALIANT AND ALETA SIT OFTEN TOGETHER, SAYING LITTLE, BOTH OCCUPIED WITH THEIR OWN THOUGHTS.

FOR PERHAPS THE HUNDREDTH TIME ALETA AIRS ARN'S CLOTHES AND REARRANGES HIS BOYISH POSSESSIONS.

AND WHEN HIS PRINCELY DUTIES ARE DONE VAL SADDLES ARVAK AND, ACCOMPANIED BY ARN'S OLD DOG, RIDES OUT FOR EXERCISE. OFTTIMES HE LIKES TO BE ALONE WITH HIS THOUGHTS.

NOT THAT HE IS WORRIED ABOUT HIS SON, FOR HAS HE NOT TAUGHT HIM SKILL AT ARMS? AND HAS NOT THE LAD PROVED HIMSELF BRAVE AND SELF-SUFFICIENT? BUT THEN HE IS VERY YOUNG AND SO FAR, FAR AWAY.

"YOU WORRY TOO MUCH," REMARKS THE WISE OLD KING. "ARN IS WELL ABLE TO LOOK AFTER HIMSELF." "WORRY! WHO'S WORRIED?" SCOFFS VAL. "HE IS PROBABLY HAVING THE TIME OF HIS LIFE AND HAS FORGOTTEN ALL ABOUT US." "WHAT NONSENSE," ANSWERS ALETA, "IT'S JUST THAT HE REFUSES TO WEAR WARM GARMENTS AND MIGHT CATCH COLD." THE KING SMILES... NOT WORRIED, INDEED!

1502

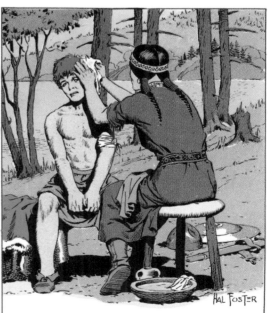

THEY MIGHT WELL HAVE REASON TO WORRY IF THEY KNEW THAT ARN HAS JUST GONE THROUGH A TRIBAL WAR AND EVEN NOW TILLICUM IS DRESSING HIS WOUNDS.

NEXT WEEK— **The Empty Storehouse**

11-21

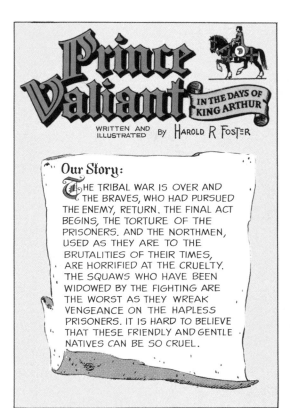

Prince Valiant

IN THE DAYS OF KING ARTHUR

WRITTEN AND ILLUSTRATED BY HAROLD R. FOSTER

Our Story:

THE TRIBAL WAR IS OVER AND THE BRAVES, WHO HAD PURSUED THE ENEMY, RETURN. THE FINAL ACT BEGINS, THE TORTURE OF THE PRISONERS. AND THE NORTHMEN, USED AS THEY ARE TO THE BRUTALITIES OF THEIR TIMES, ARE HORRIFIED AT THE CRUELTY. THE SQUAWS WHO HAVE BEEN WIDOWED BY THE FIGHTING ARE THE WORST AS THEY WREAK VENGEANCE ON THE HAPLESS PRISONERS. IT IS HARD TO BELIEVE THAT THESE FRIENDLY AND GENTLE NATIVES CAN BE SO CRUEL.

THE VIKINGS TOO HAVE TAKEN PRISONERS, BUT THESE HAVE BEEN SET TO WORK HELPING TO FINISH THE GREAT HOUSE, AND THEY WORK HARD AND WILLINGLY, FOR THEY HAVE BEEN PROMISED FREEDOM WHEN THE JOB IS FINISHED.

WITH SO MANY WILLING HANDS AT WORK THE BUILDING IS SOON FINISHED. BUT THE TRIBE'S CHIEFTAIN OBJECTS. THE PRISONERS ARE ENEMIES AND SHOULD BE MADE TO SUFFER.
"NO! WE PROMISED THEM THEIR FREEDOM FOR THEIR WORK," ANSWERS ARN FIRMLY, "IT WILL BE KNOWN THAT WE NORTHMEN KEEP OUR PROMISES OF EITHER PEACE OR WAR."

THE PRISONERS ARE ESCORTED TO THE PLACE WHERE THEY FIRST LANDED AND, AFTER MANY SIGNALS HAVE BEEN EXCHANGED, CANOES ARE SENT ACROSS THE GREAT RIVER FOR THEM.
"LET YOUR PEOPLE KNOW THAT WE KEEP OUR GIVEN WORD. WE ARE FRIENDS IN PEACE, TERRIBLE IN BATTLE. LET NO MORE BLOOD BE SPILLED."

NOW THE HOUSE MUST BE FURNISHED WITH BENCHES, SLEEPING STALLS, TABLES AND DRYING RACKS, STRONGLY MADE AND PLAIN. DURING THE LONG WINTER THE VIKINGS WILL OCCUPY THEIR TIME DECORATING THEM WITH INTRICATE CARVINGS.

THE STOREHOUSE STANDS EMPTY NOW, BUT IT MUST BE FILLED BEFORE THE SNOW COMES, NOT ONLY WITH FOOD FOR THE WINTER BUT WITH ENOUGH TO CARRY THEM OVER THE LONG JOURNEY HOME.

NEXT WEEK—*The Harvest*

1503

11-28

Our Story: *"THE STOREHOUSE IS FINISHED AND MUST BE FILLED, FOR THE WINTER HERE IS LONG AND OUR SHIP MUST BE PROVISIONED FOR THE VOYAGE HOME,"* ANNOUNCES ARN. *"OUR INDIAN FRIENDS WILL ADVISE US WHERE AND HOW TO OBTAIN FOOD."*

THE LAKE TROUT HAVE DESCENDED TO THE COOLER DEPTHS OF THE LAKE, OUT OF REACH OF INDIANS' LINES, BUT THE NORTHMEN SINK THEIR GREAT GILL-NETS TO THE BOTTOM AND EACH DAY BRING THEM UP BY THE THOUSANDS.

THEIR SMOKEHOUSE IS BUSY DAY AND NIGHT, AND THE STOREHOUSE IS NO LONGER EMPTY. THE INDIANS ARE AMAZED AT THIS HOARDING, FOR SUMMER IS A TIME FOR TAKING THEIR EASE. THE SQUAWS BRING IN RIPE BLUEBERRIES BY THE BASKETFUL, AND THE FISH NEAR SHORE ARE EASY TO CATCH.

OTHER FISH ARE SPLIT, THE BACKBONES REMOVED; THEN, AFTER BEING SOAKED IN BRINE THEY ARE SPREAD TO DRY IN THE SUN.

AS SUMMER ENDS THE DUCKS GATHER IN EVER-GROWING FLOCKS AND THE NETS ARE USED TO MAKE A TRAP. THE DUCKS ARE ENTICED IN BY A WAVING FOX-SKIN. AS THEY APPROACH, THE LURE DISAPPEARS AND THEN APPEARS AGAIN FARTHER INTO THE TRAP.

AFTER THE FIRST FROST IT IS TIME TO HARVEST THE WILD RICE. THIS IS DONE BY BENDING THE STALKS OVER THE BOAT WITH ONE STICK AND BEATING THE KERNELS FREE WITH ANOTHER. THE VIKINGS DO A THOROUGH JOB.

THE GREAT CHIEF CALLS A COUNCIL. *"YOU HOARD TOO MUCH,"* HE SCOLDS, *"YOU TAKE FROM OUR HUNTING GROUNDS THE FOOD THAT IS TO KEEP MY PEOPLE THROUGH THE WINTER, AND MY PEOPLE GRUMBLE."*

"THIS IS BAD," WORRIES ARN. *"THE INDIANS WILL NOT SUBMIT QUIETLY IF THEY SUFFER FAMINE WHILE WE HAVE PLENTY."* TILLICUM AND GUNDAR SAY NOT A WORD. IF PRINCE ARN IS TO BE THE LEADER, HE MUST PROVE HIMSELF EQUAL TO THIS CRISIS.

NEXT WEEK— **The Huckster**

Prince Valiant
IN THE DAYS OF KING ARTHUR
WRITTEN AND ILLUSTRATED BY HAROLD R FOSTER

Our Story: PRINCE ARN FACES HIS PROBLEM ALONE, FOR NEITHER TILLICUM NOR GUNDAR OFFERS ANY SOLUTION. WELL, IF THEY THINK HIM CAPABLE OF LEADERSHIP, HE MUST EARN THEIR CONFIDENCE.

FOOD THEY MUST HAVE FOR THEIR HOMEWARD VOYAGE, BUT ALREADY THEIR INDIAN FRIENDS COMPLAIN THAT THE NORTHMEN ARE STRIPPING THEIR HUNTING GROUNDS.
ARN EXAMINES THEIR STORE OF TRADE GOODS, AND THERE IS MORE THAN ENOUGH TO CARRY OUT THE PLANS HE HAS MADE.

HE SEEKS ADVICE FROM THE CHIEF. "ABOVE THE FALLS OF THE GREAT MANITOU IS THE LAND OF THE HURONS, AND YOU MAY TRADE WITH THEM, FOR OUR TRIBES ARE AT PEACE," HE SAYS.

NEXT DAY THE CANOES ARE CARRIED UP THE LONG PORTAGE AND LAUNCHED ABOVE NIAGARA. SEVERAL DAYS OF HARD PADDLING LIE AHEAD.

THE HURONS MEET THE LITTLE BAND IN FORCE, FOR THEY HAVE HEARD HOW THESE TERRIBLE FAIR-HAIRED WARRIORS IN THE SHINING ARMOR HAVE TURNED BACK THE IROQUOIS RAID WITH GREAT SLAUGHTER. ARN, IN HIS CEREMONIAL ROBES, GIVES THE SIGN OF PEACE.

ARN LAYS OUT HIS TRADE GOODS; AXES OF STEEL, KNIVES, SPEAR AND ARROW-HEADS, CLOTH DYED IN BRIGHT COLORS, AMBER BEADS.

1505

AFTER MANY DAYS OF HAGGLING, FEASTING AND CEREMONY, THE CANOES ARE LOADED WITH QUANTITIES OF MILLET, MAPLE SUGAR, DRIED FRUIT AND BERRIES, HONEY AND PEMMICAN. A MEETING PLACE IS ARRANGED FOR FURTHER TRADE WITH THE HURONS, AND THE HOMEWARD JOURNEY BEGINS.

NEXT WEEK— Changing Ways

12-12

HAL FOSTER

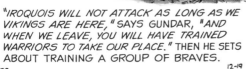

Our Story: ONCE AGAIN ARN LEADS HIS BAND ACROSS THE NIAGARA PORTAGE, BUT THIS TIME THEY ARE LOADED DOWN WITH FOODSTUFFS, THE RESULT OF THEIR TRADING VENTURE WITH THE HURONS. AND THERE IS A PROMISE OF FURTHER TRADING BEFORE WINTER COMES.

THE INDIANS LOOK ON ENVIOUSLY AS THE STOREHOUSE BEGINS TO FILL UP. SUCH A WEALTH OF FOOD THEY HAVE NEVER EVEN DREAMED OF. THE CHIEF TELLS THE REASON:

"WE, THE ALGONQUINS, ARE A POOR, WEAK TRIBE. THE HURONS TO THE WEST AND THE OTTAWAS TO THE EAST LIMIT OUR HUNTING GROUNDS. WE ARE WEAK FROM HUNGER IN THE SPRING, AND OUR ENEMIES, THE IROQUOIS ACROSS THE RIVER, RAID US AT WILL, AND OUR NUMBERS DECREASE. OUR TRIBE IS ABOUT TO VANISH!"

"NOT SO!" DECLARES ARN, REMEMBERING HIS MOTHER'S PROPHECY. ONCE MORE THE NETS ARE SET, FOR IN THE LAKE IS AN INEXHAUSTIBLE SUPPLY OF FOOD, AND THE INDIANS ARE SET TO WORK SMOKING THE FISH. AS THE SUPPLY INCREASES THE CHIEF WORRIES: "SHOULD THE IROQUOIS HEAR OF THIS THEY WILL MAKE A RAID AND TAKE OUR CACHE, AND MANY OF OUR BRAVES WILL DIE."

"IROQUOIS WILL NOT ATTACK AS LONG AS WE VIKINGS ARE HERE," SAYS GUNDAR, "AND WHEN WE LEAVE, YOU WILL HAVE TRAINED WARRIORS TO TAKE OUR PLACE." THEN HE SETS ABOUT TRAINING A GROUP OF BRAVES.

NOW ARN DONS HIS ARMOR AND CROSSES THE RIVER INTO IROQUOIS TERRITORY. HE SOUNDS A HORN AT INTERVALS UNTIL TWO CURIOUS HUNTERS APPEAR. THEY SHOW GREAT FEAR OF THE WHITE-FACED STRANGER, BUT ARN COAXES THEM TO COME CLOSER.

ARN LAYS OUT HIS TRADE GOODS AND SETS A PRICE: THREE STEEL FISHHOOKS FOR A DEER, AN AXE FOR A MOOSE, AND FOR THE STRING OF AMBER BEADS, PEMMICAN TO THE WEIGHT OF ONE MAN.

NEXT WEEK — **The Bootleggers**

Prince Valiant
IN THE DAYS OF KING ARTHUR
WRITTEN AND ILLUSTRATED BY HAROLD R. FOSTER

Our Story: PRINCE ARN HAS CONTACTED TWO OF THE IROQUOIS AND HAS MADE A BARGAIN WITH THEM; SO MUCH MEAT AND SO MUCH PEMMICAN FOR ITEMS OF TRADE GOODS. THE INDIANS ARE DELIGHTED, FOR THE DEER AND THE MOOSE ARE FREE FOR THE TAKING AND IN RETURN THEY GET STEEL AXES, KNIVES, SPEARS, BRIGHT RIBBONS AND BEADS.

THEY SEND FOR THEIR FAMILIES. THE SQUAWS POUND OUT THE DRIED MEAT INTO PEMMICAN; THE BOYS BRING IN THE VENISON AND BUTCHER IT; THE BRAVES DO ALL THE HUNTING, AND COLLECT THE PRICE.

WORD COMES TO THE IROQUOIS CHIEF THAT GAME IS GETTING SCARCE IN THE REGION OF THE NIAGARA RIVER MOUTH. HE SUSPECTS THE ALGONQUINS ARE POACHING ON THE HUNTING GROUNDS, AND SENDS SCOUTS TO FIND OUT.

AND THE SCOUTS SEE SOME OF THEIR OWN PEOPLE BRING PROVISIONS TO A ROCKY POINT, AND LATER, THE WHITE-SKINNED WARRIORS COME AND TAKE IT AWAY, LEAVING AXES, KNIVES AND OTHER ARTICLES IN PAYMENT.

THE BOOTLEGGING BRAVES ARE BROUGHT BEFORE THE CHIEF. A PAINFUL DEATH IS IN STORE FOR THOSE SELLING TO THE HATED ALGONQUINS PROPERTY THAT RIGHTFULLY BELONGS TO THE TRIBE. BUT THE BRAVES HAVE AN EXCUSE READY: *"DECOY THE BLOND WARRIORS AWAY, AND WE CAN RAID THEIR STOREHOUSES OF ALL THEY GOT FROM US AND THE HURONS AND ALSO THEIR TRADE GOODS!"*

GUNDAR HARL SHOWS THE ALGONQUINS HOW TO FIGHT AS A UNIT IN THE SUCCESSFUL ROMAN WAY. AT FIRST THEY SHOW THEIR USUAL ENTHUSIASM FOR ANYTHING NEW..... THEN TIRE OF THE GAME AND SOME QUIT.

1507   12-26

THEN GUNDAR STAGES A MOCK BATTLE WITH WOODEN WEAPONS, AND HIS TRAINED BAND MAKES A SHAMBLES OF THE MOB THAT FIGHTS AS INDIVIDUALS.

GUNDAR'S TROOP RECEIVES GREAT HONOR: THEY HAVE THEIR OWN LONG HOUSE FOR WINTER QUARTERS AND WEAR A WOLF'S HEAD RE-ENFORCED WITH METAL. MANY BRAVES NOW TRY TO JOIN THE BAND, BUT ONLY THE MOST STEADFAST ARE CHOSEN.

NEXT WEEK—**The Gathering Storm**

Prince Valiant
IN THE DAYS OF KING ARTHUR
WRITTEN AND ILLUSTRATED BY HAROLD R. FOSTER

Our Story: FAR ACROSS THE RIVER'S MOUTH ARN CAN SEE THE SACKS OF PEMMICAN ON THE ROCKY POINT. THIS TRADING WILL NOT LAST MUCH LONGER, FOR SKIM ICE IS ALREADY FORMING AND SOON FLOATING ICE CAKES WILL MAKE THE CROSSING IMPOSSIBLE.

UNTIL NOW TRADING HAS BEEN HONEST, BUT THESE SACKS, THOUGH HEAVY, ARE SMALL... AND NO WONDER, SAND AND ROCKS HAVE BEEN ADDED TO INCREASE THEIR WEIGHT.

HIDDEN IN THE NEARBY WOODS THE FIERCE IROQUOIS SEE THE FAIR-HAIRED ONES DEPART, LEAVING THE PEMMICAN AND NO TRADE GOODS. IN THEIR ARROGANCE THEY CURSE THE LOWLY ALGONQUINS.

NOW IT BECOMES TIME TO BEACH THEIR SHIP FOR THE WINTER, AND ARN GOES ALOFT TO LOOSE THE RIGGING. IN THE CLEAR FROSTY AIR HE CAN SEE FOR MILES, AND AS HE LOOKS UP THE COAST HE CAN SEE FLASHING LIGHTS IN THE DISTANCE, LIKE SUNLIGHT ON THE SPEAR POINTS OF A MARCHING ARMY.

HE SEEKS OUT TILLICUM: "THERE WERE HUNDREDS OF FLASHING LIGHTS CLOSE ALONG THE SHORE BUT TOO FAR AWAY TO SEE ANYTHING ELSE. THE FLASHES STOPPED WHEN THE SUN SET BEHIND THE HILLS."
"SUNLIGHT ON WET PADDLES!" SAYS TILLICUM. "THE IROQUOIS ARE GATHERING."

TWO COUNCILS MEET THAT NIGHT. IN THE IROQUOIS CAMP IT IS PLANNED TO MAKE A FEINT ABOVE THE FALLS TO DRAW THE TERRIBLE WHITE FACES THERE, THEN FALL UPON THE VILLAGE.

AT THE OTHER COUNCIL GUNDAR SAYS: "WE KNOW THAT MANY CANOES TRIED TO COME UP THE SHORE UNOBSERVED. I AM SURE THE MAIN ATTACK WILL COME FROM ACROSS THE RIVER MOUTH."

1508   1-2

NEXT DAY MANY CANOES ARE SEEN GATHERING ABOVE THE GREAT FALLS. THERE IS NO ATTEMPT AT CONCEALMENT. ARE THE IROQUOIS SO CONFIDENT OF VICTORY, OR IS IT A RUSE?

NEXT WEEK— **The Marathon**

Prince Valiant
IN THE DAYS OF KING ARTHUR
WRITTEN AND ILLUSTRATED BY HAROLD R FOSTER

Our Story: DAWN IS BREAKING AS PRINCE ARN REACHES THE END OF THE PORTAGE ABOVE THE FALLS. TEN VIKINGS AND THIRTY INDIANS CARRY THE THREE MANGONELS AND THE BUNDLES OF SPEARS.

AS THEY SET UP THE WEAPONS THE IROQUOIS COME SWARMING OUT FROM THE OPPOSITE SHORE MAKING A FRIGHTFUL DIN. JUST OUT OF BOWSHOT THEY HALT TO MAKE SURE THE TERRIBLE WHITE WARRIORS HAVE BEEN DECOYED AWAY FROM THE VILLAGE.

BUT THEY ARE WITHIN EASY RANGE OF MANGONELS, AND THE HEAVY SPEARS FALL AMONG THE CLOSELY-PACKED CANOES. FEW ENEMIES ARE HIT BUT MANY CANOES ARE PUNCTURED AND, WHEN THEY FILL WITH WATER, ARE CARRIED TOWARD THE FALLS BY THE SWIFT CURRENT.

THEIR ENEMIES RETREAT IN TERROR AND THE LITTLE BAND UNDER ARN'S COMMAND LEAVE THEIR MACHINES AND BEGIN THEIR LONG TWO-HOUR RUN, HOPING TO ARRIVE AT THEIR VILLAGE BEFORE THE FIGHTING THERE IS OVER.

AS HAD BEEN EXPECTED, THE MAIN ATTACK IS AT THE VILLAGE. AS THE IROQUOIS SWARM ACROSS THE RIVER THE ARCHERS TAKE A HEAVY TOLL, BUT ONCE ASHORE THE ALGONQUINS CANNOT WITHSTAND THEIR FEROCITY. THE CHIEFTAIN GIVES HIS COMMAND OVER TO GUNDAR.

1509   1-9

AND HE CALLS UPON HIS TRAINED TROOP. STEP BY STEP IN ROMAN FASHION THEY MOVE FORWARD BEHIND THE SHIELD-WALL, THEIR AXES RISING AND FALLING, WHILE BETWEEN THE SHIELDS THE SPEARMEN THRUST THEIR GLEAMING POINTS.

THE TIDE OF BATTLE IS TURNING. PANIC IS GRIPPING THE RAIDERS WHEN ARN FINALLY ARRIVES. HIS VIKINGS ARE EAGER TO ENTER THE BATTLE BUT HE SAYS: "NO, LET THE ALGONQUINS HAVE THE VICTORY UNASSISTED. IT MAY BE THEIR TURNING POINT."

NEXT WEEK— A Prophecy nears Fulfillment

Prince Valiant
IN THE DAYS OF KING ARTHUR
WRITTEN AND ILLUSTRATED BY HAROLD R FOSTER

Our Story: THE IROQUOIS CHARGE COMES LIKE AN ANGRY WAVE, BUT THE ALGONQUINS' SHIELD-WALL HOLDS FIRM AND THE ATTACK FALLS BACK SHATTERED. THE BRAVES RUSH IN TO THE SLAUGHTER. GUNDAR HOLDS BACK HIS TRAINED SHIELD-BEARERS: *"HOLD FIRM YOUR RANKS IN CASE OF A COUNTERATTACK. THE VICTORY IS YOURS. LET LESSER MEN SLAY THE FUGITIVES IN THEIR PANIC!"*

THOSE WHO ESCAPE THE MASSACRE AND CROSS THE RIVER WATCH AS THE ALGONQUINS CELEBRATE THEIR VICTORY. ALL NIGHT THE DANCE GOES ON TO THE THROBBING TOM-TOMS AND THE SCREAMS OF THE PRISONERS. DEFEAT IS AN AWFUL THING.

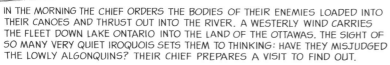

IN THE MORNING THE CHIEF ORDERS THE BODIES OF THEIR ENEMIES LOADED INTO THEIR CANOES AND THRUST OUT INTO THE RIVER. A WESTERLY WIND CARRIES THE FLEET DOWN LAKE ONTARIO INTO THE LAND OF THE OTTAWAS. THE SIGHT OF SO MANY VERY QUIET IROQUOIS SETS THEM TO THINKING: HAVE THEY MISJUDGED THE LOWLY ALGONQUINS? THEIR CHIEF PREPARES A VISIT TO FIND OUT.

AND HE DOES FIND OUT. HIS HOSTS HAVE LEARNED TO FIGHT IN THE MANNER OF THE TERRIBLE FAIR-HAIRED STRANGERS. HE GIVES BACK ALL THE TERRITORY HIS TRIBE HAS TAKEN FROM THE ALGONQUINS AND IS GLAD THEY DO NOT ASK FOR MORE.

THE CHIEF OF THE HURONS HEARS OF THE SURPRISING VICTORY OVER THE DREADED IROQUOIS AND, IN SPITE OF APPROACHING FREEZE-UP, PAYS A VISIT. THE ARMY IS DRILLED FOR HIS EDIFICATION.

1510

1-16

"WE WILL EXCHANGE GIFTS OF FRIENDSHIP," SMILES ARN. *"THIS STRING OF BRIGHT BEADS MEANS PEACE. BUT HOW CAN YOU WEAR IT IN PEACE WHEN YOU HOLD BY FORCE SO MUCH OF THE ALGONQUIN FORESTS AND RIVERS?"*

HAL FOSTER

TILLICUM SEES THE GROWING STRENGTH OF THE TRIBE. ARN'S MOTHER, THE SUN-WOMAN, HAD SAID: *"SOMEDAY MY SON MAY RETURN AND LEAD YOUR TRIBE TO GREATNESS."* THAT PROPHECY MAY WELL BE FULFILLED!

NEXT WEEK— The Map

Prince Valiant
IN THE DAYS OF KING ARTHUR
WRITTEN AND ILLUSTRATED BY HAROLD R FOSTER

Our Story: AFTER THEIR GREAT VICTORY OVER THE IROQUOIS THE NEIGHBORING TRIBES GIVE BACK TO THE ALGONQUINS THE LANDS THAT HAVE HEMMED THEM IN. IT IS LIKE OPENING A GATE TO THE NORTH WHERE GAME IS PLENTIFUL. MANY FAMILIES LEAVE THE VILLAGE WHILE THE RIVERS ARE STILL FREE OF ICE.

A LEAN-TO IS BUILT ON ONE WALL OF THE LOG HOUSE TO KEEP THE FIREWOOD DRY AND STORE EQUIPMENT, BUT MOST OF ALL TO MAKE ROOM FOR THE BREWMASTER. FOR WHAT HARDY VIKING COULD SPEND THE LONG WINTER WITHOUT HIS MEAD AND ALE?

EACH DAY THE ICE GROWS THICKER, LAKES AND MARSHES CAN BE CROSSED, RIVERS BECOME AS PAVED HIGHWAYS. WITH SO MANY TRIBESMEN GOING TO THE NEWLY-OPENED NORTH COUNTRY FOOD WILL BE PLENTIFUL THIS WINTER.

SNOW FALLS, COVERING THE FORESTS UNDER A WHITE BLANKET OF SILENCE. ARN OFTEN TAKES HIS DEERSKIN TO THE CHIEF'S TEPEE AND SLOWLY, INCH BY INCH, HE PAINTS A MAP OF THE NEW ROUTE TO THE SEA.

FIRST THE GREAT LAKES, THEN EASTWARD TO THE ISLAND OF THE MOUNTAIN. TWO DAYS' PADDLING DOWNSTREAM A RIVER ENTERS FROM THE SOUTH. ARN SKETCHES THESE THINGS IN, BEING CAREFUL TO NOTE DISTANCES AND DIRECTIONS.

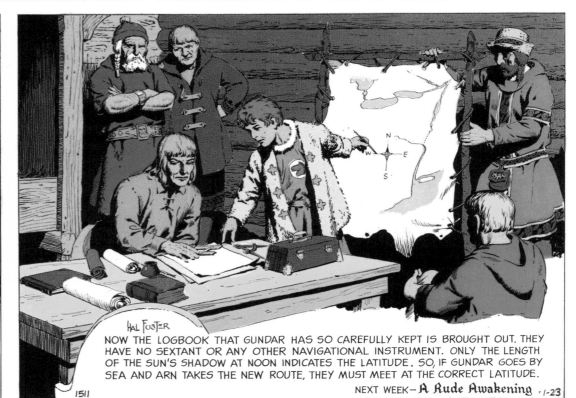

HAL FOSTER

NOW THE LOGBOOK THAT GUNDAR HAS SO CAREFULLY KEPT IS BROUGHT OUT. THEY HAVE NO SEXTANT OR ANY OTHER NAVIGATIONAL INSTRUMENT. ONLY THE LENGTH OF THE SUN'S SHADOW AT NOON INDICATES THE LATITUDE. SO, IF GUNDAR GOES BY SEA AND ARN TAKES THE NEW ROUTE, THEY MUST MEET AT THE CORRECT LATITUDE.

NEXT WEEK— **A Rude Awakening** · 1-23

1511

Prince Valiant

IN THE DAYS OF KING ARTHUR

WRITTEN AND ILLUSTRATED BY HAROLD R FOSTER

Our Story: EVER SINCE THE VICTORY OVER THE IROQUOIS THE OLD CHIEFTAIN HAS SOUGHT TO LEARN FROM THE NORTHMEN THEIR TACTICS IN BATTLE AND THEIR FORM OF GOVERNMENT. AND HE LEARNS MANY THINGS THAT WILL INCREASE THE POWER OF HIS TRIBE.

PRINCE ARN HAS CHANGED GREATLY IN THE PAST FEW MONTHS. HE HAS ACCEPTED RESPONSIBILITY FOR THE WELFARE OF HIS BAND OF VIKINGS AND IS OFTEN IN CONFERENCE WITH HIS TWO ADVISORS, GUNDAR AND TILLICUM.

LEFT OUTSIDE OF THIS CIRCLE IS HATHA, SON OF BOLTAR, ARN'S CLOSE COMPANION UNTIL MORE SERIOUS MATTERS PUT AN END TO BOYISH PLAY. HE CAN JOIN IN THE SPORTS OF THE INDIAN LADS, BUT HE LONGS FOR THE OLD FRIENDSHIP.

HE GOES HUNTING ALONE NOW, A SOLITARY FIGURE. HIS MOTHER TILLICUM WATCHES HIM GO. SHE KNOWS HIS DISTRESS BUT SAYS NOTHING. HER MAN-CHILD MUST GAIN STRENGTH BY SOLVING HIS OWN PROBLEMS.

DEEP IN THE FOREST HE COMES ACROSS SNOWSHOE TRACKS. AS HE GOES ALONG HE 'READS SIGN': THE SNOWSHOES ARE SMALL, THE IMPRESSION LIGHT, PROBABLY SOME CHILD ROAMING THE WOODS....

.....TO SNARE RABBITS, FOR HE FINDS A NUMBER OF 'SETS' RATHER EXPERTLY MADE ON RUNWAYS THE CONEYS MAKE GOING TO AND FROM THEIR WARRENS. A CRY OF FEAR MAKES HIM HASTEN FORWARD.

A CHILD IS SWAYING ON THE TOP OF A SLENDER BIRCH, AND A BEAR IS TRYING TO REACH HER. TRACKS IN THE SNOW TELL THE STORY. IN SETTING A SNARE SHE HAS DISTURBED AND AWAKENED A HIBERNATING BEAR. AND THE BEAR, THOUGH ONLY HALF AWAKE, IS FAR FROM FRIENDLY.

NEXT WEEK – 'A Girl'

HAL FOSTER

1512

1-30

Prince Valiant
IN THE DAYS OF KING ARTHUR

WRITTEN AND ILLUSTRATED BY HAROLD R FOSTER

Our Story: HATHA, SON OF BOLTAR, FITS AN ARROW TO HIS BOW. THE BEAR, ANGERED AT BEING AWAKENED FROM ITS WINTER SLEEP, IS TRYING SLEEPILY TO REACH THE INDIAN GIRL, AND SHE IS TRYING TO SWAY HER SLENDER PERCH AWAY FROM THE MENACING CLAWS.

THE ARROW THUDS HOME AND THE BEAR TURNS TO A MORE ANNOYING ENEMY. TWO MORE ARROWS REACH THEIR TARGET BEFORE IT REACHES THE GROUND.

HATHA SETS HIS SPEAR FIRMLY ON THE GROUND AND KNEELS ON THE BUTT TO HOLD IT. THE ANIMAL LUNGES FORWARD INTENT ONLY TO RIP, TEAR AND KILL.

THE WEIGHT OF THE BEAR AND THE FEROCITY OF ITS CHARGE SENDS THE SPEAR HOME. HATHA SWINGS THE BUTT END UPWARD, TURNS THE BEAST OVER ON ITS BACK AND DRIVES ANOTHER STROKE INTO ITS HEART.

EXHAUSTED AND NUMBED WITH THE COLD THE INDIAN GIRL HAS ONLY STRENGTH ENOUGH TO SWING AROUND ON HER FRAIL PERCH AND SWAY IT TOWARD THE SPRUCE WHERE HATHA WAITS.

HE CARRIES HER DOWN, FOR SHE IS TREMBLING WITH COLD AND CANNOT EVEN STAND. HE STANDS THERE BEWILDERED, STILL HOLDING HER IN HIS ARMS. 'SO THIS...THIS...IS A GIRL!'

1513   2-6

SHE MUST DEPEND ON HIM, HATHA, FIRST BORN OF TILLICUM, FOR PROTECTION. DEFTLY HE OPENS THE BEAR, REMOVES THE ENTRAILS AND PLACES HER IN THE STILL-WARM CAVITY.

INTO THE WINTER DEN HE DRAGS ITS FORMER OCCUPANT AND BUILDS A FIRE. SOMEHOW HE FEELS VERY COMPETENT AND MANLY. WE HAVE IT ON GOOD AUTHORITY THAT GIRLS SOMETIMES DO BRING ABOUT THIS FEELING.

NEXT WEEK— The Man-Squaw

Our Story: DAWN, AND HATHA LOOKS AT THE INDIAN GIRL HE HAS RESCUED. *"THE BEAR HAS SERVED US WELL,"* HE SAYS, *"WE FIND SHELTER IN ITS DEN, ITS WARM BODY HAS KEPT YOU FROM FREEZING, AND WE BREAKFAST ON ITS MEAT."*

HE HAS NEVER HAD MUCH TO DO WITH GIRLS, BUT NOW HE FINDS IT NICE TO HAVE ONE AROUND AS A STARRY-EYED WITNESS TO HIS MANLY DEEDS.

HE HAD NO IDEA THAT HE HAD BEEN SO VERY BRAVE AND STRONG UNTIL HE HEARS THE GIRL TELL HER PARENTS OF THEIR ORDEAL. HATHA RECEIVES THEIR GRATITUDE WITH BECOMING MODESTY.

A WEEK GOES BY. HATHA SEES THE GIRL OFTEN BUT AT A DISTANCE. HER NAME IS STARLIGHT AND SHE SEEMS VERY SHY.... BUT NOT TOO SHY TO INVITE HIM TO GO INTO THE FOREST WITH HER AND TEND HER SNARES.

ALWAYS EAGER TO LEARN MORE OF THE WAYS OF HIS MOTHER'S PEOPLE, HATHA HELPS STAR CUT THE RABBIT SKINS INTO LONG STRIPS. THESE ARE THEN TWISTED INTO FURRY CORDS AND USED TO WEAVE WARM UNDERGARMENTS.

HELPING WITH A SQUAW'S WORK IS NOT A MANLY THING TO DO AND THE INDIAN BOYS MAKE FUN OF HATHA, CALLING HIM A MAN-SQUAW. THAT IS THE WRONG THING TO DO TO THE SON OF BOLTAR.

1514   2-13

STAR, NO LONGER THE SHY LITTLE MAID, RUSHES FORWARD, EYES BLAZING, AND THRUSTS HIS SPEAR INTO HATHA'S HAND, AND, FLOURISHING HER FATHER'S TOMAHAWK, OFFERS TO KILL ANYONE WHO HARMS HER FRIEND.

UNTIL NOW HE HAD BEEN ON FRIENDLY TERMS WITH EVERYONE. THEN HE MET A GIRL AND EVERYTHING CHANGED. GIRLS! (THE AUTHOR HAS IT FROM RELIABLE SOURCES THAT THIS HAS BEEN HAPPENING SINCE TIME BEGAN).

NEXT WEEK— **The Betrothal**

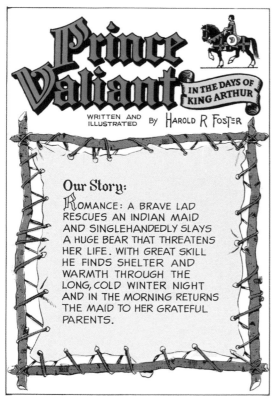

Prince Valiant
IN THE DAYS OF KING ARTHUR
WRITTEN AND ILLUSTRATED BY HAROLD R FOSTER

Our Story:

ROMANCE: A BRAVE LAD RESCUES AN INDIAN MAID AND SINGLEHANDEDLY SLAYS A HUGE BEAR THAT THREATENS HER LIFE. WITH GREAT SKILL HE FINDS SHELTER AND WARMTH THROUGH THE LONG, COLD WINTER NIGHT AND IN THE MORNING RETURNS THE MAID TO HER GRATEFUL PARENTS.

BUT THE LAD KNOWS NOTHING OF ROMANCE. HE IS ONLY TWELVE AND THIS IS THE FIRST GIRL HE HAS EVER NOTICED. THE GIRL, STARLIGHT, WILL NO DOUBT FURTHER HIS EDUCATION.

STAR HAS ALREADY CAUSED A FIGHT BETWEEN HATHA AND THE INDIAN BOYS HE USED TO PLAY WITH. NOW IN HIS LONELINESS HE HAS NO FRIEND BUT HER.

THEN ONE DAY SHE PRESENTS HIM WITH THE GARMENT SHE HAS BEEN WEAVING OF RABBIT-SKIN STRIPS. HE IS PLEASED WITH THE GIFT AND IN RETURN GIVES HER THE STEEL KNIFE SHE HAS ADMIRED.

STARLIGHT'S PARENTS INVITE HIM TO A FEAST, AND HE IS SURPRISED WHEN TOLD THAT HE IS ACCEPTABLE AS A SON-IN-LAW. ONLY THEN DOES HE LEARN THAT AN EXCHANGE OF GIFTS BETWEEN GIRL AND BOY MEANS THEY ARE BETROTHED!

HATHA GOES TO HIS MOTHER: "I AM A VIKING AND THEREFORE NOT BOUND BY INDIAN CUSTOMS," HE DECLARES. "BUT I AM AN ALGONQUIN," SAYS TILLICUM, "AND IN MY TRIBE CHILDREN BELONG IN THE FEMALE LINE."

15/5   2-20

PRINCE ARN BLAMES HIMSELF FOR HATHA'S TROUBLES. "I'VE BEEN TOO CONCERNED WITH OTHER THINGS AND HAVE NEGLECTED OUR CLOSE COMPANIONSHIP. IT IS MY RESPONSIBILITY TO GET HIM OUT OF THIS WITHOUT OFFENDING THE INDIANS."

ARN AND HATHA GO HUNTING TOGETHER AND TALK THINGS OVER. IT IS EASY FOR HATHA TO REFUSE THE HAND OF STARLIGHT, BUT THEY MUST NOT OFFEND AGAINST THE CUSTOMS AND HONOR OF THEIR HOSTS.

NEXT WEEK— A Hint of Trouble

Our Story: HATHA TELLS PRINCE ARN HOW HE CAME TO EXCHANGE GIFTS WITH STARLIGHT, AN INDIAN GIRL, AND LEARNED TO HIS DISMAY THAT THIS ACT MEANT A BETROTHAL ACCORDING TO TRIBAL CUSTOM. HIS PROBLEM: HOW TO BREAK IT OFF WITHOUT OFFENDING THE INDIANS' TOUCHY SENSE OF HONOR.

SPRING IS NOT FAR OFF. THE CANOES AND GEAR MUST BE MADE READY FOR THEIR VOYAGE OF EXPLORATION. HATHA IS GIVEN ENOUGH WORK AND RESPONSIBILITY TO KEEP HIM SO BUSY HE WILL NOT HAVE TIME TO ASSOCIATE WITH THE INDIANS.

ARN'S FIFTEENTH BIRTHDAY IS THE SIGNAL FOR A GREAT FEAST TO WHICH THE INDIANS ARE INVITED. ON THIS OCCASION THE NORSEMEN, IN FULL ARMOR, SWEAR ON THEIR SWORDS THE OATH OF ALLEGIANCE. HATHA ALSO TAKES THE OATH TO FOLLOW HIS PRINCE WHEREVER HE MAY LEAD.

THE FATHER OF STARLIGHT IS NOT PLEASED. HE CALLS IN THE MEMBERS OF HIS FAMILY. "I DO NOT LIKE THIS OATH! HATHA HAS BUT ONE DUTY, TO MARRY MY DAUGHTER WHEN HE BECOMES SIXTEEN. HE WILL BRING HONOR TO OUR CLAN, FOR HE IS GRANDSON TO OUR CHIEF AND MAY ONE DAY RULE OUR TRIBE. ALSO HE IS VERY RICH IN WHAT THEY CALL 'TRADE GOODS'."

"TELL ALL WHO WILL LISTEN THAT THE HONOR OF OUR TRIBE WILL BE TRAMPLED IN THE DUST IF HE REFUSES TO ABIDE BY OUR ANCIENT CUSTOMS. HINT THAT TROUBLE MAY COME OF THIS."

1516

GRAY FOX, THE FATHER OF STARLIGHT, MAKES HIS MEANING CLEAR. "HATHA, MY FUTURE SON-IN-LAW, HAS TAKEN THE OATH TO OBEY YOUR ORDERS," HE SAYS TO ARN. "YOU MUST ORDER HIM TO FULFILL HIS DUTY ACCORDING TO THE ANCIENT LAWS OF OUR TRIBE, ELSE TROUBLE WILL FOLLOW."

2-27

SOON THE SNOW WILL MELT, THE WATERS RISE. THEIR SHIP MUST BE PROTECTED FROM THE CRUSH OF FLOATING ICE.

NEXT WEEK— The Showdown

Our Story: "YOU HAVE DONE WELL IN YOUR TRADING FOR FURS AND WILL DO EVEN BETTER WHEN THE INDIANS TO THE NORTH RETURN," SAYS PRINCE ARN. "BUT GRAY FOX HAS STARTED TROUBLE THAT MAY END PEACEFUL RELATIONS. TILLICUM, GO TO YOUR FATHER, THE GREAT CHIEF, AND ASK HIM TO HOLD A HEARING THAT GRAY FOX CAN MAKE PUBLIC HIS GRIEVANCE."

GRAY FOX IS QUITE CONFIDENT AS HE HARANGUES THE MEETING, FOR HE IS A NOTED ORATOR. THEY MUST HOLD TRUE TO THE WISDOM OF THE ANCIENTS WHO MADE THE LAWS, HE INSISTS, OR ELSE THE GHOSTS OF LONG-DEAD ANCESTORS WILL BE TROUBLED AND BRING THEM BAD LUCK. TO CHANGE TO NEW UNTRIED WAYS IS ONLY FOR CHILDREN WHO LACK MATURE EXPERIENCE.

WHEN HIS LONG SPEECH IS ENDED ARN RISES: "GRAY FOX SPEAKS WITH MOUTH FULL OF WIND. HE WOULD HAVE YOU FOLLOW THE OLD WAYS. BUT DID THE SPIRITS OF LONG-DEAD ANCESTORS HELP YOU WHEN THE HURONS AND OTTAWAS ROBBED YOU OF YOUR HUNTING GROUNDS? DID THE OLD WAYS PREVENT THE IROQUOIS FROM STEALING YOUR WOMEN AND ENSLAVING YOUR CHILDREN? YOUR GREAT CHIEFTAIN LOOKS FORWARD TO A BRIGHT FUTURE. GRAY FOX TURNS BACK TO THE SHADOWY PAST."

NEXT WEEK— The Stubborn One

1517

3-6

Our Story: THE ALGONQUINS TALK AMONG THEM-SELVES: IT IS TRUE THESE FAIR-HAIRED STRANGERS HAVE TAUGHT THEM NEW WAYS. THEY HAVE WON A VICTORY OVER THEIR OPPRESSORS, THE IROQUOIS, AND REGAINED ALL THEIR LOST TERRITORY FROM THEIR NEIGHBORS. THEY ENJOY PEACE THROUGH STRENGTH.

BUT GRAY FOX IS STUBBORN. PRIDE AND GREED MAKE HIM RECKLESS. "ONLY YOU CAN GIVE THE ORDER THAT WILL MAKE HATHA ACCEPT MY DAUGHTER AS HIS PROMISED BRIDE. YOUR MEN FIGHT WELL, BUT THEY ARE TOO FEW TO PREVAIL AGAINST A WHOLE NATION, ANGERED BECAUSE YOU OFFEND AGAINST THEIR ANCIENT CUSTOMS!"

"AND WILL YOU ALSO ABIDE BY OUR CUSTOMS?" ASKS ARN CALMLY, "FOR HATHA IS THE SON OF BOLTAR, THE SEA-KING, A GREAT WARRIOR. HE WILL DEMAND A SUITABLE DOWRY, AND STARLIGHT MUST APPEAR BEFORE HIM TO PROVE HERSELF WORTHY TO BE HIS DAUGHTER-IN-LAW."

"BEWARE OF OFFENDING BOLTAR. HIS RAGE WILL BE TERRIBLE WHEN HE HEARS THAT HIS SON, IN HIS INNOCENCE, HAS BEEN TRICKED BY A SLY INDIAN!" AND ARN DESCRIBES BOLTAR IN HIS GREAT DRAGON SHIPS LEADING HIS BERSERKERS TO WAR.

HIS CLEVERNESS HAS GOTTEN GRAY FOX IN DEEP TROUBLE. HE TRIES TO SCRAMBLE OUT OF HIS DILEMMA BY MAKING A NOBLE GESTURE. THE BETROTHAL GIFTS ARE RETURNED AND, IN A LONG-WINDED SPEECH, HE DECLARES THAT HE HAS SACRIFICED HIS FAMILY'S HONOR FOR THE GOOD OF THE TRIBE, EVEN THOUGH IT BREAK THE HEART OF HIS BELOVED DAUGHTER.

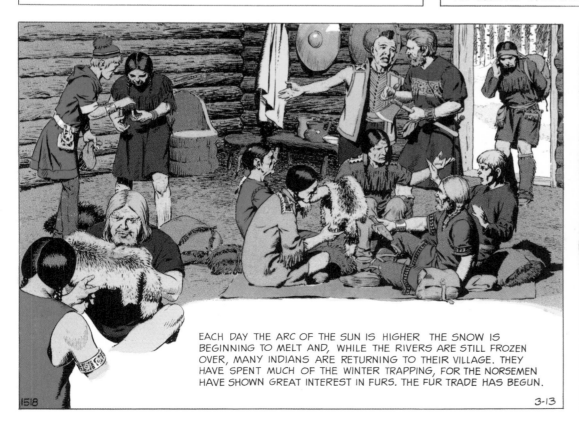

EACH DAY THE ARC OF THE SUN IS HIGHER. THE SNOW IS BEGINNING TO MELT AND, WHILE THE RIVERS ARE STILL FROZEN OVER, MANY INDIANS ARE RETURNING TO THEIR VILLAGE. THEY HAVE SPENT MUCH OF THE WINTER TRAPPING, FOR THE NORSEMEN HAVE SHOWN GREAT INTEREST IN FURS. THE FUR TRADE HAS BEGUN.

1518

3-13

NOW THE NORSEMEN MUST PREPARE THEIR SHIP FOR THE LONG VOYAGE HOME. SHE IS SCRAPED AND CAULKED, TARRED AND PAINTED. REMEMBERING THE PERILS OF THEIR LAST JOURNEY, GUNDAR HARL DEMANDS PERFECTION.

NEXT WEEK— The Promise Fulfilled.

Prince Valiant

IN THE DAYS OF KING ARTHUR

WRITTEN AND ILLUSTRATED BY HAROLD R FOSTER

Our Story: AS THE TIME FOR DEPARTURE DRAWS NEAR, PRINCE ARN OFTEN LIES AWAKE WONDERING IF HE HAS FULFILLED HIS MOTHER'S PROPHECY. THEY HAVE TAUGHT THE ALGONQUINS MANY NEW METHODS, BUT WILL THEY DRIFT BACK TO THEIR OLD WAYS AND ONCE MORE BECOME THE VICTIMS OF THEIR MORE POWERFUL NEIGHBORS?

FIFTEEN YEARS HAVE PASSED SINCE 'THE GREAT SEA VOYAGE', BUT THE INDIANS STILL REMEMBER ALETA, HER BRIGHT HAIR LIKE SUNLIGHT, EYES GRAY AS RAIN, AND THEY HAD BELIEVED HER TO BE THE 'SUN-GODDESS, BRINGER OF HARVESTS'. AND SHE HAD SAID: "SOME DAY MY SON MAY RETURN AND LEAD YOU TO GREATNESS."

WELL, THE TROOP OF SHIELD BEARERS GUNDAR HAS TRAINED IN THE ROMAN MANNER WILL ASSURE THEM SAFETY, FOR THEY HAVE PROVED THEMSELVES INVINCIBLE IN BATTLE AND THEIR FAME HAS SPREAD FAR AND WIDE.

THE INDIANS WERE FIERCELY INDEPENDENT, EACH ONE SUFFICIENT UNTO HIMSELF. IN THE SPRING WHEN GAME WAS BOTH SCARCE AND POOR THEY RETURNED TO THE VILLAGE AND FAMINE. BUT THEY HAVE LEARNED CO-OPERATION AND NOW RETURN WITH VENISON, KILLED AND FROZEN IN EARLY WINTER WHEN GAME WAS PLENTIFUL, AND FAMINE IS NO LONGER A MENACE.

THE HURONS MOVE WESTWARD TO THE LAKE THAT NOW BEARS THEIR NAME AND MAKE TREATY WITH THE IROQUOIS. FOR THEY FEAR THAT NOW THE VICTORIOUS ALGONQUINS MIGHT SEEK REVENGE FOR THE MANY WRONGS DONE THEM.

HAL FOSTER

WHEN AT LAST THE ICE GOES OUT A GREAT FLEET OF CANOES ARRIVES. THE OTTAWAS FROM THE EAST AND NORTH COME TO PROPOSE A UNION OF THEIR TRIBES. OTHER TRIBES ARE ANXIOUS TO JOIN; THE ALGONQUIN NATION HAS BEEN BORN.

"FROM A LOWLY TRIBE FACED WITH EXTINCTION YOUR TRIBE HAS, IN ONE YEAR, FOUND GREATNESS AND WILL GATHER MANY TRIBES INTO A POWERFUL NATION."

NEXT WEEK— The Last Farewell

Prince Valiant
IN THE DAYS OF KING ARTHUR
WRITTEN AND ILLUSTRATED BY HAROLD R FOSTER

Our Story: WITH THE FIRST FAVORABLE WIND GUNDAR HARL SETS SAIL FOR THE HOMEWARD VOYAGE. THE DECKS ARE CROWDED WITH PASSENGERS, FOR ALL THE CHIEFTAINS WANT TO RIDE ON THE GREAT WINGED CANOE. WITH THE CHIEF OF THE OTTAWAS TO POINT OUT THE WAY, THE THOUSAND ISLANDS ARE PASSED.

THE SHIP PLUNGES DOWN THE LACHINE RAPIDS IN A WILD RIDE, FOR THE SPRING RUN-OFF HAS FILLED THE RIVER BANK FULL.

AT THE TREATY GROUNDS ON THE ISLAND OF THE MOUNTAIN A FEAST IS HELD, FOR HERE THEIR WAYS MUST PART. THERE ARE MANY INDIANS HERE FROM DISTANT TRIBES AND ARN SEEKS A GUIDE FOR THE LONG CANOE ROUTE TO THE SEA.

TILLICUM'S FATHER, NOW THE GREAT CHIEFTAIN OF AN EMERGING NATION, TRIES TO FORM AN ALLIANCE WITH THE DIFFERENT TRIBES. THE MOHEGANS ARE WILLING BUT THE MOHAWKS PREFER TO JOIN THE WARLIKE IROQUOIS. BOTH PARTIES ARE RETURNING HOME BY THE ROUTE ARN INTENDS TO TAKE.

TILLICUM AND HER FATHER WALK AMID THE FRESH GREEN OF THE SPRING. THEY HAVE LITTLE TO SAY, FOR EACH KNOWS THAT THIS IS THEIR LAST FAREWELL!

1520

3-27

ONCE MORE THE SHIP IS BORN SEAWARD ON THE SWIFT CURRENT OF THE ST. LAWRENCE. ARN IS FILLED WITH EXCITEMENT AS HE SELECTS HIS COMPANIONS FOR THE ADVENTURE AHEAD. TWO DAYS LATER THEY DROP ANCHOR AT THE MOUTH OF THE RICHELIEU RIVER.

HERE THEY ARE TO MEET THE MOHEGAN TRADING PARTY WHO WILL ACT AS GUIDES. AS THE SHIP WILL GO AROUND BY SEA, AND ARN OVERLAND BY CANOE, THEIR MEETING PLACE IS VERY IMPORTANT. AS YET THEY HAVE NO LANDMARK TO INDICATE WHERE THIS WILL BE.

NEXT WEEK – Troubled Waters

Prince Valiant
IN THE DAYS OF KING ARTHUR

WRITTEN AND ILLUSTRATED BY Harold R Foster

Our Story: THE INDIANS HAVE NO SENSE OF TIME, SO IT IS SEVERAL DAYS BEFORE THEY APPEAR AT THE MEETING PLACE. NOT ONLY DO THEIR FRIENDS THE MOHEGANS ARRIVE BUT THE MOHAWKS AS WELL. AND THE TWO TRIBES DO NOT TRUST EACH OTHER.

THEY HAVE NEVER SEEN A MAP BEFORE, BUT WHEN ARN EXPLAINS THE LAKES AND RIVERS SOME RECOGNIZE THE ROUTE. THE JOURNEY CAN BE MADE IN THE TIME BETWEEN TWO FULL MOONS, SAY SOME. OTHERS CLAIM THE LEAVES WILL TURN BEFORE THE SEA IS REACHED.

THEY ALL AGREE ON ONE IMPORTANT LANDMARK: WHERE THE RIVER MEETS THE SEA GREAT CLIFFS COME DOWN TO THE WATER'S EDGE.

ARN AND HATHA HAVE BECOME GOOD CANOEMEN, BUT THE OTHER NORTHMEN HAVE NO SKILL IN THE LIGHT CRAFT AND ZIGZAG ALL OVER THE RIVER UNTIL SOME OF THE MOHEGANS OFFER HELP. WITH EXPERTS AT THE BOW AND STERN PADDLES, THE VIKINGS' GREAT STRENGTH IS NO LONGER WASTED.

EACH DAY IT BECOMES MORE NOTICEABLE THAT THE MOHAWKS ARE KEEPING TO THEMSELVES. WHEN A MIDDAY STOP IS MADE AT THE FIRST RAPIDS ARN SUGGESTS THAT HIS MEN WEAR THEIR SWORDS AND HELMETS.

THEY REACH LAKE CHAMPLAIN LYING BETWEEN TWO MOUNTAIN RANGES, ITS ISLANDS LIKE BRIGHT JEWELS IN THEIR FRESH SPRING GREENERY. THE MOHAWKS SEEK THEIR OWN ISLAND TO CAMP ON.
"THIS IS AS FAR AS THE TREATY GROUNDS EXTEND," SAYS THE MOHEGAN CHIEF. "FROM NOW ON WE ARE IN MOHAWK TERRITORY AND I FEAR TROUBLE."

1521   4-3

AT DAWN THE MOHAWK CAMP IS VACANT. "THEY HAVE GONE AHEAD," THE CHIEF SAYS. "THAT CAN ONLY MEAN THEY INTEND TO SET UP AN AMBUSH FOR US."

NEXT WEEK – Ticonderoga

Prince Valiant
IN THE DAYS OF KING ARTHUR
WRITTEN AND ILLUSTRATED BY HAROLD R FOSTER

Our Story: PRINCE ARN, HIS VIKINGS AND THEIR MOHEGAN GUIDES PADDLE HARD BUT ONLY ONCE DO THEY SEE ANY SIGN OF THE MOHAWKS. AT NOON THE SMOKE OF THEIR COOKING FIRES FLOATS ABOVE A FAR DISTANT POINT.

"WE ARE MORE THAN A MATCH FOR THAT GROUP," ARN SAYS. "THEY OFFER DANGER ONLY IF THEY AMBUSH US WHILE STRUNG OUT ALONG A PORTAGE. BUT IF THEY CAN FIND OTHERS OF THEIR TRIBE, THEY WILL ATTACK. LET US PADDLE FAST AND LONG SO THEY WILL NOT HAVE MUCH TIME TO GATHER STRENGTH."

THEIR LITTLE FLEET ROUNDS A HIGH POINT, NOW NAMED TICONDEROGA, AND COMES IN SIGHT OF A MOHAWK ENCAMPMENT WITH MANY CANOES DRAWN UP ON THE SHORE. ARN GIVES A COMMAND AND THEY HEAD STRAIGHT FOR THE LANDING.

THIS IS A BOLD STROKE THAT IS VERY PLEASING TO THE VIKINGS AS THEY FOLLOW THEIR YOUNG CHIEFTAIN UP THE SLOPE. THEIR FIERCE, CONFIDENT GRINS ARE NOT LOST ON THE MOHAWKS.

"WE COME IN PEACE AND WISH TO GO IN PEACE," SAYS ARN TO THE CHIEF. "WE ALSO LOVE WAR!"

1522   4-10

THE CHIEF'S FACE IS DARK WITH ANGER AS ARN CONTINUES: "THOSE OF YOUR TRIBE WHO SURVIVE WILL HAVE WONDROUS TALES TO TELL OF THE TERRIBLE WARRIORS WITH WHITE SKINS AND FAIR HAIR, WHO WIELD GREAT DEATH-DEALING WEAPONS."

LOTTI-THE-AXEMAN BREAKS THE SPELL. HE WALKS UP TO THE GROUP OF WARRIORS, LOOKS THEM IN THE EYE, GRINS AND, WITH A SHRUG, TURNS HIS BACK.

NEXT WEEK— Two heads better than one

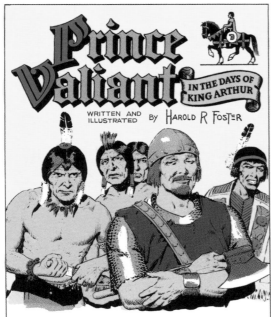

Prince Valiant
IN THE DAYS OF KING ARTHUR
WRITTEN AND ILLUSTRATED BY HAROLD R FOSTER

Our Story: THE NORTHMEN DEARLY LOVE BRAVE AND DARING DEEDS AND THEY SEE ONE DEVELOPING AS LOTTI—THE-AXEMAN INSOLENTLY WALKS UP TO THE MOHAWK WARRIORS, SNEERS AND TURNS HIS BACK CONTEMPTUOUSLY.

HE LOOKS ANYTHING BUT DANGEROUS AS HE CUDDLES HIS FAVORITE WEAPON LOVINGLY IN HIS ARMS. ALTHOUGH HIS COMPANIONS SEEM TO PAY LITTLE ATTENTION, THEY ARE ADVISING HIM IN THE NORTHMEN'S TONGUE OF WHAT IS HAPPENING BEHIND HIM.

AT THE INSTANT THE MOHAWK RAISES HIS KEEN FLINT KNIFE LOTTI EXPLODES INTO ACTION. THE TERRIBLE AXE FLASHES IN THE SUN AND AN EAGLE FEATHER IS SPLIT IN TWO, AMONG OTHER THINGS.

THIS INTERRUPTS ARN'S TALK WITH THE CHIEFTAIN. "LOTTI, THAT IS NO WAY TO MAKE FRIENDS!" HE CAUTIONS. "BUT, ARN, HE DID NOT THINK WELL WITH ONE HEAD," GRINS LOTTI, "AND YOU KNOW TWO HEADS ARE BETTER THAN ONE, EVEN TWO HALF-HEADS."

THE MOHAWKS HAD BEEN WARNED IN ADVANCE, BUT BEFORE THEY COULD PREPARE TO ATTACK, THE WHITEFACES HAD LANDED AND MARCHED RIGHT INTO THEIR MIDST, UNAFRAID, CONFIDENT, ALTHOUGH OUTNUMBERED TEN TO ONE. NOTHING CAN WITHSTAND THE STROKE OF THOSE GLEAMING WEAPONS WIELDED BY HUGE MEN WHO SEEM TO HAVE EYES IN THE BACK OF THEIR HEADS. FEAR MOUNTS STEADILY.

"I TOLD YOU WE CAME IN PEACE, BUT IF IT IS WAR YOU WANT, LET BUT ONE BRAVE TAKE A STEP TOWARDS US AS WE LEAVE, AND OUR AWFUL WEAPONS WILL SATISFY THEIR TERRIBLE THIRST."

WAS THIS A BLUFF? NONE OF THE BEWILDERED MOHAWKS SEEM TO HAVE ANY DESIRE TO FIND OUT. ARN LEADS THE WAY TO THEIR CANOES, AND ON THE WAY A SPEAR THRUST OR AXE STROKE GUARANTEES THEY WILL NOT BE FOLLOWED FOR SOME TIME.

NEXT WEEK— The Portage

1523

4-17

Prince Valiant

IN THE DAYS OF KING ARTHUR

WRITTEN AND ILLUSTRATED BY HAROLD R FOSTER

Our Story: FROM THE HIGH POINT (NOW KNOWN AS TICONDEROGA) THE MOHAWKS WATCH THE TERRIBLE FAIR-HAIRED STRANGERS SLASH THEIR CANOES AND DEPART. NEVER BEFORE HAVE THEY SEEN MEN FACE DANGER *AND LAUGH!*

ONE OF THE MOHEGANS, WHO HAVE BEEN THEIR FRIENDS AND GUIDES, POINTS TO THE RIGHT: "THAT WAY (LAKE GEORGE) LEADS TO A GOOD PORTAGE BUT IT IS DEEPER IN MOHAWK COUNTRY. TO THE LEFT (WOOD CREEK) IS A SAFER PORTAGE IF NO RAIDING PARTIES ARE OUT."

IT IS A RELIEF TO COME IN FROM THE WINDY LAKES TO A CALM, WINDING RIVER. AS SUMMER ADVANCES THE WATER BECOMES LOWER, BUT THEIR GUIDES ASSURE THEM THAT THERE WILL BE PLENTY TO FLOAT THEM TO THE PORTAGE.

ARN AND HATHA, IN THEIR LIGHT CANOE, ARE FIRST TO ARRIVE AT THE PORTAGE (FORT ANNE). "SLOWLY," CAUTIONS HATHA. "MANY CANOES HAVE LANDED HERE LATELY. THERE ARE FRESH KEEL MARKS AND FOOTPRINTS."

AXE MARKS AND CHIPS ARE STILL FRESH. THE ASHES, THOUGH COLD, SMELL STRONGLY. "THREE OR FOUR DAYS OLD," HATHA ESTIMATES. "THEY MUST HAVE BEEN MOHAWKS. HOW OTHERWISE COULD THEY HAVE PASSED THE ENCAMPMENT ON THE HIGH POINT?"

A COUNCIL IS HELD. "IS THERE ANY OTHER PORTAGE?" ASKS ARN. "YES," HE IS TOLD, "FAR UP THE CREEK AND USED IN WINTER WHEN THE RIVER IS FROZEN. THE WAY WILL BE ROUGH, THE WATER SHALLOW AND HAMPERED BY BEAVER DAMS."

1524

THE LIGHT CANOE GOES AHEAD AND THE FIRST DAY'S TRAVEL IS EASY, THEN THE STREAM NARROWS, OBSTACLES BECOME NUMEROUS..... SO DO THE MOSQUITOES.

NEXT WEEK — *The Winter Road*

4-24

Prince Valiant

IN THE DAYS OF KING ARTHUR

WRITTEN AND ILLUSTRATED BY HAROLD R. FOSTER

Our Story: EVER SINCE THE VOYAGE STARTED THE WEATHER HAS BEEN FINE, BUT NOW PRINCE ARN WISHES IT HAD RAINED EVERY DAY AND KEPT THE RIVER FULL. HOWEVER, HE AND HATHA WORK HARD TO CLEAR THE WAY FOR THE LARGER AND HEAVIER CANOES.

THE CREEK RUNS THROUGH A MARSHY PLAIN BETWEEN MOUNTAIN RANGES. ALDER BUSHES SHUT OUT THE BREEZE, AND MOSQUITOES HAVE THEIR WAY WITH THE STRUGGLING NORTHMEN AND THEIR MOHEGAN ALLIES.

ALDERS GIVE WAY TO POPLARS AND HERE THE BEAVERS ARE AT WORK. THREE DAMS IN SUCCESSION ARE OPENED AND THE IMPOUNDED WATERS SPILL DOWNSTREAM.

ONCE AGAIN THE PADDLES COME INTO PLAY AS THEY STRAIN TO GAIN AS MUCH DISTANCE AS POSSIBLE, FOR THE BEAVERS WILL REPAIR THE BREAKS WITHIN HOURS.

WHEN THE ALTERNATE PORTAGE IS REACHED IT IS A GREAT DISAPPOINTMENT. THIS IS A WINTER ROAD USED ONLY WHEN RIVERS, PONDS AND SWAMPS ARE FROZEN. NOW, IN THE SUMMER, THESE PRESENT FORMIDABLE OBSTACLES.

1525   5-1

THEY WILL LONG REMEMBER THEIR FIRST DAY ON THE PORTAGE.

FINALLY THE HEIGHT-OF-LAND IS REACHED. BEHIND THEM THE RIVERS ALL FLOW NORTH TO THE ST. LAWRENCE; AHEAD THEY HOPE TO FIND A RIVER (THE HUDSON) FLOWING SOUTHWARD TO THE SEA.

NEXT WEEK— The Worried Ones

Our Story: PRINCE ARN AND HIS BAND OF VIKINGS HAVE COME A LONG WAY. BEHIND THEM THE WATERS FLOW NORTH, AHEAD HE HOPES TO FIND A RIVER RUNNING SOUTH TOWARD THE SEA. BUT THE COUNTRY IS SO IMMENSE, CAN HE BE SURE OF MEETING THE SHIP THAT IS COMING AROUND BY SEA? FOR THE FIRST TIME ARN HAS MISGIVINGS.

HE BRINGS OUT HIS CRUDE SEXTANT; THEY ARE TO AWAIT THE SHIP WHERE THE ANGLE OF THE SUN'S SHADOW TOUCHES THE MARK. THEY STILL HAVE A LONG WAY TO GO SOUTHWARD.

GUNDAR HARL SAILS ALONG AN UNKNOWN COAST AND ENCOUNTERS MANY DANGERS ON THE LONG ROUNDABOUT VOYAGE. HE HAS AN INSTRUMENT THAT IS THE DUPLICATE OF ARN'S AND JUST AS PRIMITIVE. AN ERROR OF A HAIR'S BREADTH MAY MAKE A DIFFERENCE OF A HUNDRED MILES IN THEIR MEETING PLACE.

IN FAR-OFF THULE THERE IS ALSO ANXIETY. BOLTAR IS LONELY. HIS WIFE TILLICUM AND HIS SON HATHA ARE AWAY ACROSS THE GREAT SEA. THERE WILL BE NO RAIDING THIS SUMMER. PRINCE VALIANT WOULD LIKE TO BE IN CAMELOT WITH THE FELLOWSHIP OF THE ROUND TABLE, BUT HE MUST AWAIT NEWS OF ARN.

SCOUTS RETURN AND REPORT THE MOHAWKS HAVE CROSSED THE PORTAGE AND GONE ON THEIR WAY.

NEXT DAY THE NORTHMEN AND THEIR MOHEGAN GUIDES LOAD THEIR CANOES BELOW THE GREAT FALLS OF THE HUDSON AND HOPES ARE HIGH FOR A QUICK JOURNEY TO THE SEA. FOR THEY ARE OVERAWED BY THIS VAST LAND WHERE HUGE LAKES AND RIVERS SUGGEST THAT IT MUST STRETCH TO THE VERY ENDS OF THE WORLD.

NEXT WEEK— On to the Sea

1526   5-8

Prince Valiant IN THE DAYS OF KING ARTHUR

WRITTEN AND ILLUSTRATED BY HAROLD R FOSTER

Our Story: THEY PROCEED CAUTIOUSLY UNTIL ONE OF THE MOHEGANS POINTS TO THE MOUTH OF A WIDE RIVER AND SAYS TO ARN: "THAT IS KNOWN AS THE MOHAWKS' RIVER AND LEADS TO THEIR LANDS. FROM NOW ON WE ARE SAFE IN MOHEGAN TERRITORY."

AS THE END OF THEIR JOURNEY NEARS, HATHA, SON OF BOLTAR, IS VERY QUIET. FOR HE IS HALF INDIAN AND THE GRANDEUR OF THE RIVER, THE SILENT MOUNTAINS AND WIDE, FREE FORESTS CALL TO HIM. HE PLANS TO STAY.

TOWERING PALISADES RISE FROM THE WATER'S EDGE. THIS IS THE LANDMARK AS IT WAS DESCRIBED TO THEM. JUST BEYOND, THE BLUE SEA SPARKLES IN THE SUN. HERE THE MOHEGANS LEAVE THEM. THEY TOO HAVE COME A LONG WAY AND ARE ANXIOUS TO GET HOME.

ON THE SEAWARD POINT OF A LARGE ISLAND HUTS ARE BUILT AND A WATCH TOWER ERECTED. DAYS DRAG ON INTO WEEKS AND THE WEEKS MULTIPLY.

ARN IS HARD PUT TO KEEP HIS MEN BUSY, FOR AN IDLE VIKING IS A QUARRELSOME ONE. ON EITHER SIDE OF THE HARBOR ENTRANCE THERE IS A SANDSPIT, AND THERE HE RAISES GREAT STONE CAIRNS.

FOR MANY DAYS GUNDAR HAS BEEN SAILING NEAR THE SHORE HOPING FOR SOME SIGN OF THE EXPLORERS. THERE IS NO MISTAKING THE CAIRNS. HE TURNS HIS SHIP INTO THE HARBOR.....

.....AND TO A NOISY WELCOME. THERE ARE MANY TALES TO TELL BEFORE THE HOMEWARD VOYAGE BEGINS.

NEXT WEEK— *The Younger Generation*

1527

5-15

Our Story: PRINCE ARN HAS COMPLETED HIS GREAT ADVENTURE AND MAPPED A ROUTE FROM THE ST. LAWRENCE TO THE SEA. GUNDAR HAS SAILED THE LONG ROUTE AROUND BY SEA AND THEY HAVE MET AT THE ISLAND OF MANHATTAN. WHILE THE SHIP IS BEING PREPARED FOR THE HAZARDOUS VOYAGE ACROSS THE SEA GUNDAR TELLS OF A GREAT DISCOVERY......

...."WE WERE DRIVEN OFFSHORE BY A GALE AND FOUND A STRONG CURRENT COMING UP FROM THE SOUTH. IT MOVED SWIFTLY AND WAS QUITE WARM. SHOULD WE USE IT TO HELP US ON OUR WAY?" (HE HAS FOUND THE GULF STREAM).

TO TRY SOMETHING NEW IS A CHALLENGE THEY ACCEPT, AND SAIL OUT ONTO THE WIDE UNKNOWN SEA. BY TESTING THE TEMPERATURE OF THE WATER, THEY ARE ABLE TO KEEP IN THE CURRENT AS IT GRADUALLY TURNS EASTWARD. THE WIND HOLDS FAIR AND HOPES ARE HIGH.

PRINCE VALIANT AND BOLTAR ARE NOT WORRIED ABOUT THEIR SONS, THEY INSIST, BUT THEY AGREE ON ONE THING: THE YOUNGER GENERATION ARE SCATTERBRAINED AND DASH OFF EVERYWHERE WITHOUT GIVING A THOUGHT TO THEIR PARENTS. THEY HAVE BEEN GONE FOR FOURTEEN MONTHS AND MOST LIKELY HAVE FORGOTTEN ALL ABOUT HOME.

ALETA HAS LITTLE TIME TO WORRY ABOUT ARN'S LONG ABSENCE, FOR VAL HAS THOUGHTFULLY PROVIDED HER WITH A LARGE FAMILY TO KEEP HER BUSY.

1528   5-22

EVEN THEN THE ADVENTURERS ARE ROUNDING THE NORTHERN TIP OF IRELAND. COMPARED WITH THE RIGORS OF THE LONG WESTERLY VOYAGE THIS HAS BEEN A SMOOTH, QUICK JOURNEY WITH ONLY A FEW STORMS, AND IF THE WIND HOLDS FAIR THEY SHOULD BE HOME IN A FEW WEEKS.

NEXT WEEK—The Tournament

Prince Valiant
IN THE DAYS OF KING ARTHUR
WRITTEN AND ILLUSTRATED BY HAROLD R FOSTER

Our Story: PRINCE ARN NEARS THE END OF HIS GREAT ADVENTURE. THE WIDE SEA HAS BEEN CROSSED, IRELAND LEFT BEHIND, AND NOW THE MISTY COAST OF CALEDONIA LOOMS AHEAD. THEY CANNOT STOP TO REST, FOR THIS IS THE HOME OF THE WARLIKE PICTS.

ALL SUMMER LONG VAL HAS LINGERED IN VIKINGHOLM AWAITING THE RETURN OF HIS SON BUT, OH, HOW HE LONGS FOR CAMELOT AND THE COURT OF KING ARTHUR. ALREADY HE HAS MISSED THREE BIG TOURNAMENTS. THEN HE GETS A BRIGHT IDEA.

WHY NOT HOLD A VIKING TOURNAMENT AND CROWN THE MIGHTIEST CHAMPION? HERALDS ARE SENT OUT TO INVITE THE WARRIORS TO A TEST OF SKILL.

AND THEY COME IN GREAT NUMBERS, BRINGING THEIR WEAPONS, A GREAT THIRST AND MANY A BOAST. FOR EACH VIKING BELIEVES HIMSELF TO BE THE HARDIEST OF FIGHTING MEN AND ANNOUNCES IT LOUD AND CLEAR.

WHILE AGUAR, THEIR KING, AND QUEEN ALETA ARE PRESENT THE FEAST IS QUIET AS A SMALL RIOT, BUT WHEN THEY LEAVE, THE MEAD BOWL AND ALE FIRKIN PASS AROUND MORE RAPIDLY AND THE FUN AND FIGHTING BECOME DEAFENING.

IN THE MORNING PRINCE VALIANT READS THE TOURNAMENT RULES HE HAS DRAWN UP. IT IS DOUBTFUL IF ANY LISTEN TO HIM.

FOR THE VIKING WARRIORS WERE HARDENED IN BATTLE AND KNOW BUT ONE WAY TO FIGHT: TO WHACK AN OPPONENT UNTIL HE BECOMES STILL. SADLY VAL TEARS UP THE RULES.

NEXT WEEK— The Viking Way

1529

5-29

Prince Valiant
IN THE DAYS OF KING ARTHUR
WRITTEN AND ILLUSTRATED BY HAROLD R FOSTER

Our Story: PRINCE VALIANT, LONGING FOR CAMELOT AND THE GAY TOURNEYS, DECIDES TO HOLD A VIKING TOURNAMENT. VAL AND HIS FATHER, KING AGUAR, WATCH IN HORROR AS THEIR HARDY WARRIORS ABANDON THE RULES AND TURN A SPORTING EVENT INTO A REAL WAR.

THE TRUMPETER IS ORDERED TO SOUND THE RETREAT AND END THE GAMES, BUT WHAT VIKING WOULD LEAVE UNFINISHED BUSINESS WHEN THEIR MOTTO IS, *"NEVER PUT OFF FOR TOMORROW WHAT CAN BE DONE TODAY"*?

EVEN THOUGH PRACTICE WEAPONS WITH DULLED EDGES ARE BEING USED, THEIR ENTHUSIASM FOR COMBAT IS SHARP. KING AGUAR PULLS HIS BEARD NERVOUSLY. THE NUMBER OF HEALTHY WARRIORS IS GROWING LESS BY THE MINUTE.

THE DANGER OF TURNING THE CASTLE INTO AN EMERGENCY WARD SPURS VAL TO ACTION. *"SET UP THE TRESTLE TABLES, LOAD THEM WITH MEATS,"* HE BELLOWS. *"BRING MEAD AND ALE, LOTS OF ALE!"*

THEN VAL WALKS FEARLESSLY BETWEEN THE COMBATANTS, CONFIDENT THAT NO THIRSTY NORTHMAN WOULD RISK SPILLING A WASSAIL BOWL FILLED WITH COOL ALE. THE BOWL IS FILLED AND FILLED AGAIN, FOR NOW THE WARRIORS FIND CONQUERING A BURNING THIRST MORE IMPORTANT THAN WHACKING AN OPPONENT.

VAL SUGGESTS THEY STAND A BIT CLOSER TO THE LOADED TABLES, AND VERY SOON A WARM AND FRIENDLY FEELING PREVAILS. THE HOUSECARLS BRING IN THE LOSERS TO BE PATCHED UP WHILE STABLE HANDS GO TO WORK WITH THEIR SHOVELS.

GUNDAR HARL SKILLFULLY STEERS HIS SHIP THROUGH THE ORKNEY ISLANDS, AND PRINCE ARN CAN MEASURE HIS HOMECOMING IN DAYS NOW, INSTEAD OF MONTHS AND WEEKS.

NEXT WEEK—**The Signal Fires**

1530

6-5

Our Story: PRINCE VALIANT AND THE KING LOOK ON SADLY AS THE LOSERS ARE CARRIED IN TO BE PATCHED UP. THE TOURNAMENT HAD SEEMED SUCH A GOOD IDEA AT FIRST BUT THE VIKINGS ENTERED THE GAMES WITH SUCH ENTHUSIASM THAT THE RULES WERE IGNORED IN FAVOR OF A FREE-FOR-ALL.

NOR DID THE WINNERS FARE MUCH BETTER. DAWN REVEALS MANY SUFFERERS IN THE DINING HALL, AND IT IS AGREED THAT THEY HAD, PERHAPS, EATEN TOO MUCH.

QUEEN ALETA GOES ABOUT HER DUTIES WITH CALM CHEERFULNESS AS IF SHE IS CONFIDENT HER SON WILL ARRIVE ANY DAY NOW. NO ONE KNOWS HOW OFTEN SHE SITS GAZING TOWARD THE DISTANT OCEAN.

THE SHETLAND ISLANDS FADE INTO THE DISTANCE. AHEAD LIES THULE, AND PRINCE ARN SPENDS THE DAYLIGHT HOURS IN THE BOW STRAINING TO CATCH THE FIRST GLIMPSE OF THE TOWERING CLIFFS OF HIS HOMELAND.

ONE DAY THE LOOKOUT GIVES A GLAD SHOUT. TRUMPETS BLARE AND THE ROYAL FAMILY GATHERS ON THE BATTLEMENT. ALL EYES TURN TO WHERE THE FJORD MEETS THE SEA.
THE SMOKE OF A SIGNAL FIRE RISES IN THE DISTANCE. THEN, ONE BY ONE, THE MOUNTAINTOPS CARRY THE MESSAGE THAT GUNDAR HARL'S SHIP IS IN SIGHT.

THE WANDERERS COME HOME. THERE IS A LUMP IN ARN'S THROAT SO HE DARE NOT SPEAK. AND HATHA, WHO HAD WISHED TO STAY IN THAT WILD LAND ACROSS THE SEA, FINDS HE LOVES HIS BIRTHPLACE BETTER.

NEXT WEEK - Homecoming

1531   6-12

Our Story: THE RETURNING ADVENTURERS SAIL UP TRONDHEIM FJORD. SIGNAL FIRES ON THE MOUNTAINTOPS HERALD THEIR COMING AND OUT FROM THE SHORE COME THE BOATS BEARING FRIENDS, PARENTS AND WIVES OF THE CREW TO FORM A PROCESSION UP THE FJORD.

SOME SAY THERE ARE TEARS IN VAL'S EYES AS HE WATCHES HIS FIRST-BORN APPROACH, BUT HE INSISTS THAT HE HAS CAUGHT A COLD AND HAS THE SNIFFLES.

WOMEN MUST BE ALLOWED MANY PRIVILEGES, SO ARN SUBMITS TO ALETA'S HUGS AND KISSES BEFORE HIS GRINNING COMPANIONS. IT IS NICE TO BE LOVED. THEN HE GREETS HIS FATHER AND THE KING WITH A DIGNITY BEFITTING A YOUNG WARRIOR. BUT VAL CAN READ IN HIS EYES HOW HE FEELS AND IS CONTENT.

BOLTAR IS ABOUT TO TOSS HIS SON INTO THE AIR AS USUAL, BUT THIS IS NOT THE BOY WHO WENT AWAY. HATHA IS A YOUNG MAN. HE GREETS HIM AS MAN TO MAN.

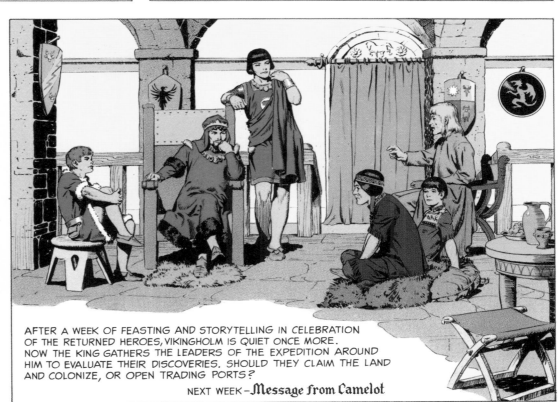

ARN BRINGS HIS MOTHER THE GIFTS HE HAS FOR HER; FURS SUCH AS NO ONE HAS HAD BEFORE. HER DELIGHT BRINGS HIM SUCH HAPPINESS, HE WONDERS WHY HE HAS NOT TRIED IT OFTENER.

1532   6-19

AFTER A WEEK OF FEASTING AND STORYTELLING IN CELEBRATION OF THE RETURNED HEROES, VIKINGHOLM IS QUIET ONCE MORE. NOW THE KING GATHERS THE LEADERS OF THE EXPEDITION AROUND HIM TO EVALUATE THEIR DISCOVERIES. SHOULD THEY CLAIM THE LAND AND COLONIZE, OR OPEN TRADING PORTS?

NEXT WEEK— *Message from Camelot*

Prince Valiant IN THE DAYS OF KING ARTHUR

WRITTEN AND ILLUSTRATED BY Harold R Foster

Our Story: PRINCE VALIANT AND BOLTAR FORESEE A PLEASANT FUTURE. THEIR SONS HAVE RETURNED FROM THEIR GREAT ADVENTURE ACROSS THE SEA, MATURE AND SELF-RELIANT, WELL ABLE TO ACCOMPANY THEIR FATHERS INTO THE MAN'S WORLD.

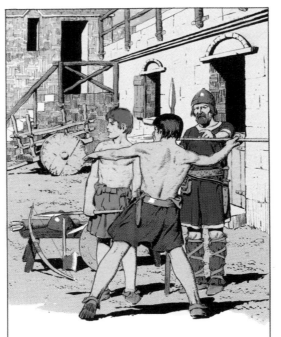

NO MORE DO ARN AND HATHA PLAY AT MAKE-BELIEVE, BUT PRACTICE THE SKILLS OF WARRIORS.

A SIGNAL FIRE WARNS THAT A STRANGE SHIP IS ENTERING THE FJORD AND HEADING TOWARD VIKINGSHOLM.

TOWARD EVENING IT APPROACHES THE LANDING, AND ON ITS SAIL IS THE DRAGON CREST OF KING ARTHUR.

A YOUNG KNIGHT, BARELY OUT OF HIS TEENS, STEPS ASHORE: "I AM HOWARD OF FINNMOOR, AND BEAR A MESSAGE FROM KING ARTHUR TO PRINCE VALIANT OF THULE," AND HE HANDS VAL A SCROLL BEARING ARTHUR'S SEAL.

"TO PRINCE VALIANT, GREETINGS. OUR COURT HAS GROWN DULL OF LATE AND CAN BE BRIGHTENED ONLY BY THE DELIGHTFUL PRESENCE OF THE LOVELY ALETA. ESCORT HER TO CAMELOT, VAL, ERE WE PERISH OF BOREDOM. HOWARD WILL GIVE YOU THE GOSSIP."

1533   6-26

HAL FOSTER

"THE KING'S MESSAGE IS BUT A RUSE, IN CASE IT FALL INTO OTHER HANDS," SAYS HOWARD. "HE BIDS ME TELL YOU THERE IS TROUBLE BREWING AT 'THE WALL', WHERE THE PICTS AND CALEDONIANS ARE GATHERING FOR WAR. NOT AGAINST EACH OTHER, AS IN THE PAST, BUT. COMBINING TOGETHER FOR AN ASSAULT ON BRITAIN. THE KING WILL NOT ADMIT IT, BUT GOSSIP HAS IT THAT MORDRED IS BEHIND THE SCHEME, AND HE IS CLEVER."

NEXT WEEK— **Back To Work**

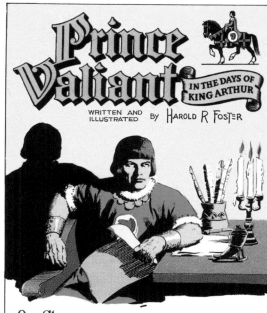

Prince Valiant
IN THE DAYS OF KING ARTHUR
WRITTEN AND ILLUSTRATED BY HAROLD R FOSTER

Our Story: PRINCE VALIANT HAS RECEIVED A MESSAGE FROM KING ARTHUR BIDDING HIM RETURN TO CAMELOT WHERE THE KNIGHTS OF THE ROUND TABLE ARE GATHERING. FOR RUMOR HAS IT THAT THE WARLIKE TRIBES BEYOND 'THE WALL' ARE UNITING FOR AN INVASION.

THE KING'S MESSENGER, HOWARD OF FINNMOOR, CAN GIVE BUT LITTLE INFORMATION. "ALL THAT IS KNOWN IS THAT THE CLANS ARE UNITING WITH THE PICTS FOR THE FIRST TIME AND ARE PREPARING FOR WAR. MORDRED IS REPORTED TO BE WITH THEM AND IS SUSPECTED OF BEING THE LEADER."

ALETA IS DELIGHTED THAT THEY ARE GOING TO CAMELOT. THERE WILL BE NEW FASHIONS, NEW GOSSIP, AND SHE CAN SHOW OFF HER GROWING DAUGHTERS.

VAL HAS ALREADY MADE PLANS. HE AND HIS FAMILY WILL TRAVEL IN THE KING'S WARSHIP, BOLTAR TO AWAIT THEM IN THE ORKNEYS WHERE VAL WILL TRANSFER TO HIS LONGSHIP. DEFINITE INFORMATION ON THE SUSPECTED ENEMY MUST BE GATHERED.

DURING THE SEA VOYAGE VAL BIDS GOOD-BY TO VANITY. HE NEITHER COMBS HIS HAIR, SHAVES OR BATHES. THE JEWELED SCABBARD AND HILT OF THE 'SINGING SWORD' ARE HIDDEN IN A LEATHER SHEATH. HE OBTAINS RAGGED CLOTHES FROM THE CREW.

IT IS A SORRY-LOOKING RASCAL THAT BOLTAR WELCOMES ABOARD HIS SHIP AT THE MEETING PLACE.

ARN LONGS TO BE PART OF THIS ADVENTURE, BUT VAL TELLS HIM: "YOUR MOTHER, THE QUEEN, MUST HAVE A NOBLE ESCORT WHEN SHE ENTERS CAMELOT. THIS IS YOUR DUTY."

THERE WILL BE NO GAY COURT LIFE FOR VAL. THE RUGGED COAST OF CALEDONIA LOOKS GRIM, BUT ADVENTURE IS THERE AND HE FEELS THAT OLD FAMILIAR THRILL

NEXT WEEK— Louse Town

1534   7-3

Prince Valiant
IN THE DAYS OF KING ARTHUR
WRITTEN AND ILLUSTRATED By HAROLD R FOSTER

Our Story: THE ROMANS BUILT 'THE WALL' ACROSS BRITAIN TO HOLD BACK THE FIERCE NORTHERN TRIBES. BEYOND THE EASTERN END OF THE WALL A TOWN SPRANG UP, EVIL, WITHOUT LAW, DIRTY. HERE CAME THE CRIMINALS, THE BANISHED, SAFE FROM THE KING'S JUSTICE. THE ARRIVAL OF A VIKING SHIP CAUSED NO INTEREST.

THE UNKEMPT PASSENGER WHO COMES ASHORE IS A WARRIOR BY HIS BEARING, MUCH LIKE THE MANY OTHERS WHOSE SWORD IS FOR THE HIGHEST BIDDER.

VAL TAKES LODGINGS IN A TAVERN, ONE OF THOSE PLACES THAT GIVES THE SETTLEMENT THE NAME OF 'LOUSE TOWN.' HE SITS IN A CORNER ALONE, DRINKING. ALTHOUGH HE APPEARS DRUNK HE IS LISTENING, LISTENING FOR ANY MENTION OF THE COMING RAIDS.

FINALLY HE IS INVITED TO ENTER A DICE GAME. THE DICE ARE CROOKED AND THE PLAYERS ARE TRYING TO FLEECE HIM. "ENOUGH," HE GROWLS, "THAT'S ALL I CAN AFFORD TO LOSE. TIMES ARE HARD AND NO ONE SEEMS TO WANT TO HIRE A GOOD SWORD."

LATE THAT NIGHT ONE OF THE PLAYERS APPROACHES HIM: "JOIN US IF YOU ARE ANXIOUS TO EXERCISE THAT GREAT SWORD FOR PROFIT."
"I WANT MORE THAN EXERCISE," ANSWERS VAL. "WHO WILL SUPPLY THE PROFIT AND HOW MUCH?"

HE SPEAKS LIKE A TRUE MERCENARY. "THERE WILL BE NO PAY EXCEPT WHAT YOU CAN TAKE IN THE PLUNDERING OF CITIES, EITHER GOLD OR SLAVES TO BE SOLD," ANSWERS HIS NEW ACQUAINTANCE.

1535

7-10

VAL HAS HIS ANSWER IN 'THE PLUNDER OF CITIES,' FOR THERE ARE NO WALLED CITIES NORTH OF 'THE WALL! THEREFORE A RAID INTO BRITAIN IS PLANNED.

NEXT WEEK — The Slave Buyer

Our Story: PRETENDING TO BE A MERCENARY WHOSE SWORD IS FOR HIRE, PRINCE VALIANT LOITERS IN THE TAVERNS OF 'LOUSE TOWN' WITH DUBIOUS COMPANIONS AND LEARNS MANY THINGS. THE RUMORS HE HAS HEARD PROVE TO BE TRUE. THE CALEDONIANS ARE JOINING WITH THEIR ANCIENT ENEMIES, THE PICTS, AND PLAN A GREAT RAID ON BRITAIN.

AND MORDRED IS BEHIND THE SCHEME. BECAUSE OF THE MYSTERY OF KING ARTHUR'S BIRTH MORDRED BELIEVES HE HAS A BETTER RIGHT TO THE THRONE. HIS AMBITION IS LIKE A FLAME AND WILL EXCUSE ANY TREACHERY TO GAIN HIS ENDS.

VAL WOULD BE JUSTIFIED IN RIDING TO CAMELOT WITH THE INFORMATION HE HAS GATHERED.... AND BE WITH HIS FAMILY AGAIN. THEN HE GETS AN IDEA.

IN THESE ROBUST DAYS PRISONERS ARE PART OF THE SPOILS OF WAR AND ARE SOLD AS SLAVES. VAL BUYS TWO PICTS.

HE BECOMES TALKATIVE AMONG HIS TAVERN CRONIES: "THE COMING RAID WILL BE PROFITABLE TO US. THE PICTS WILL DO MOST OF THE FIGHTING AND WE WILL TAKE THE LOOT FROM THEM WHEN IT IS OVER!" WHO CARES IF THE SLAVES OVERHEAR?

VAL OBTAINS A HORSE AND RIDES INTO THE HILLS. HE IS BRUTAL TO HIS SLAVES. "FASTER, YOU LAZY SCUM," HE GROWLS. THEN, WITH A HARSH LAUGH: "IN A FEW WEEKS THERE WILL BE PLENTY OF YOUR TRIBE TO HELP WITH THE WORK."

HE IS CARELESS WITH THE KEY TO THEIR SHACKLES, AND IT IS NOT LONG BEFORE HIS SLAVES ESCAPE. VAL MERELY CHUCKLES AT THIS LOSS.

1536   7-17

FOR HE IS SURE HIS MISSING SLAVES WILL FIND THEIR WAY TO THE PICTS' CHIEFTAIN AND REPORT THAT TREACHERY IS AFOOT

NEXT WEEK—The Seeds of Distrust

Prince Valiant
IN THE DAYS OF KING ARTHUR
WRITTEN AND ILLUSTRATED BY HAROLD R FOSTER

Our Story: THE SCOTTISH CLANS OF CALEDONIA HAVE JOINED WITH THEIR ANCIENT ENEMIES, THE PICTS, FOR AN INVASION ACROSS 'THE WALL'. THE TWO NATIONS DO NOT TRUST EACH OTHER, AND PRINCE VALIANT'S MISSION IS TO CULTIVATE THAT DISTRUST. HE IS DISGUISED AS A SOLDIER OF FORTUNE SEEKING EMPLOYMENT.

THE CLANS ARE GATHERING NEAR 'THE WALL' TO AWAIT THE SIGNAL TO MARCH. VAL MEETS MANY OF THESE BANDS AND BEGINS TO PUT HIS PLAN INTO EFFECT. *"I KNOW THE PICTS AND DO NOT TRUST THEM,"* HE SNEERS. *"THEY WILL LET YOU DO ALL THE HARD FIGHTING. WHEN THEY COLLECT ANY PLUNDER THEY WILL RUN BACK BEHIND 'THE WALL' AND LET YOU FACE KING ARTHUR'S KNIGHTS ALONE."*

HIS WANDERINGS TAKE HIM EVER WESTWARD UNTIL HE COMES TO THE LAND OF THE PICTS. THEY RISE FROM THE HEATHER WHERE THEY HAVE LAIN UNSEEN, THEIR BLUE-PAINTED FACES AND COLORED CLOAKS MAKING THEM ALMOST INVISIBLE. SILENTLY THEY LEAD HIM TO THEIR CHIEFTAIN FOR QUESTIONING.

"I SEEK SIR MORDRED, FOR I HAVE A SWORD FOR HIRE AND HE HAS THE MONEY. HE WILL ALSO HAVE MOST OF THE PLUNDER WHEN THE FIGHTING IS OVER. FOR MORDRED IS AMBITIOUS AND WILL PUSH ON TO CAMELOT AND WILL NEED GREAT WEALTH TO ATTRACT FOLLOWERS."

"CAMELOT, RICHES, POWER!" MUSES THE CHIEFTAIN. BUT VAL DAMPENS HIS ARDOR: *"MORDRED IS NOT ONE TO SHARE WEALTH OR POWER WITH ANYONE. TO CONSERVE HIS STRENGTH FOR THE FINAL EFFORT HE WILL LET THE PICTS DO MOST OF THE FIGHTING."*

1537   7-24

GUIDES LEAD HIM TOWARD HEADQUARTERS. HERE LIES REAL DANGER, FOR VAL MUST BE SURE THAT IT IS INDEED MORDRED WHO IS ORGANIZING THE INVASION.

MORDRED WOULD RECOGNIZE HIM IN SPITE OF HIS DISGUISE, AND THAT WOULD MEAN DEATH. HE SENDS HIS GUIDES BACK.

NEXT WEEK— *A Price on his Head*

Prince Valiant
IN THE DAYS OF KING ARTHUR
WRITTEN AND ILLUSTRATED BY HAROLD R FOSTER

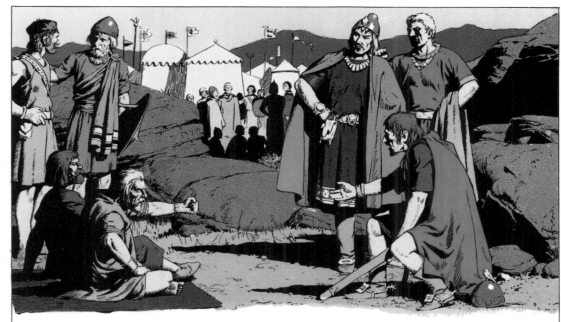

Our Story: NOW THE TIME HAS COME TO MAKE SURE THAT IT IS INDEED SIR MORDRED WHO IS BEHIND THE COMING INVASION. UNDER COVER OF DARKNESS PRINCE VALIANT MOVES CLOSER TO THE CAMP. UNDER HIS GRAY CLOAK, HIS FACE SMEARED WITH CLAY, HE IS ALMOST INVISIBLE AMONG THE ROCKS.

MORDRED IS INDEED IN COMMAND AND WITH HIM ARE TWO OF HIS HALF-BROTHERS, AGRAVAINE-THE-CRUEL AND STUPID GARETH. VAL IS RELIEVED TO NOTE THAT THE OTHER BROTHERS, GEHERIS AND GAWAINE, ARE NOT PRESENT.
HE IS TOO FAR AWAY TO HEAR WHAT IS BEING SAID, BUT BY THE ANGRY GESTURES OF THE CHIEFTAINS ALL IS NOT WELL.

MORDRED'S PLAN FOR A QUICK THRUST TOWARD CAMELOT WHILE ARTHUR'S KNIGHTS ARE SCATTERED THROUGHOUT THE LAND IS BEING HAMPERED BY A GROWING DISTRUST AMONG THE BLUE-PAINTED PICTS. THEY ARE DEMANDING IMPOSSIBLE GUARANTEES FOR THEIR HELP.

HE IS NOT WITHOUT HIS SPIES, AND THERE ARE REPORTS OF A WANDERING SOLDIER-OF-FORTUNE WHO IS SPREADING DISTRUST... AND HE HAS BLACK HAIR!

AND BLACK HAIR IS CONSPICUOUS AMONG THE FAIR HILL-PEOPLE. "FIVE MARKS OF SILVER FOR EVERY DARK HEAD BROUGHT IN," OFFERS MORDRED. "FIVE MARKS OF GOLD TO HIM WHO BRINGS THE RIGHT ONE."

1538   7-31

VAL IS NOW CERTAIN THE INVASION IS ABOUT TO BEGIN, AND THIS INFORMATION MUST GET TO KING ARTHUR IMMEDIATELY. HE DOES NOT KNOW A PRICE HAS BEEN PLACED ON HIS HEAD....

.....BUT HE SOON FINDS OUT!

NEXT WEEK— "Beware The Picts!"

Our Story: SIR MORDRED HAS PLACED A PRICE UPON THE HEAD OF THE DARK-HAIRED SOLDIER-OF-FORTUNE WHO HAS BEEN SPREADING DISTRUST AMONG HIS ALLIES WITH SUCH SUCCESS AS TO ENDANGER HIS TREACHEROUS SCHEMES.

WHEN VAL IS TOLD OF THE REWARD HE LAUGHS: "I HAD NO IDEA MORDRED THOUGHT SO MUCH OF ME!" BUT HIS HEART SINKS WHEN HE THINKS OF HIS FATE AT MORDRED'S CRUEL HANDS.

HIS CAPTORS ARE HEADING FOR THE CAMP TO COLLECT THEIR REWARD WHEN THEY MEET A BAND OF PICTS GOING IN THE SAME DIRECTION, AND THEY TOO HAVE A CAPTIVE WITH BLACK HAIR.

VAL SEEMS QUITE INDIGNANT AS HE SHOUTS: "CHEATS! WILL YOU TRY TO PASS OFF THAT BLACK-HAIRED VAGABOND AS ME AND STEAL THE REWARD? YOU SCURVY PICTS CANNOT RECOGNIZE QUALITY, HAVING NONE YOURSELVES."

THE ENRAGED PICTS, GREEDY FOR THE REWARD, AND OUTNUMBERING THE SCOTS, RUSH TO THE ATTACK. WHEN HIS GUARD DROPS THE REINS TO DRAW HIS SWORD, VAL DRIVES HIS HEELS INTO HIS MOUNT'S RIBS.

HE ESCAPES, BUT UNARMED AND BOUND, AND WITH A PRICE ON HIS HEAD, HE IS FAR FROM BEING FREE.

THIS IS NOT ONE OF HIS LUCKY DAYS. EVERY HILL AND DALE SEEMS TO HOLD A WAR BAND. TOO LATE TO ESCAPE, VAL SPURS TOWARD THEM SHOUTING: "BEWARE THE PICTS! THEY ARE COMING!"

NEXT WEEK—The 'Singing Sword' Returns

1539   8-7

Our Story: BOUND AND DISARMED, PRINCE VALIANT HAS LITTLE CHANCE TO ESCAPE, BUT RECOGNIZING THIS NEW GROUP AS CALEDONIANS, HE SPURS TOWARD THEM SHOUTING: "*BEWARE! THE PICTS ARE COMING. ALREADY THEY MAKE WAR ON THE CLANS!*" HE FORGETS TO TELL THE SCOTS THAT IT WAS HE WHO CAUSED THE FIGHT.

"*HO! THE BLACK-HAIRED ONE WITH THE PRICE ON HIS HEAD,*" CRIES THE CHIEFTAIN. "*DO YOU THINK ONLY OF THE REWARD WHEN JUST OVER YONDER HILL THE PICTS ARE MURDERING YOUR COUNTRYMEN?*" ANSWERS VAL, CONTEMPT IN HIS VOICE.

UNDER CLOSE GUARD VAL IS COMMANDED TO LEAD THE WAY. JUST AS HE HAS SAID, THERE HAS BEEN A SKIRMISH AND THE VICTORIOUS PICTS ARE FINISHING OFF THE REMAINDER OF THE SCOTTISH CLAN. WITH WILD CRIES VAL'S CAPTORS RUSH INTO BATTLE.

VAL IS LEFT UNGUARDED. HE SLIPS FROM HIS MOUNT, FINDS A DISCARDED SWORD, AND SAWS AT HIS BONDS DESPERATELY, FOR ON THE HILLSIDE HE SEES THE PICT CHIEFTAIN DIRECTING HIS MEN, AND HE HAS THE 'SINGING SWORD.'!

NOW FREE AND ARMED HE SKIRTS THE BATTLE AND CHARGES UP THE SLOPE. BEING MOUNTED GIVES HIM A GREAT ADVANTAGE.....

1540   8-14-66

..... AND ONCE MORE THE 'SINGING SWORD' IS HIS! THE FIGHT IS OVER AND THE OUTNUMBERED PICTS ARE SCATTERING ACROSS THE HEATHER.

HAVING CAUSED BLOODSHED AND SET IN FLAME THE LONG ENMITY BETWEEN PICT AND SCOT, VAL GALLOPS SOUTHWARD TOWARD 'THE WALL' AND SAFETY.

NEXT WEEK— **The Grim Pursuit**

Prince Valiant

IN THE DAYS OF KING ARTHUR

WRITTEN AND ILLUSTRATED BY HAROLD R FOSTER

Our Story: PRINCE VALIANT HAS AROUSED THE OLD ENMITY BETWEEN PICT AND SCOT AND CAUSED A CLASH BETWEEN THEM. SIR MORDRED'S PLAN TO UNITE THE TWO RACES IN AN ATTACK ON BRITAIN WILL BE ALMOST IMPOSSIBLE.

HIS MOUNT GOES LAME AT THE SAME TIME THAT HE DISCOVERS HE IS BEING PURSUED. THE WIRY HILLMEN COME ON IN A TIRELESS TROT THAT WOULD WEAR DOWN EVEN A GOOD HORSE. VAL LOOKS FOR A DEFENSIVE POSITION.

ON A NEARBY HILLTOP A CIRCLE OF HUGE STONES SURROUNDS AN ANCIENT BURIAL MOUND. HERE HE CAN FACE HIS ONCOMING FOES.

THEY RACE UP THE HILLSIDE BUT STOP OUTSIDE THE STONE CIRCLE IN SUPERSTITIOUS FEAR. "BEWARE THE CURSE OF THE DEAD," CALLS THEIR LEADER. "WHEN NIGHT FALLS YOU WILL BE DRIVEN MAD!"

AT DAY'S END THE MIST TURNS TO RAIN AND VAL SEEKS SHELTER WITHIN THE MOUND. STILL HIS PURSUERS WAIT AND HE FEELS UNEASY, FOR THIS IS A DUBIOUS PLACE AND THERE JUST MIGHT BE A GOOD REASON FOR THE FEAR IN WHICH IT IS HELD. IT IS THEN THAT HE DISCOVERS THE SLAB OF STONE.

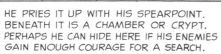

HE PRIES IT UP WITH HIS SPEARPOINT. BENEATH IT IS A CHAMBER OR CRYPT. PERHAPS HE CAN HIDE HERE IF HIS ENEMIES GAIN ENOUGH COURAGE FOR A SEARCH.

IT IS A MISCHANCY PLACE WHERE ALMOST ANYTHING MIGHT HAPPEN. IN THE FADING LIGHT VAL DISCOVERS ITS OCCUPANT, AN ANCIENT WARRIOR WHOSE DREAMS HAVE BEEN UNDISTURBED FOR CENTURIES.

NEXT WEEK— *The Voice of the Dead*

HAL FOSTER
8-21

1541

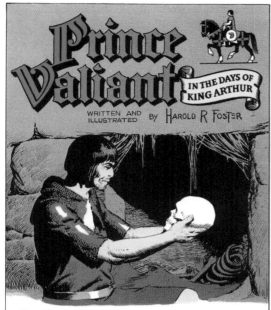

Prince Valiant
IN THE DAYS OF KING ARTHUR
WRITTEN AND ILLUSTRATED BY HAROLD R FOSTER

Our Story: PRINCE VALIANT TAKES REFUGE FROM HIS PURSUERS IN AN ANCIENT BURIAL MOUND AND FINDS HE IS NOT THE ONLY OCCUPANT. *"OLD WARRIOR, YOU HAVE RESTED THROUGH THE CENTURIES. NOW YOU MUST AID ME BEFORE RETURNING TO YOUR LONG DREAMING."*

ALL NIGHT HE STAYS ON GUARD, ARMS READY, AND AT DAWN LOOKS OUT TO FIND THE HILL PEOPLE STILL WAITING BEYOND THE STANDING-STONE CIRCLE. ARE THEY GOING TO STARVE HIM OUT?

THE ANSWER COMES. A DRUID HAS BEEN SENT FOR. OUTLAWED FROM BRITAIN BY THE ROMANS, THEY HAVE FOUND A REFUGE IN CALEDONIA AND STILL PREACH THEIR STRANGE CULT.

PRIEST OF SUPERSTITION, MASTER OF FEAR, HE ADVANCES TO A PLACE SACRED TO A PEOPLE WHO EXISTED LONG BEFORE THE DRUIDS. *"COME OUT,"* HE CHANTS, *"COME OUT OR FEEL THE OMINOUS POWER OF THE DRUIDS."*

A HOLLOW VOICE ANSWERS: *"DO NOT DESECRATE THIS SACRED PLACE. BEGONE! FOR THE CURSE OF THE DEAD IS UPON YOU!"* AND HE WHO HAD BROUGHT FEAR TO SO MANY OTHERS IS FILLED WITH DREAD.

SHUDDERING WITH FEAR HE RACES TO THE PROTECTION OF THE SCOTS..... ONLY TO FIND THEY ARE RACING AWAY FROM THE HAUNTED PLACE.

WHEN HE IS SURE ALL HAVE FLED BEYOND SIGHT, VAL ARMS HIMSELF AND HEADS SOUTHWARD.

1542

8-28

WITH A SIGH OF RELIEF HE BEHOLDS 'THE WALL'! BEYOND IT THERE IS SAFETY AND A LONG RIDE TO CAMELOT TO INFORM THE KING.

NEXT WEEK — **The Mophead**

HAL FOSTER

Our Story: PRINCE VALIANT ARRIVES AT 'THE WALL' AND HEADS FOR THE NEAREST MILE-CASTLE. WHEN THE ROMANS FAILED TO SUBDUE THE WILD PICTS AND SCOTS OF THE NORTH, EMPEROR HADRIAN HAD THIS WALL BUILT ACROSS THE NARROW PART OF BRITAIN TO HOLD THEM BACK.

VAL POUNDS ON THE GATE: *"OPEN UP!"* HE DEMANDS. *"I AM PRINCE VALIANT, KNIGHT OF THE ROUND TABLE, ON THE KING'S SERVICE."*

A SENTRY LOOKS DOWN. *"A KNIGHT? A PRINCE?"* HE LAUGHS, FOR HE FANCIES HIMSELF AS A VERY FUNNY FELLOW. *"YOU LOOK TO ME LIKE AN UNWASHED JONGLEUR, A RAGGED FOLKSINGER. HAW, HAW, WHERE IS YOUR LUTE?"*

VAL IS ABOUT TO MAKE AN ANGRY REPLY WHEN HE REMEMBERS THAT HE HAS BEEN PLAYING THE PART OF A ROUGH MERCENARY SOLDIER AND HAS NOT COMBED, SHAVED OR WASHED FOR SEVERAL WEEKS, AND MUST INDEED LOOK LIKE ANYTHING BUT A PRINCE.

SUDDENLY THE SENTRY IS JERKED BACK AND A VOICE RASPS: *"DOLT, ARE YOU SO STUPID YOU CANNOT RECOGNIZE A WARRIOR'S BEARING? THAT IS INDEED PRINCE VALIANT. GO OPEN TO HIM!"*

THE SENTRY HASTENS TO OBEY, HELPED GENEROUSLY BY A YOUNG KNIGHT.

"HOWARD!" EXCLAIMS VAL AS HE GREETS THE YOUNG KNIGHT WHO HAD BEEN THE KING'S MESSENGER WHEN VAL WAS CALLED OUT OF THULE TO SERVE ON THIS MISSION.

1543   9-4

"I WAS SENT BY KING ARTHUR TO FIND YOU, AND HAVE PATROLLED 'THE WALL' FOR MANY WEEKS. THE LADY ALETA INSISTED THAT I BRING YOUR WARHORSE, ARVAK, AND WEAPONS. SHALL WE RIDE FOR CAMELOT?"
"NO," ANSWERS VAL, *"I HAVE AN INVASION TO STOP"*
NEXT WEEK—**The Flame that Died**

Prince Valiant
IN THE DAYS OF KING ARTHUR
WRITTEN AND ILLUSTRATED BY HAROLD R FOSTER

Our Story: BEYOND 'THE WALL' AN ARMY IS WAITING TO INVADE BRITAIN. THOUGH TORN BY OLD ENMITIES AND SUSPICION IT IS STILL A FORMIDABLE THREAT.
"SIR HOWARD, RIDE WESTWARD TO CARLISLE AND ALERT THE GARRISONS ON THE WAY." PRINCE VALIANT COMMANDS. "I WILL GO EAST TO WALLSEND."

VAL STOPS AT EACH MILE-CASTLE TO WARN OF THE DANGER AND ARRANGE SIGNALS. THERE HAS BEEN PEACE ALONG THE WALL FOR MANY YEARS AND THE GARRISONS HAVE BEEN REDUCED TO A MERE GUARD.

MORDRED IS SICK WITH RAGE. HIS WELL-PLANNED CAMPAIGN TO GAIN KING ARTHUR'S THRONE IS BEING WRECKED BY THE AGE-OLD HATREDS BETWEEN PICT AND SCOT. IT IS TOO LATE TO BACK OUT NOW. HE ORDERS THE INVASION TO BEGIN.

SCOUTS WARN OF THE APPROACH AND SIGNALS ARE FLASHED FROM TOWER TO TOWER, AND WHAT STRENGTH THERE IS ALONG THE WALL GATHERS AT THE THREATENED SPOT.

AS THE WILD HILL PEOPLE ADVANCE IT IS NOTICED THAT THEY SEPARATE, THE PICTS TO ONE SIDE, SCOTS TO THE OTHER, AND WHEN THEY STAND BEFORE 'THE WALL' NEITHER SIDE IS INCLINED TO ATTACK FIRST.

VAL'S VOICE RINGS OUT: "DON'T KEEP US WAITING. WHICH SIDE WILL DIE UPON OUR WEAPONS THAT THE OTHER MAY COLLECT ALL THE SPOILS?"

1544   9-11

"PRINCE VALIANT!" EXCLAIMS MORDRED. "CAN IT BE HE WHO WAS THE BLACK-HAIRED WANDERER WHO SOWED THE SEEDS OF HATRED AND DISTRUST AMONG OUR ALLIES?"

ANGRY WORDS BREAK OUT, BLOWS ARE STRUCK. MORDRED MOUNTS HIS HORSE AND GALLOPS AWAY. EVEN AS HE RIDES HE MAKES PLANS TO GAIN SOME ADVANTAGE FROM HIS TREACHERY.

NEXT WEEK— The Hero

Prince Valiant
IN THE DAYS OF KING ARTHUR
WRITTEN AND ILLUSTRATED BY HAROLD R. FOSTER

Our Story: FROM THE WATCHTOWER PRINCE VALIANT AND THE SCANTY GARRISON WATCH THE ALLIED INVASION FORCE HESITATE AND BREAK APART WITH ANGRY GESTURES. ALL NIGHT THEY STAND BY THEIR ARMS, BUT AT DAWN THE HILLS ARE EMPTY. DISTRUST AND LONG-STANDING HATREDS HAVE BROKEN THEIR UNITY.

OVER HILL AND GLEN RIDES MORDRED AT BREAKNECK SPEED, INTENT ON REACHING CAMELOT BEFORE PRINCE VALIANT. HE MUST COVER HIS TREACHERY AND PLAY THE PART OF A HERO.

HE BOARDS HIS SWIFT GALLEY AND DRIVES THE OARSMEN RUTHLESSLY DAY AND NIGHT.

AFTER A FEW DAYS IT SEEMS SURE THE HILL PEOPLE WILL NOT RENEW THEIR INVASION, AND VAL AND SIR HOWARD SET OFF TOWARD CAMELOT AT A GALLOP.

MORDRED IS FIRST TO ARRIVE AND IMMEDIATELY SEEKS AN AUDIENCE WITH ARTHUR. "SIRE, I COME FROM CALEDONIA WHERE A GREAT RAID WAS BEING PLANNED. I AM OF THE LOTHIAN CLAN AND MY WORDS CARRY WEIGHT, SO I WAS ABLE TO DISSUADE THE WAR-LUSTING CHIEFTAINS FROM A RUINOUS WAR."

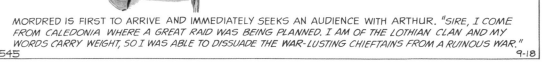

1545

WHEN VAL ARRIVES AT COURT HE IS GREATLY SURPRISED NOT ONLY TO FIND MORDRED THERE AHEAD OF HIM BUT BEING ACCLAIMED A HERO FOR PREVENTING A COSTLY WAR!

NEXT WEEK—A Fly in the Ointment

9-18

HAL FOSTER

Prince Valiant
IN THE DAYS OF KING ARTHUR

WRITTEN AND ILLUSTRATED BY HAROLD R FOSTER

Our Story: PRINCE VALIANT RIDES INTO CAMELOT TO REPORT TO KING ARTHUR THAT HIS MISSION IS A SUCCESS AND HE HAS FOILED THE PLANS OF MORDRED, WHO WAS URGING THE WILD HILL PEOPLE OF THE NORTH TO RAID ACROSS THE BORDER. TO VAL'S SURPRISE MORDRED HAS ARRIVED FIRST AND CLAIMED THAT IT WAS HE WHO PREVENTED THE RAID.

THE KING WELCOMES VAL: "WE ARE SORRY TO HAVE CALLED YOU OUT OF THULE TO NO PURPOSE. FOR MORDRED HAS REPORTED THE RAID GREATLY EXAGGERATED, AND HE WAS ABLE TO DISSUADE THE CHIEFTAINS."

AND VAL, WHO HAS WITNESSED MORDRED'S TREACHERY, REMAINS SILENT. WHAT IS THE STRANGE BOND BETWEEN THE KING AND HIS NEPHEW, THAT HE WILL FORGIVE HIM HIS MISDEEDS, OVERLOOK TREACHERIES, AND LET HIS FALSEHOODS GO UNPUNISHED?

THERE IS A PLACE IN THE SOUTH TOWER WHERE ALL CARES VANISH. ALETA HAS BUT ONE WORRY: CAN SHE STILL DELUDE HER HUSBAND INTO BELIEVING HER THE LOVELIEST PERSON IN THE WORLD? THEN SHE SIGHS CONTENTEDLY, AS THAT ADORING, FATUOUS LOOK MELTS HIS FACE.

BUT IN ANOTHER ROOM THERE IS NO LOVE. MORDRED IS TALKING TO AGRAVAINE AND GAHERIS, HIS HALF-BROTHERS: "I AM SURE THE BLACK-HAIRED SPY WAS SIR VALIANT AND HE KNOWS WE WERE BEHIND THE PLANNED INVASION. WE WILL NOT BE SAFE SO LONG AS HE LIVES!"

"HE MUST BE MADE TO SUFFER," WHISPERS AGRAVAINE-THE-CRUEL. "HE LOVES HIS WIFE AND FAMILY, AND IF SOMETHING HAPPENED TO THEM....." HE GIGGLES, THEN CONTINUES, "AFTER THAT WE CAN HIRE A DAGGER-MAN."

1546

HAL FOSTER

THE TWINS HAVE REACHED THE ROMANTIC AGE, AND AS THEIR FATHER HAS SPOKEN OF YOUNG SIR HOWARD IN GLOWING TERMS, THEY PROCEED TO LOOK HIM OVER.
AND THEY DO LOOK HIM OVER....THOROUGHLY. HOWARD SQUIRMS UNEASILY AS TWO PAIRS OF SERIOUS EYES APPRAISE HIM IN SILENCE AS IF HE WERE A HORSE THEY PLANNED TO BUY.

NEXT WEEK— First Love

9-25

Prince Valiant
IN THE DAYS OF KING ARTHUR
WRITTEN AND ILLUSTRATED BY HAROLD R FOSTER

Our Story: PRINCE VALIANT'S DAUGHTERS, KAREN AND VALETA, HAVE HEARD TROUBADORS SINGING OF ROMANCE SO OFTEN THAT THEY HAVE DECIDED TO FALL IN LOVE WITH A GOOD-LOOKING YOUTH, SIR HOWARD.

KAREN APPROACHES ROMANCE IN HER FORTHRIGHT MANNER: *"ARE YOU MARRIED?"* SHE DEMANDS. WHILE VALETA FLUTTERS HER LASHES AND SHOWS HER DIMPLES: *"HAVE YOU EVER BEEN IN LOVE BEFORE?"* *"GIVE US EACH A KEEPSAKE TO WEAR NEXT TO OUR HEARTS,"* KAREN DEMANDS.
"YOU MAY WEAR MY SCARF IN THE TOURNAMENTS OR SLAY A DRAGON IN OUR HONOR," SUGGESTS VALETA.

"THAT IS OUR WINDOW UP THERE," WHISPERS VALETA WITH A SAD, SWEET SMILE. *"IF YOU WISH TO SERENADE US TONIGHT WE WILL THROW YOU A ROSE."* HOWARD HAS NOT SAID A WORD NOR CAN HE LAUGH THE INCIDENT OFF. THE TWINS ARE SO SELF-ASSURED THAT HE FEELS AS IF HE HAS BEEN ANNEXED.

PRINCE ARN, RETURNING FROM THE PRACTICE FIELD, LOOKS DOWN ON THIS SCENE, BUT IT IS NOT THE BUDDING ROMANCE THAT HOLDS HIS ATTENTION; IT IS THE OTHER WATCHER. MORDRED IS WATCHING THE TWINS LIKE A HUMAN HAWK.

VAL AND HIS FAMILY HAVE SEVERAL TIMES THWARTED MORDRED'S TREACHEROUS SCHEMES, AND WELL THEY KNOW HIS CRUEL, UNFORGIVING NATURE. HE WILL LET NOTHING DETER HIM FROM HIS REVENGE.

1547   10-2

ANOTHER INCIDENT ALSO CALLS FOR REVENGE. FROM A BALCONY FROM WHICH THE TWINS ARE TRYING TO DROP WORMS ON THE PEOPLE IN THE GARDEN, THEY WITNESS A DASTARDLY EXAMPLE OF DECEIT: HOWARD IS WALKING WITH A WOMAN, AND WORSE, IS ENJOYING IT!

HAL FOSTER

"HE IS FALSE. WE GAVE HIM OUR LOVE AND HE HAS BROKEN OUR HEARTS!" CRIES KAREN TRAGICALLY.
"SHE IS A TEMPTRESS," SAYS GENTLE VALETA, *"WE WILL DROWN HER IN THE LILY POND. IT IS MORE ROMANTIC."*
NEXT WEEK— **Love's Labor**

Prince Valiant
IN THE DAYS OF KING ARTHUR
WRITTEN AND ILLUSTRATED BY HAROLD R FOSTER

Our Story: REVENGE IS IN THE AIR. THE TWINS GO IN SEARCH OF SIR HOWARD, WHOM THEY HAVE CHOSEN AS THEIR CHAMPION TO DO GREAT DEEDS OF BRAVERY IN THEIR HONOR. NOT ONLY HAS HE BROKEN THEIR HEARTS BY WALKING WITH SOME WOMAN, BUT HE SEEMS TO ENJOY IT!

AND MORDRED, EVER SEEKING TO FURTHER HIS AMBITIONS OR ENJOY SOME CRUEL VENGEANCE, IS ALWAYS UNDER THE WATCHFUL EYE OF PRINCE ARN.

AS MORDRED NEVER NOTICES THE PEASANTS UNLESS HE CAN USE THEM IN HIS DARK SCHEMES, ARN TAKES A GOOD LOOK AT THE MAN IN GREEN, AN OBVIOUS FOOTPAD.

THEY FIND THE WOMAN. KAREN, AS USUAL, COMES RIGHT TO THE POINT.
"SIR HOWARD IS OUR ROMANTIC HERO, TO DO WONDROUS SERVICE IN OUR HONOR....... LIKE KILLING GIANTS AND OGRES AND WINNING TOURNAMENTS. IF HE BREAKS OUR HEARTS OUR FATHER WILL CUT HIM IN LITTLE PIECES!"
"AND WE WILL HAVE YOUR HEAD CUT OFF," ADDS SWEET LITTLE VALETA WITH A DIMPLED SMILE, "YOUR BLOOD WILL SQUIRT ALL OVER EVERYTHING."

"WHAT BLOODTHIRSTY LITTLE IMPS YOU ARE," SAYS THE GIRL WITH A QUIET SMILE. "TELL ME, HAVE YOU EVER HAD YOUR LITTLE PANTIES WARMED?"
THE TWINS INSTINCTIVELY PUT THEIR HANDS BEHIND THEM. "YOU TALK JUST LIKE OUR MOTHER," COMPLAINS KAREN.

DAUGHTERS OF A QUEEN AND A WARRIOR PRINCE, THEY ARE THOROUGHLY SPOILED BY EVERYONE...... EXCEPT THIS ONE. AND SHE HAS NOT ONLY THREATENED THEM WITH BODILY HARM BUT LOOKS AS IF SHE WOULD DO IT, TOO.

1548

10-9

HAL FOSTER

"HERE COMES SIR HOWARD NOW. LET HIM CHOOSE BETWEEN US," LAUGHS THE GIRL.
HOWARD, A MERE STRIPLING, AS YET UNTRIED IN BATTLE, FACES A MOST EMBARRASSING SITUATION.
"OUR FATHER'S SWORD WILL PROTECT OUR HONOR," KAREN REMINDS HIM. "I HAVE NO ONE TO PROTECT ME," SAYS THE GIRL, AND THEN FOR SOME STRANGE REASON BURSTS OUT LAUGHING.
"I MUST GO ON GUARD DUTY," STAMMERS THE BLUSHING YOUTH AS HE HASTENS AWAY.

NEXT WEEK—*Vengeance*

Prince Valiant

IN THE DAYS OF KING ARTHUR

WRITTEN AND ILLUSTRATED BY HAROLD R FOSTER

Our Story: A SMALL CORNER OF CAMELOT SEETHES WITH INTRIGUE AND SUSPICION. PRINCE VALIANT'S TWIN DAUGHTERS KEEP AN EYE ON SIR HOWARD, THEIR CHOSEN KNIGHT ERRANT, TO MAKE SURE HE DOES NOT AGAIN WALK WITH 'THAT WOMAN'.

AND FRAYDA, 'THAT WOMAN,' HAS FOUND IT PLEASANT TO WALK WITH HOWARD. BUT SHE HAS LAUGHED AT HIM AND HURT HIS FEELINGS, AND NOW SHE SEEKS MEANS TO MAKE AMENDS.

MORE DEADLY IS THE HATRED OF MORDRED, FOR HE SUSPECTS VAL KNOWS OF HIS TREACHERY. HE PLANS TO SEEK REVENGE THROUGH VAL'S LOVED ONES.

MORDRED SPENDS AN ANXIOUS HOUR AS KING ARTHUR QUESTIONS THEM ABOUT THE THREATENED RAID; WILL VAL DISCLOSE HIS TRAITOROUS LEADERSHIP?
"I RODE NORTH OF 'THE WALL' AND SAW THE WAR BANDS GATHERING," SAYS VAL. "AND DID YOU SEE MORDRED IN YOUR WANDERINGS?" ASKS ARTHUR.
"YES," VAL REPLIES, "HE WAS TALKING WITH THE CHIEFTAINS." THE KING SMILES: "OUR THANKS TO YOU, MORDRED, FOR INDUCING THE CHIEFTAINS TO GIVE UP THE RAID."

VAL COULD HAVE ADDED THAT MORDRED WAS PLANNING THE RAID, NOT STOPPING IT. BUT WHY ADD ANOTHER WORRY TO THE ALREADY-OVERBURDENED KING?

WHY HAS NOT VAL ACCUSED HIM OF TREACHERY; DOES HE HAVE OTHER SCHEMES; WHAT IS HE PLANNING?
NOW MORDRED IS REALLY FRIGHTENED. SELFISHNESS AND REVENGE HE CAN UNDERSTAND, BUT NOT GENEROSITY.

WHEN ARN ENTERS THE STABLES HE GETS A SURPRISE. AT MORDRED'S STALLS THERE ARE STRANGE HOSTLERS, AND ONE OF THEM IS THE MAN IN GREEN TO WHOM MORDRED HAS PASSED A PURSE.

1549

10-16

ARN HAS A NARROW ESCAPE. ON HIS FIRST CHARGE AT THE PRACTICE QUINTAIN HIS STIRRUP LEATHER BREAKS AND HE VERY NEARLY CRASHES INTO THE POST. HIS STIRRUP LEATHER HAS BEEN CUT ALMOST THROUGH!

NEXT WEEK— *Kidnaper*

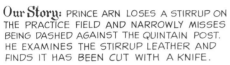

Prince Valiant
IN THE DAYS OF KING ARTHUR
WRITTEN AND ILLUSTRATED BY HAROLD R FOSTER

Our Story: PRINCE ARN LOSES A STIRRUP ON THE PRACTICE FIELD AND NARROWLY MISSES BEING DASHED AGAINST THE QUINTAIN POST. HE EXAMINES THE STIRRUP LEATHER AND FINDS IT HAS BEEN CUT WITH A KNIFE.

HE SHOWS IT TO HIS HOSTLER WHO SAYS, *"IT MIGHT BE THE WORK OF SIR MORDRED'S NEW STABLE HANDS."* HE FROWNS. *"THEY ARE TAVERN LOAFERS FROM THE TOWN AND WERE NOT ALLOWED IN THE CASTLE UNTIL MORDRED HIRED THEM."*

ONE OF MORDRED'S MEN, THE ONE IN GREEN, SPENDS MUCH TIME ON THE STABLE ROOF PRETENDING TO REPAIR THE THATCH. FROM HERE HE CAN WATCH THE COMINGS AND GOINGS OF PRINCE VALIANT'S FAMILY. ARN IS QUICK TO NOTE THIS.

HE FINDS IT HARD TO CONVINCE HIS FATHER THAT THE FAMILY IS IN DANGER, THAT ANYONE COULD SINK SO LOW AS TO SEEK VENGEANCE THROUGH INNOCENT CHILDREN. *"BUT, SIRE, SIR MORDRED DOES NOT GO BY THE STANDARDS OF OTHERS,"* ARGUES ARN. *"BY YOUR OWN TELLING HE HAS THE SOUL OF A VIPER."*

VAL TAKES THE FAMILY OUT FOR A PICNIC. THEY WAVE GOOD-BYE TO GALAN WHO IS TOO YOUNG TO RIDE, AND CLATTER OUT OF THE COURTYARD.

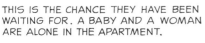

THIS IS THE CHANCE THEY HAVE BEEN WAITING FOR. A BABY AND A WOMAN ARE ALONE IN THE APARTMENT.

1550   10-23

IN A SHELTERED CORNER OF THE BALCONY KATWIN PREPARES GALAN FOR HIS AFTERNOON NAP.

A LADDER TOUCHES THE WALL GENTLY AND THE MAN IN GREEN PEERS OVER. HE GRINS. THIS IS AN EASY WAY TO WIN THE PROMISED REWARD.

NEXT WEEK — **The Reward**

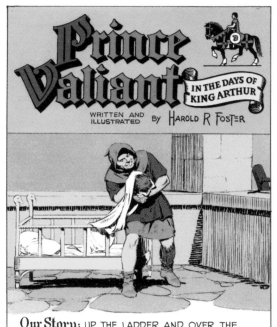

Prince Valiant

IN THE DAYS OF KING ARTHUR

WRITTEN AND ILLUSTRATED BY HAROLD R FOSTER

Our Story: UP THE LADDER AND OVER THE PARAPET GLIDES THE SINISTER MAN IN GREEN. HE GLANCES RIGHT AND LEFT AS HE APPROACHES GALAN'S CRIB. THEN, SNATCHING UP THE COVERS TO MUFFLE THE INFANT'S CRIES, HE SLIPS DOWN THE LADDER.

THE DEED IS DONE. THEY HAVE EARNED MORDRED'S REWARD AND NOW THE DESPERATE NEED TO ESCAPE BECOMES NEAR PANIC. TO SPEED THE GETAWAY THE INFANT IS THROWN DOWN TO WAITING HANDS.

AS THEY TURN TO ESCAPE, A HORRIFYING SIGHT MEETS THEIR EYES. PRINCE VALIANT BLOCKS THEIR WAY AND IS DRAWING THE FEARFUL 'SINGING SWORD.' WORST OF ALL IS THE LOOK IN HIS EYES.

THE OMINOUS SILENCE IS BROKEN BY THE TWINS. "ROBBERS! STOP THIEF!", THEY SCREAM. "HO, THE GUARD! THEY ARE STEALING OUR DOLL!" VAL ALLOWS THE GUARD TO REMOVE THE RUFFIANS.

SIR KAY, THE SENESCHAL, CONDUCTS THE TRIAL. SIR MORDRED IS THE PICTURE OF VIRTUE BETRAYED. "YES, THESE VARLETS ARE MY MEN, AND IF IT PLEASE YOU, SIR KAY, RELEASE THEM TO ME AND I WILL SEE THAT THEY ARE FITTINGLY PUNISHED."
"THEY ARE FORBIDDEN TO ENTER THE CASTLE EVER AGAIN." THE SENTENCE PLEASES MORDRED. HE WILL SEE THAT THEY NEVER HAVE A CHANCE TO BETRAY HIM.

KATWIN TELLS HOW SHE STOOD JUST INSIDE THE DOOR WITH A WAR AX IN CASE THE KIDNAPPER DISCOVERED THE HOAX AND TRIED TO ENTER. AND KATWIN, A CHIEFTAIN'S DAUGHTER, SEEMS SORRY HE HAD NOT. VAL REMAINS SILENT. LATER HE ARMS AND GOES OUT, HIS FACE GRIM.

"SIR MORDRED, I HOLD YOU RESPONSIBLE FOR THE DEEDS OF YOUR MEN," AND HIS VOICE IS FULL OF MENACE. "KINDLY SEE THAT NO DANGER THREATENS MY FAMILY.....EVER!" THE HAND THAT CARESSES THE HILT OF THE 'SINGING SWORD' SEEMS ALL TOO EAGER.

NEXT WEEK — The Mermaid

1551   10-30

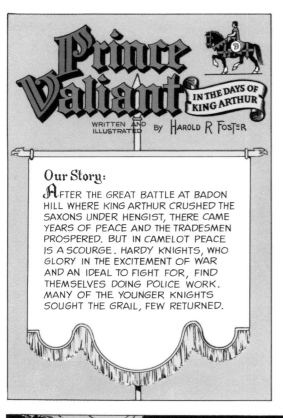

Prince Valiant

IN THE DAYS OF KING ARTHUR

WRITTEN AND ILLUSTRATED BY HAROLD R FOSTER

Our Story:

AFTER THE GREAT BATTLE AT BADON HILL WHERE KING ARTHUR CRUSHED THE SAXONS UNDER HENGIST, THERE CAME YEARS OF PEACE AND THE TRADESMEN PROSPERED. BUT IN CAMELOT PEACE IS A SCOURGE. HARDY KNIGHTS, WHO GLORY IN THE EXCITEMENT OF WAR AND AN IDEAL TO FIGHT FOR, FIND THEMSELVES DOING POLICE WORK. MANY OF THE YOUNGER KNIGHTS SOUGHT THE GRAIL, FEW RETURNED.

THE SUMMER IS HOT, CAMELOT IS DULL, SO ALETA TAKES HER FAMILY TO THE SEASHORE. BORN ON AN AEGEAN ISLAND THE SEA HAS ALWAYS BEEN HER PLAYGROUND AND ITS CALL IS IRRESISTIBLE

HER BROOD HAS BEEN TAUGHT TO SWIM EVEN AS THEY LEARNED TO WALK AND THEY SPEND HOURS OF DELIGHT IN THE SHELTERED COVE. THEN ALETA WOULD SEND THEM ASHORE AND GLIDE FAR OUT TO SEA.

THEN ONE DAY SHE DISCOVERS A GROTTO ON A LONELY POINT THAT STRETCHES FAR OUT INTO THE WAVES. AS A PRINCESS SHE HAD HAD HER OWN PRIVATE BEACH WHERE SHE COULD SWIM UNHAMPERED BY THE GARMENTS FASHION DECREES. NOW, FAR FROM PRYING EYES, SHE CAN ONCE AGAIN SWIM FREE.

PRINCE VALIANT IS BUSY AND, AT FIRST, PAYS LITTLE ATTENTION TO THE RUMORS THAT ARE EXCITING ALL CAMELOT. NYMPHS, MERMAIDS AND WATERMAIDS HAVE BEEN SEEN AT LLANTWIT, AND SOME CLAIM TO HAVE BEEN WITNESSES TO THE APPEARANCES.

A— "A PEASANT LED ME TO THE TOP OF THE CLIFF AND WITH MY OWN EYES I SAW A MERMAID RISE FROM THE OCEAN DEPTHS AND GLIDE OUT TO SEA!"

B— "AND I SAW THIS MAGICAL NYMPH COME IN FROM THE WAVES AND DISAPPEAR INTO THE DEPTHS."

C— "BEWARE THESE WATERMAIDENS! ONE LURED ME DOWN TO THE WATER'S EDGE BY HER POTENT CHARM, THEN VANISHED FROM SIGHT. I SCRAMBLED UP THE CLIFF IN HASTE AND SO AVOIDED HER SPELL."

1552

"SIRE, THERE MUST BE SOME INFORMATION OF THESE APPEARANCES AMONG MERLIN'S BOOKS AND SCROLLS."

"MERLIN'S TOWER HAS BEEN LOCKED SINCE HIS DISAPPEARANCE, BUT AS YOU WERE HIS FAVORITE PUPIL, I GIVE YOU THE KEY."

HAL FOSTER

NEXT WEEK— Proof

11-6

Prince Valiant
IN THE DAYS OF KING ARTHUR
WRITTEN AND ILLUSTRATED BY HAROLD R FOSTER

Our Story: WILD STORIES REACH CAMELOT. MERMAIDS, WATER NYMPHS AND OTHER MAGICAL CREATURES HAVE BEEN SEEN OFF THE COAST NEAR LLANTWIT. PRINCE VALIANT IS WORRIED, FOR HIS FAMILY IS ON A HOLIDAY NEAR THERE. HE ASKS KING ARTHUR FOR THE KEY TO MERLIN'S LABORATORY.

NO ONE HAS ENTERED THIS TOWER ROOM SINCE THE GREAT WIZARD DISAPPEARED, BUT VAL, A PUPIL OF MERLIN'S IN BYGONE DAYS, IS FAMILIAR WITH THE LIBRARY.

IN DUSTY TOMES AND YELLOWED SCROLLS HE FINDS MANY REFERENCES TO THESE SEAGOING LADIES AND MAKES A LONG LIST....

....APHRODITE AROSE FROM THE SEA WITH AN ESCORT OF MERMAIDS. LEDA WAS A WATER NYMPH. THEN THERE WAS THE SIREN, LORELEI; ANOTHER SIREN ALMOST OVERCAME ULYSSES. THE LADY OF THE LAKE GAVE EXCALIBUR TO ARTHUR.

VAL SETS OUT FOR LLANTWIT TAKING WITH HIM AS GUIDES THE KNIGHTS WHO CLAIMED TO HAVE SEEN THESE MYTHOLOGICAL BEINGS. IN HIS ANXIETY FOR THE SAFETY OF HIS FAMILY HE HAS FORGOTTEN MERLIN'S TEACHING.

WHEN THEY ARRIVE AT THE CLIFF'S EDGE QUITE A CROWD HAS FOLLOWED. THE SEA, SPARKLING IN THE SUNLIGHT, IS EMPTY SAVE FOR A FEW GULLS.

"THERE SHE IS!" THEN, AS SHE GLIDES IN CLOSER, "SHE HAS A TAIL ALL COVERED WITH GOLDEN SCALES!" "NOT SO," EXCLAIMS ANOTHER. "IT IS HER GOLDEN HAIR." "LET US DRAW BACK LEST SHE BE A SIREN AND LURE US TO OUR DOOM!"

STRAIGHT FOR THE FOOT OF THE CLIFF THE CREATURE COMES. THEY CANNOT TELL IF IT BE A MERMAID, FOR HER GOLDEN HAIR FLOWS OUT BEHIND LIKE A CLOAK. THEN, BEFORE THEIR VERY EYES, SHE RETURNS TO THE DEPTHS.
NEXT WEEK- Can Mermaids Blush?

1553   11-13

Prince Valiant
IN THE DAYS OF KING ARTHUR
WRITTEN AND ILLUSTRATED BY HAROLD R FOSTER

Our Story: IN AWED SILENCE THE GROUP ON THE CLIFF WATCH THE MERMAID RETURN TO THE DEPTHS OF THE SEA. IT IS THEN THAT PRINCE VALIANT REMEMBERS MERLIN SAYING: *"THE SUPERNATURAL ALWAYS HAS A RATIONAL EXPLANATION."* HE DETERMINES TO SEEK THE ANSWER TO THIS MYSTERY.

AS HE CLIMBS DOWN THE CLIFF HIS COMPANIONS WARN HIM OF THE DANGER OF MEDDLING IN THE AFFAIRS OF THE MAGICAL BEINGS.

CLIMBING AMONG THE ROCKS AT THE WATER'S EDGE NEAR THE SPOT WHERE THE MAID DISAPPEARED, HE DISCOVERS AN ENTRANCE TO A GROTTO. HERE HE SITS DOWN TO WAIT, FOR THERE IS A DEEP SUSPICION IN HIS MIND.

IN A FEW MINUTES HIS SUSPICIONS ARE CONFIRMED. ALETA POPS OUT, NOW CLOTHED IN BATHING ATTIRE THAT EVEN THE MOST PRUDISH WOULD APPROVE.
"SO, MY WIFE HAS NOW BECOME A LEGEND," HE SCOLDS, *"A MYTHICAL DENIZEN OF THE DEEP. THANK HEAVEN FOR YOUR LONG HAIR!"*

"I SWIM AS I PLEASE," SHE SNAPS. *"I HAVE THE WHOLE WIDE SEA TO MYSELF."*
"BUT NOT THE LAND," VAL ANSWERS. *"LOOK TO THE TOP OF THE CLIFF."* ALETA TAKES A PEEK AND BLUSHES A BRIGHT PINK.
"OH, DEAR ME," SHE EXCLAIMS WEAKLY.

VAL CLIMBS UP TO HIS COMPANIONS. *"IT WAS NOT A SIREN,"* HE ANNOUNCES. *"POSSIBLY A MERMAID WHO LIVES IN A SEA CAVE UNDER THE CLIFF. PERFECTLY HARMLESS. SHALL WE GO?"*

1554

11-20

VAL THOROUGHLY ENJOYS THE NEXT FEW DAYS. HIS WIFE IS NOT AS ROYALLY AUTOCRATIC AS USUAL, BUT CHASTENED AND ALMOST DEMURE. HE MAKES THE MOST OF IT, FOR IT WILL NOT LAST LONG.

NEXT WEEK— **Back to Romance**

HAL FOSTER

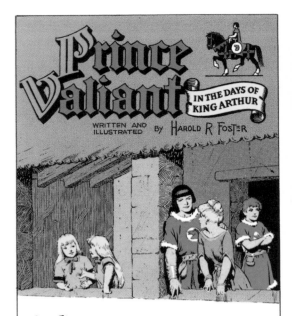

Prince Valiant

IN THE DAYS OF KING ARTHUR

WRITTEN AND ILLUSTRATED BY HAROLD R. FOSTER

Our Story: A COLD MISTY RAIN SPOILS THEIR SEASHORE HOLIDAY AND PRINCE VALIANT SUGGESTS THEY RIDE BACK TO CAMELOT. AT THE MENTION OF CAMELOT THE TWINS SUDDENLY REMEMBER THEIR UNDYING LOVE FOR THEIR CHOSEN KNIGHT CHAMPION, SIR HOWARD.

ROMANCE ALWAYS COMES TO PRINCESSES, (SO THE TROUBADORS SING) BUT KAREN AND VALETA DO NOT INTEND TO LEAVE IT TO CHANCE. THEY WANT ROMANCE NOW. HOWARD IS THEIR TARGET WHETHER HE LIKES IT OR NOT.

IN THEIR ABSENCE 'THAT WOMAN' HAS HOWARD SO BEMUSED THAT HE HAS FORGOTTEN TO SLAY EVEN A SMALL DRAGON IN HONOR OF HIS TWO ROMANTIC LADIES.

THE TWINS FIND THEIR FAITHLESS CHAMPION IN THE MIDST OF HIS GUILT AND DEMAND A SHOWDOWN. "WILL YOU MARRY US OR FACE OUR FATHER IN A DUEL FOR OUR HONOR?" ASKS KAREN WRATHFULLY. 'THAT WOMAN' ANSWERS — "IT IS UNLAWFUL TO HAVE TWO WIVES, EVEN TWINS. YOU MUST CHOOSE BETWEEN YOU."

"THEN HE CAN MARRY ME AND VALETA CAN BE MY LADY-IN-WAITING." TO KAREN THE MATTER IS SETTLED.
"WHAT! BE YOUR LADY-IN-WAITING!" SCREAMS VALETA. "YOU DON'T EVEN WASH BEHIND YOUR EARS AND YOU HAVE FLEAS!" AND THE FIGHT IS ON ...... AND OVER AS QUICKLY.

THEY SEEK OUT THE COURT MUSICIAN WHO HAS SUNG SO BEAUTIFULLY OF ROMANCE. HE UNDERSTANDS; NOW HE SINGS OF BLIGHTED LOVE, THE SMILE THAT HIDES A BROKEN HEART, THE GAY LAUGH THAT COVERS TRAGEDY.

1555   11-27

ALL DAY THEY ENJOY THEIR SWEET SORROW. THERE IS TALK OF ENDING THEIR PAIN WITH POISON OR ENTERING A CONVENT, BUT A LOST LOVE CANNOT COMPETE WITH AN EMPTY STOMACH. BY DINNER TIME THEY ARE BACK TO NORMAL.

HOWEVER, SOME TRAGEDIES ARE REAL, AND SORROW MARKS THE FACE OF AN AGED WARRIOR WHO RIDES INTO CAMELOT WITH A STORY TO TELL.

NEXT WEEK— The Missing Heir

Prince Valiant
IN THE DAYS OF KING ARTHUR
WRITTEN AND ILLUSTRATED BY HAROLD R FOSTER

Our Story: AN AGED WARRIOR ENTERS CAMELOT AND SEEKS AUDIENCE WITH THE KING. SOON THEREAFTER PRINCE VALIANT IS SUMMONED AND ARTHUR SAYS: "BALA BURWULF ASKS OUR HELP. BUT LET HIM REPEAT HIS STORY TO YOU."
"I AM CHANCELLOR TO KING BEDWIN OF DINMORE, LONG A FAITHFUL FOLLOWER OF KING ARTHUR," BEGINS THE OLD MAN. "KING BEDWIN IS FULL OF YEARS AND HIS DAYS ARE NUMBERED. HIS SON, PRINCE HARWICK, HAS DISAPPEARED AND THIS POSES A PROBLEM."

"SHOULD THE KING DIE AND THE THRONE BE UNOCCUPIED HIS TWO BROTHERS WILL CONTEND FOR IT AND A RUINOUS WAR WILL FOLLOW. PRINCE HARWICK MUST BE FOUND!"

"I CAN CALL UPON LAUNCELOT TO LEAD AN ARMY OR SIR GAWAIN FOR SINGLE COMBAT," ARTHUR SAYS, "BUT THIS CALLS FOR SUBTLETY, FOR HARWICK MUST BE THERE TO FILL THE THRONE WHEN THE KING DIES. SO I HAVE CHOSEN YOU, VAL."

WHEN HE GOES TO BID FAREWELL TO ALETA SHE IS SHARING AN AFTERNOON NAP WITH GALAN. FOR A LONG WHILE HE FEASTS HIS EYES ON HER SERENE FACE, FOR HE MUST STORE UP MEMORIES TO LAST UNTIL HIS RETURN.

THEN HE TIPTOES OUT SO AS NOT TO DISTURB HER DREAMS.

"IS THERE ANYTHING YOU CAN TELL ME ABOUT PRINCE HARWICK THAT MIGHT AID ME IN MY SEARCH FOR HIM?" ASKS VAL. "YES, HE HATED COURT LIFE," ANSWERS THE OLD CHANCELLOR, "AND SPENT HIS TIME FISHING FOR SALMON AND TROUT OR HAWKING."

1556   12-4

"HIS FATHER, THE KING, WAS STRICT AND VERY SEVERE. THE TWO QUARRELED OFTEN, THEN THE BOY WOULD TAKE HIS NEW-FANGLED FISHING TOOLS AND SPEND THE DAY ON THE RIVER."
NEXT WEEK— The Salmon Fisherman

HAL FOSTER

Prince Valiant
IN THE DAYS OF KING ARTHUR
WRITTEN AND ILLUSTRATED BY HAROLD R. FOSTER

Our Story: THE OLD CHANCELLOR LEADS PRINCE VALIANT INTO THE TINY KINGDOM OF DINMORE, AND WHEN THE KING'S CASTLE COMES IN SIGHT VAL HALTS. "HERE I MUST LEAVE YOU," HE SAYS. "IF I AM TO SEARCH FOR PRINCE HARWICK IT IS BEST I REMAIN UNKNOWN."

AS THE MISSING HEIR SPENDS ALL HIS TIME HAWKING AND FISHING FOR SALMON, VAL FOLLOWS THE RIVERS, ASKING ALL HE MEETS ABOUT THE FISHING. "THIS RIVER IS FAMOUS FOR ITS SALMON," A WOODCUTTER TELLS HIM, "EVEN NOW A FISHERMAN IS USING STRANGE METHODS TO CATCH THEM."

COULD THIS BE THE RUNAWAY PRINCE? FROM A DISTANCE VAL OBSERVES A PLUMP YOUNG MAN CASTING WITH ROD AND LINE. UP TO NOW SALMON HAVE BEEN TAKEN ONLY BY SPEAR OR NET, BUT THIS FELLOW HOOKS AND LANDS ONE!

VAL, AN ARDENT FISHERMAN HIMSELF, MUST LEARN THE SECRET OF THIS SPORTING WAY OF TAKING SALMON. HE FOLLOWS THE YOUTH AND HIS COMPANION AND TAKES LODGINGS AT THE SAME INN. THE INNKEEPER TELLS HIM THE YOUTH IS A TROUBADOR NAMED OWEN.

DURING HIS WANDERINGS VAL HAS OFTEN PROVIDED A TROUT DINNER BY TRAILING A HOOK DECORATED WITH SMALL FEATHERS IN A TROUT STREAM. NOW HE BEGINS TO TIE A FEW FLIES, KNOWING THIS WILL BE IRRESISTIBLE TO ANOTHER FISHERMAN.

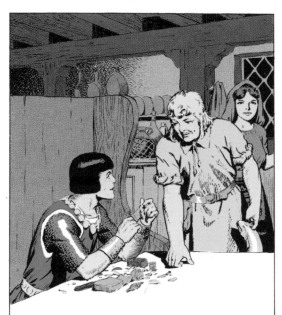

"PARDON MY INTRUSION. MY NAME IS OWEN AND I SEE YOU KNOW MY SECRET OF TAKING SALMON." "NOT SO," ANSWERS VAL. "THESE FEATHERED HOOKS REPRESENT INSECTS AND ARE USED FOR TROUT. SALMON WILL NOT TAKE THEM."

"OH, BUT THEY WILL!" CRIES OWEN. "IN THE MORNING I WILL SHOW YOU, FOR YOU ARE A FISHERMAN AND THEREFORE A BROTHER."

CAN THIS CHUBBY LITTLE MAN BE THE CROWN PRINCE? VAL MUST BE SURE BEFORE HE SENDS A MESSAGE TO THE CHANCELLOR.

NEXT WEEK— **The Promise**

1557   12-11

Our Story: TRUE TO HIS PROMISE, OWEN, THE TROUBADOR, TAKES PRINCE VALIANT TO THE STREAM TO TEACH HIM HOW TO TAKE SALMON ON A FEATHERED HOOK. THE INNKEEPER'S DAUGHTER INSISTS ON CARRYING THE RODS AND LUNCH HAMPER.

EACH HAS HIS OWN PRIVATE THOUGHTS: "CAN THIS HAPPY YOUTH BE THE MISSING HEIR TO THE THRONE OF DINMORE?" DESPITE HIS PLAIN GARMENTS AND SIMPLE WAYS HIS BEARING IS THAT OF A GENTLEMAN BORN.

OWEN MEASURES HIS COMPANION: "NO ORDINARY WARRIOR IS HE. GOLD ARM BANDS AND NECKLACE, JEWELS IN THE HILT OF HIS GREAT SWORD, AND HIS CREST, THE CRIMSON STALLION. WHERE HAS HE HEARD OF THAT CREST? HE IS OBVIOUSLY A FELLOW OF THE ROUND TABLE."

"STRIP ENOUGH LINE TO REACH ACROSS THE RIVER," INSTRUCTS OWEN. "THE ROD IS AS A BOW, THE HEAVY LINE THE ARROW. THROW AND THE HEAVY LINE WILL TAKE OUT THE SLACK." VAL IS SO INTERESTED IN LEARNING TO CAST THAT HE ALMOST FORGETS THERE ARE SALMON THERE.

HE TRIES TO HALT THE LEAPING RUN BY HOLDING THE LINE AND IS REWARDED WITH SEVERELY BURNED FINGERS. TWO MORE SALMON ARE LOST ERE HE LEARNS TO PLAY THEM.

VAL IS MOST ENTHUSIASTIC AND WANTS TO KNOW WHAT WOOD IS BEST FOR A ROD, HOW TO BRAID A LINE AND WHIP ON THE GUIDES, ETC.

AFTER DINNER THEY ARE DISCUSSING TACKLE WHEN OWEN SAYS: "I WILL TELL YOU SOMETHING IF YOU GIVE YOUR KNIGHTLY WORD TO KEEP IT A SECRET."
"OF COURSE," VAL PROMISES.
WITH A SLY GRIN OWEN ANSWERS: "I AM PRINCE HARWICK, HEIR TO THE DINMORE THRONE."
"AND," VAL SAYS, "I WAS SENT TO FIND YOU AND BRING YOU BACK. BUT YOU HAVE MY OATH; YOUR SECRET IS SAFE."

NEXT WEEK— *Harwick's Story*

1558

12-18

Prince Valiant
IN THE DAYS OF KING ARTHUR
WRITTEN AND ILLUSTRATED BY Harold R Foster

Our Story: PRINCE VALIANT HAS BEEN TRICKED! HE IS SENT ON A MISSION TO FIND THE RUNAWAY PRINCE HARWICK, AND THAT CLEVER YOUNG MAN SECURES VAL'S PROMISE TO KEEP HIS WHEREABOUTS A SECRET. WHICH COURSE SHOULD HE FOLLOW: HIS DUTY TO THE KING OR HIS OWN GIVEN WORD?

"YOU MAY WONDER WHY I GIVE UP RICHES AND POWER FOR THE LIFE OF SIMPLE LEISURE. WELL, AFTER MY MOTHER DIED, MY SIRE TOOK OVER MY SCHOOLING. DAY AFTER DAY I SAT IN A STUFFY ROOM AND STUDIED GOVERNMENT, LAW AND HISTORY...."

"AND UNDER HIS STERN EYE I WAS FORCED TO PRACTICE AT ARMS UNTIL TOO WEARY FOR PLAY WITH OTHER BOYS."

"WHEN I ATTAINED MANHOOD THE VERY THOUGHT OF ASCENDING TO THE THRONE OF DINMORE WAS HATEFUL. I REBELLED AND SOUGHT PEACE AND PLEASURE IN FIELD AND STREAM. MY FATHER, THE KING, SCOLDED ME ENDLESSLY."

"ONCE I WANDERED FAR FROM HOME AND FOUND THIS PLEASANT LITTLE INN AND MET RUTH, THE INNKEEPER'S DAUGHTER. I FELL IN LOVE WITH HER FRESH YOUNG BEAUTY. THE PERFUMED LADIES AT COURT COULD NOT MATCH HER SIMPLE, FRANK HONESTY. I INTEND TO MARRY HER AND SETTLE IN THIS LITTLE HEAVEN."

IN HIS GREAT BED KING BEDWIN OF DINMORE LIES PALE AND WEAK AS IF RESTING FOR HIS LONG JOURNEY INTO THE UNKNOWN. SHOULD THE THRONE BE VACANT WHEN HE DIES, TWO CLAIMANTS WILL CONTEND AND CIVIL WAR WILL DRENCH THE SMALL KINGDOM IN BLOOD.

1559   12-25

THE OLD CHANCELLOR HAS SPENT HIS LIFE IN FAITHFUL SERVICE TO HIS KING AND COUNTRY, BUT NOW, UNLESS THE CROWN PRINCE IS FOUND AND BROUGHT BACK, ALL HIS WORK WILL GO DOWN IN RUIN.

NEXT WEEK- Dark Clouds Gather

Above: The cover for *Prince Valiant in the Days of King Arthur*, Vol. #1 (Hastings House, 1951). This original cover by Foster is one of the most reprinted image of Val that never appeared in the strip. Beginning with this volume, Hastings House published six additional illustrated novelizations of Foster's strip. The first five books contained text adapted by Max Trell and the last two by James Flowers.

NOT JUST FOR SUNDAYS:
Prince Valiant's Adventures Beyond the Fourth Estate

Compiled and annotated by Brian M. Kane

While *Prince Valiant* continues to entertain readers for over 80 years in the weekend color comics (*Happy Birthday, Val!*), it has also enjoyed a robust, global reprint history as well. Before Fantagraphics' current *Prince Valiant* reprint series there was a previous one that began in 1984; filling 50 volumes over a 20-year period. The Danish publisher, Interpresse had already printed the first 25 volumes by the time Kim Thompson convinced Fantagraphics to become involved in the venture with Volume #26. Fantagraphics printed four more sequential issues before backtracking, and printing Volume #1 in Fall, 1987.

In 2008, Gary Groth approved my idea for *The Revised Prince Valiant Companion* (later rebranded *"Definitive"* by Kim Thompson). *The Companion* fit into Fantagraphics' plans to once more reprint the entire run of *Prince Valiant* using restored pages from a European publisher. A short time after Gary's approval I went to Syracuse University to study their Hal Foster collection in order to finish my research. At the end of my last day I still had an hour before closing. The online catalogue listed 40 volumes of "tear sheets"; the term for pages cut from printed comics sections. I was specifically looking for original material, but what better way is there to unwind then to spend time reading comics? As soon as I opened the volume I was shocked. These were broadsheet-sized color engraver's proof sheets, printed so Foster could make final corrections before the plates would be duplicated and sent to the various newspapers. Furthermore, they were printed on white boards, so they had not yellowed or browned with age, and had been stored in hand-crafted books away from sunlight in a climate-controlled room for over 40 years. The colors were vibrant; almost too sensual. Yellows and reds jumped off the page. There were subtle, nuanced color variations that I had never noticed before—and the black line art was thin and elegant; unlike the blotched blacks of all the other reprints I had previously seen. Because King Features had folded the pages twice to mail them to Foster they were never used for previous reprints; however, this is the digital age, so correcting creases and chips was not a problem. I ordered several pages for *The Companion* to be scanned and sent to my home then immediately left the building and called Gary Groth; imploring him not to sign the contract with the European publisher until he had a chance to see the proofs. The rest, as they say,…

The following is a gallery of American *Prince Valiant* reprint books containing Hal Foster's art. Some are good; some not so much, but all are,…uh…*Valiant* attempts.

Below: Errol Edward "Butch" Foster reading the adventures of his grandfather's greatest creation.

Right: The first reprints of *Prince Valiant* pages appeared in David McKay Company's *Ace Comics* #26 (May 1939), and ran as a 4-page feature through issue #134. Two years after that premiere, McKay also published Val's first solo reprint book, *Prince Valiant, Feature Book* No. 26 (1941) containing strip pages #1-28, & 30-63. The inside front cover has a short biography, "Meet Harold R. Foster and Prince Valiant" by Edgar W. Brown, which has been reprinted quite often.

Above and opposite: The covers for Hastings House's Prince Valiant's, Books #2-4. The cover for Book #2 was an original piece.

Below left: King Features' Executive Editor and General Manager Jimmy "Ward" Greene and Milton Caniff at the 1952 Silver Lady Awards dinner honoring Hal Foster. Under Caniff's left arm (and insert) is a slipcased set of the first two *Prince Valiant* Hastings House volumes given to all attendees by King Features.

Below right: *Prince Valiant in the Days of King Arthur by Hal Foster* (Treasure Books #874, 1954). Using panels from the strip, this 28-page children's book tells how Val became a Knight. The title page art is a Foster original—the knighting of Sir Valiant, which appears on this series' masthead.

POPULAR RESPONSE TO THE EARLIER BOOKS IN THE PRINCE VALIANT SERIES BY HAL FOSTER:

"Has the endorsement of parents, and educators and appeals to youngsters. Mr. Foster's drawings make this the picture-book at its best, and the story is genially and pleasantly told."
—Boston Post

"A story of action-packed days when knights were bold and life was cheap."
—Christian Herald

"Prince Valiant's pages take the reader back to the gallant days of King Arthur . . . make him feel an actual spectator."
—The New York Journal-American

"This edition of the valiant Prince will be eagerly read by boys and girls of today."
—The Oklahoma Teachers

"Prince Valiant recreates the Middle Ages with their romance and excitment that appeals to all—"
—Abilene, Texas, Morning Reporter News

"Splendid story-telling by a master-illustrator."
—Baltimore, Md., News-Post

"In Foster's superb drawings the gay, grim and roistering days of old are recaptured."
—San Francisco Examiner

"A very modern interpretation of Arthurian times which should lead to the reading of Malory."
—The Queens Borough (N. Y. City) Public Library

"A magnificent revelation of the days of King Arthur . . . For Valiant's old fans this volume marks a warm reunion and will make him many new friends."
—Morristown (N. J.) Daily Record

Prince Valiant's PERILOUS VOYAGE

HAL FOSTER

HASTINGS HOUSE

BOOK 4

PRINCE VALIANT BOOK 4

By HAL FOSTER
Text by MAX TRELL
adapted from the original story.

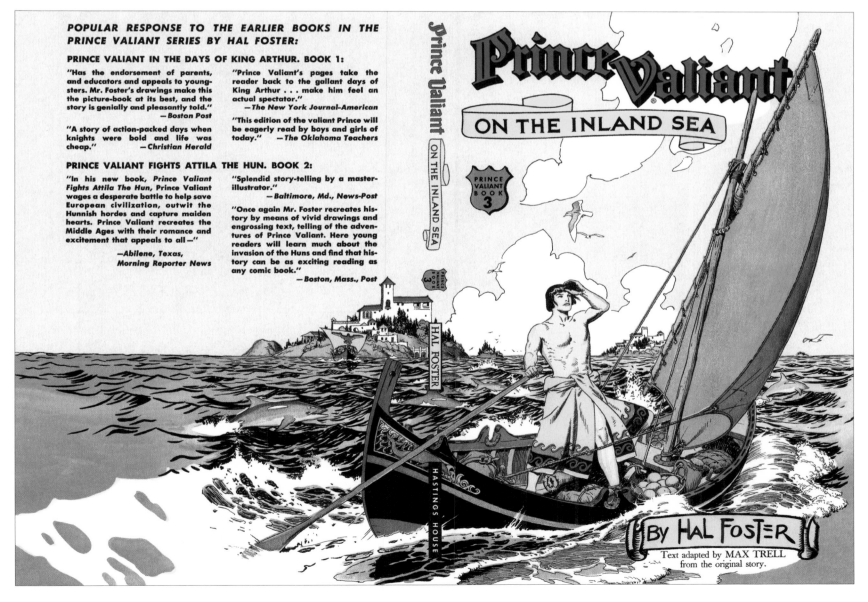

POPULAR RESPONSE TO THE EARLIER BOOKS IN THE PRINCE VALIANT SERIES BY HAL FOSTER:

PRINCE VALIANT IN THE DAYS OF KING ARTHUR. BOOK 1:

"Has the endorsement of parents, and educators and appeals to youngsters. Mr. Foster's drawings make this the picture-book at its best, and the story is genially and pleasantly told."
—Boston Post

"A story of action-packed days when knights were bold and life was cheap."
—Christian Herald

PRINCE VALIANT FIGHTS ATTILA THE HUN. BOOK 2:

"In his new book, Prince Valiant Fights Attila The Hun, Prince Valiant wages a desperate battle to help save European civilization, outwit the Hunnish hordes and capture maiden hearts. Prince Valiant recreates the Middle Ages with their romance and excitement that appeals to all—"
—Abilene, Texas, Morning Reporter News

"Prince Valiant's pages take the reader back to the gallant days of King Arthur . . . make him feel an actual spectator."
—The New York Journal-American

"This edition of the valiant Prince will be eagerly read by boys and girls of today."
—The Oklahoma Teachers

"Splendid story-telling by a master-illustrator."
—Baltimore, Md., News-Post

"Once again Mr. Foster recreates history by means of vivid drawings and engrossing text, telling of the adventures of Prince Valiant. Here young readers will learn much about the invasion of the Huns and find that history can be as exciting reading as any comic book."
—Boston, Mass., Post

Prince Valiant ON THE INLAND SEA

PRINCE VALIANT BOOK 3

HAL FOSTER

HASTINGS HOUSE

BY HAL FOSTER
Text adapted by MAX TRELL
from the original story.

AT LAST! OWN THIS RARE SET OF PRINCE VALIANT ADVENTURE PICTURE BOOKS!

HARD-COVER BOOKS LARGE 7" x 10" SIZE 128 EXCITING PAGES.

Here is your once in a lifetime opportunity to own this fascinating set of original, authentic adventure books. You'll thrill to the daring exploits of Prince Valiant, popular comics hero!

Every Page Fully ILLUSTRATED By The Great HAL FOSTER

Follow Prince Valiant, Knight of King Arthur's Round Table as he wields the mighty Singing Sword for justice everywhere. Follow him in his travels as he seeks out tyrants, thieves and marauding armies, engaging them in heroic battles.

QUALITY MADE BOOKS TO LAST A LIFETIME

From Book #5—"PRINCE VALIANT AND THE GOLDEN PRINCESS" No. 2733 .... $3.95

From Book #1—
"PRINCE VALIANT IN THE DAYS OF KING ARTHUR"
The youthful prince at the famous round-table.
No. 2729 .... $3.95

From Book #2—
"PRINCE VALIANT FIGHTS ATTILA THE HUN"
In gallant battle against barbaric plundering hordes.
No. 2730 .... $3.95

From Book #3—
"PRINCE VALIANT ON THE INLAND SEA"
Expedition across the gleaming expanse of the mysterious inland sea.
No. 2731 .... $3.95

From Book #4—
"PRINCE VALIANT'S PERILOUS VOYAGE"
Golden treasures lure him to harrowing adventures in the jungles of darkest Africa.
No. 2732 .... $3.95

From Book #6—
"PRINCE VALIANT IN THE NEW WORLD"
Crosses the sea, to the new world before the days of Columbus.
No. 2734 .... $3.95

From Book #7—
"PRINCE VALIANT AND THE THREE CHALLENGES"
The Great Prince faces a ruthless king, black magic and a horde of savages!
No. 2735 .... $3.95

SPECIAL OFFER: ORDER 6 BOOKS & GET BOOK #7 FREE!

ADD 35¢ POSTAGE AND HANDLING FOR EACH BOOK, AND MAIL TO: CAPTAIN COMPANY P.O. BOX 5987, GRAND CENTRAL STATION NEW YORK, N.Y. 10017 U.S. ORDERS ONLY NO C.O.D.'S

In the 1970s, Nostalgia Press reprinted the Hastings House series. This ad (above) is from *Creepy 1970 Yearbook's* back cover. The marketing of *Prince Valiant* on *Creepy* is significant because Foster influenced many of artists featured in the Warren magazines.

Other than the copyright information the only real difference between the two series is the publisher's name on the spine of volumes as seen on Books #5 & 6 on the opposite page.

POPULAR RESPONSE TO THE EARLIER BOOKS
IN THE PRINCE VALIANT SERIES BY HAL FOSTER:

"Has the endorsement of parents and educators and appeals to youngsters. Mr. Foster's drawings make this the picture-book at its best, and the story is genially and pleasantly told."
—Boston Post

"A story of action-packed days when knights were bold and life was cheap."
—Christian Herald

"Prince Valiant's pages take the reader back to the gallant days of King Arthur . . . make him feel an actual spectator."
—New York Journal-American

"This edition of the valiant Prince will be eagerly read by boys and girls of today."
—The Oklahoma Teachers

"Prince Valiant recreates the Middle Ages with their romance and excitement that appeals to all—"
—Abilene, Texas, Morning Reporter News

"Splendid story-telling by a master-illustrator."
—Baltimore, Md., News-Post

"In Foster's superb drawings the gay, grim and roistering days of old are recaptured."
—San Francisco Examiner

"A very modern interpretation of Arthurian times which should lead to the reading of Malory."
—The Queens Borough (N. Y. City) Public Library

"A magnificent revelation of the days of King Arthur . . . For Valiant's old fans this volume marks a warm reunion and will make him many new friends."
—Morristown (N.J.) Daily Record

Prince Valiant
and the Three Challenges
HAL FOSTER
HASTINGS HOUSE

Prince Valiant
AND THE THREE CHALLENGES

PRINCE VALIANT BOOK 7

by HAL FOSTER

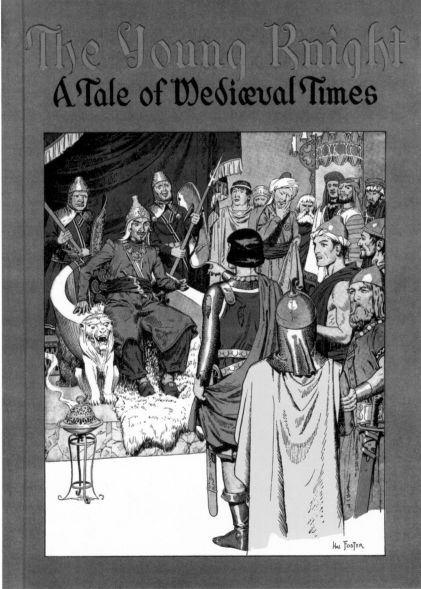

The Young Knight
A Tale of Mediæval Times

HAL FOSTER

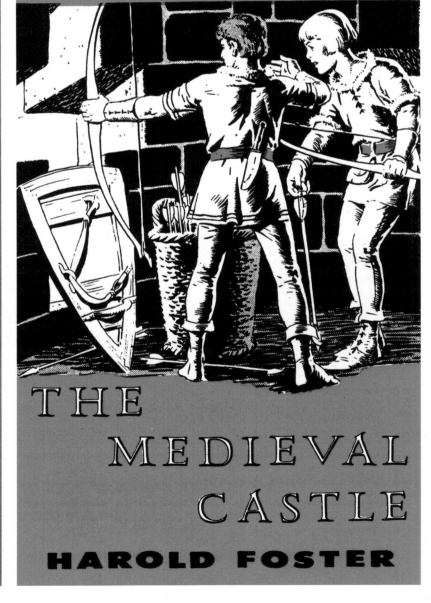

THE MEDIEVAL CASTLE

HAROLD FOSTER

Opposite top: The seventh and last Hastings House *Prince Valiant* book. The book concludes with *Prince Valiant*, page #683, March 12, 1950. However, while the American editions ended with Book #7, the series continued in Germany.

Opposite bottom left: Although Prince Valiant is prominently displayed on the cover of *The Young Knight: A Tale of Mediæval Times* (1945), the story is actually a children's book adaptation of Hal Foster's *Mediæval Castle* footer strip.

Opposite bottom right: *The Medieval Castle* (1957) is an illustrated novelization of Foster's footer strip. Published by Hastings House it is similar in format to their *Prince Valiant* books.

Clockwise from top right: *Prince Valiant's* volumes #3, 4, 2 & 1. Published by Nostalgia Press from 1974-1978, these four volumes are the worst reprints ever produced. Pages are awash with garish colors that never reference Foster's originals— or even the art in the panels. Combined with a black plate that devolves the artwork into blotchy, indecipherable splotches it is amazing to think that this series ever sold.

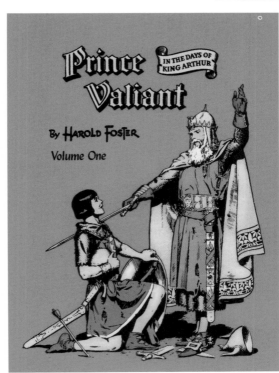

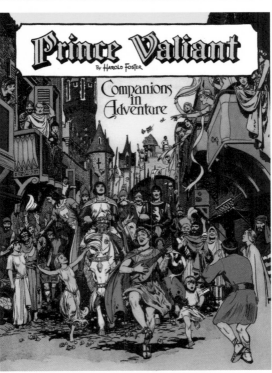

From 1978-1983, Pacific Comics Club published 8 volumes of *Prince Valiant*. Edited by Tony Raiola, each volume had a print run of only 1,000 copies. With color separations and printing by Microlito in Genoa, Italy, these 9.5" x 13.5" volumes marked the first time in the United States that reprints of *Prince Valiant* were available in a larger format with colors approaching the original pages.

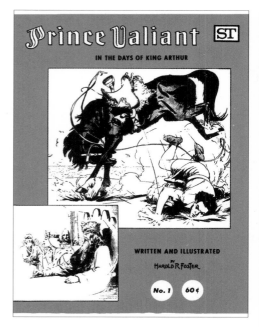

Above: This one-shot *Prince Valiant's* (August, 1972) comic book from Street Enterprises was produced by *The Menomonee Falls Gazette*'s Jerry Sinkovec and Mike Tiefenbacher.

Above middle: *Prince Valiant* (1973) was published by King Comics, a short-lived imprint of King Features Syndicate.

Above right: Fantagraphics published the *Prince Valiant: Free Comic Book Day Special Edition* in 2013.

In the 1980s, Pioneer Comics, produced several *Prince Valiant* comic books. Most covers featured Foster's or John Cullen Murphy's art, however, these two were by Mike Grell.

"Doing covers for *Prince Valiant* was a huge challenge because I grew up in the era when comic strips were a huge part of everyone's Sunday morning. Hal Foster's unsurpassed artistry and masterful storytelling became the standard by which I judged all others. There will simply never be another comic strip to compare with *Prince Valiant*."

—Mike Grell

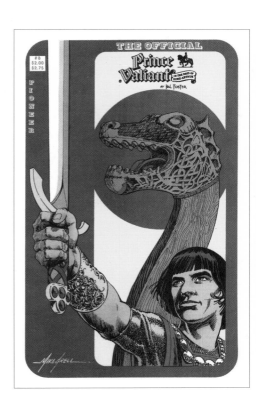

Though not a reprint series, we could not pass on the opportunity of showcasing Michael Wm Kaluta's beautiful cover art for this 4-issue *Prince Valiant* mini-series published in 1994-1995 by Marvel Comics. The issues were plotted by Charles Vess and scripted by Elaine Lee with art by John Ridgway, colors by Curtis Woodbridge, and lettering by John Workman. The cover for issue #4 is presented on the opposite page. Starting on this page above left and moving clockwise are the covers for issues #1, 2 and 3.

Prince Valiant
An American Epic
VOLUME ONE: 1937
by Hal Foster

Edited by Rick Norwood

Manuscript Press

Perhaps the most ambitious reprint project to date was *Prince Valiant: An American Epic*, edited by Rick Norwood, and published by his imprint, Manuscript Press from 1982-1990. Norwood produced the first two volumes using black proof plates, and color separations by the company that provided the original color engravings for *Prince Valiant*. For Volume #3, Norwood enlisted the help of long-time Foster fan, Murphy Anderson to recolor the entire book. Unfortunately, lack of sales for the third volume made the endeavor unprofitable, and the plans for additional volumes were abandoned.

Special thanks to: Michael Wm Kaluta, Mike Grell, Rick Norwood, Axel M. Wulff, Sander de Vries and Stephen R. Bissette for their help in preparing this gallery.

Prince Valiant
An American Epic
VOLUME TWO: 1938
by Hal Foster

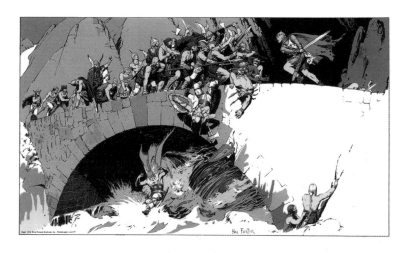

Edited by Rick Norwood

Manuscript Press

Prince Valiant
An American Epic
VOLUME THREE: 1939
by Hal Foster

Edited by Rick Norwood

Manuscript Press

IN OUR NEXT VOLUME:

PRINCE VALIANT

VOL. 16: 1967–1968

In Fantagraphics' 16th volume of the legendary Prince Valiant series, King Arthur sends our eponymous hero tries to rescue Sir Gawain who is being held for ransom in the Middle Eastern land of Dathram. Upon arrival Val too is enslaved, and the two champions must lead a revolt to escape their captors. Returning to the Misty Isles, Aleta is faced with her small empire on the verge of collapse due to greed and laziness of the nobles she had left in charge. Knowing Aleta's island paradise is ill prepared for war a neighboring kingdom plans an invasion that only Arn can stop.